MYSTERY MEN
(& WOMEN)

AIRSHIP 27 PRODUCTIONS

Mystery Men (& Women) Volume Four

A Waltz in Scarlet ©2017 Tomas Deja
Cult of the Strangler ©2017 Joel Jenkins
The Cult of Kali Kill ©2017 B.C. Bell
The Grey Mantis Strikes ©2017 C. William Russette

An Airship 27 Production
www.airship27.com
www.airship27hangar.com

Cover illustration © 2017 Zachary Brunner
Interior illustrations © 2017 Rob Davis

Editor: Ron Fortier
Associate Editor: Gordon Dymowski
Marketing and promotion: Michael Vance
Production and design by Rob Davis.

ISBN-10:1-946183-13-X
ISBN-13: 978-1-946183-13-2

Printed in the United States of America

10 9 8 7 6 5 4 3 2 1

MYSTERY MEN
(& WOMEN) VOLUME 4
—TABLE OF CONTENTS—

THE FERRYMAN IN:
"A WALTZ IN SCARLET"

By Thomas Deja

Alan Dennings had long since gotten used to waking up to the presence of new arrivals in the waiting room inside his head. Since that terrible night in 1941, he had worked very hard to gain revenge for each of the grey, dull shapes trapped between this world and the next. He had watched each of these indistinct shades pass on to the next life once their thirst for vengeance was slaked, bore witness to their time in this limbo.

But as he emerged from a sleep filled with dreams of blood and screams and the dark haired woman he had to deny himself lest this alliance to save Nocturne fall apart, Alan knew this new arrival was different.

He sat up in his hard bed, only the plainest and meanest of linens providing any comfort. Although his body, well-sculpted from the intense physical training he undertook since becoming the instrument of vengeance for Nocturne's ghosts, was stock still, his mind was already active. His consciousness moved inwards to the place in his head where the spirits waited for his help. The initial multi-toned darkness melted away and coalesced into walls of steel that reached up into infinity. As he envisioned himself walking into this edifice, tables and chairs and equipment; all without any touch of artistry to make it seem less like a dwelling and more like a home. With each step, Alan's bedclothes shifted and reconfigured around him until he was garbed in the black suit and tattered cloak of his Ferryman self. His eyes, ruined and scarred empty sockets in the early morning sunlight, were now smoldering crimson energy.

Slowly, hesitantly, his tenants emerged. Grey shades of ectoplasmic life; they pulled themselves into the light. The majority of them lacked details; Alan had come to assume that they became more indistinct the more tenuous their connection to this plane was. Some of them, the ones he was closest to avenging, were little more than dusty outlines.

Then there was the little girl standing near one of the blackboards. The one fighting back tears.

The one in vivid color. She was short with long white blonde hair falling past her shoulders and down her back. She wore a nightgown of pale, delicate pink that hung down to her ankles. Her feet were stained reddish brown. As Alan approached the child, he could sense her struggling to hold back a sob.

Reflexively, he let his heroic outfit slough away into mist for a simple white shirt and slacks. The red lights in his sockets became wisps of smoke that solidified into a pair of dark glasses. Briefly, he wondered why he ceased wearing those glasses long ago.

Some of the shades drew closer to the little girl. Small eyes darted around warily. Alan could feel the fear coming off her in waves. He motioned them emphatically to move away from the girl before getting down on one knee in front of her.

He reached out and gently pushed the hair away from her face. "Shh-hhh....it's alright, it's alright...you're fine."

"Nooooo," the girl replied in a half whisper.

"Yes. I won't let my friends hurt you. And I work hard to make sure little boys and girls like you are safe. My name is Alan. What's yours?"

Her eyes, glistening with tears that were about to fall, darted around. As if on instinct, Alan's tenants drifted further away from them. "K-Katie...."

"Katie," he said in a soft, comforting voice he realized he hadn't used since the evening he lost his sight. "You are welcome here, but I need to ask...why did you come see me?"

"I...I'm hiding."

"Hiding from what?"

She shook her head, pointedly not looking at him. "Don't wanna."

Alan wondered why he was behaving like this. For years after that night where he lost his sight and became a conduit into the next world, he had been bombarded with horror and despair and violence as a succession of shades wailed out the story of their individual demises. And he had struggled to give those shades rest by avenging their murders, only to have new ghosts step in to demand their own justice. It had hardened him. Nowadays, as he saw through the spectral eyes of these murdered souls, Alan noticed how everyone, even his allies in the so-called Shadow Legion, avoided, sometimes actively shunned him. And Alan had welcomed that solitude, as it allowed him to focus on the endless tasks put in front of him.

But he was softening in front of this tiny, doll-like girl. Alan reached out with a hand that trembled slightly and squeezed her shoulder. "Katie, dear... you came to my home to hide. That was the right thing to do. My job is to fight for little boys and girls like you and chase away the bad things. But for me to do that, I need to know what you're hiding from."

At first, Alan feared that this girl had withdrawn from him completely. But slowly she raised her head to look right in his eyes. "I'm hiding from The Red Lady."

Alan's mental sanctuary dimmed around him. His ghostly tenants wailed a chilling noise that began as a low thrum and rose gradually until it became an audible howl. He stood up, a chill sliding from the base of his skull all the way down his spine. Around him, the details of the headquarters he built out of his own dream stuff lost detail and blurred. "The Red Lady?"

She nodded.

It took a moment for him to stop the digression lest it scare the child. He allowed his appearance to shift slightly; the cloak appeared sans the tattered edges, the hood drawn down. "I know who this lady is. I promise you, Katie...I will *never* let her get you."

"You promise?"

Now it was his turn to nod. Slowly, carefully he pulled his surroundingsback into full detail. "She is a very bad lady. I've stopped her in the past, and I will stop her again for you."

Impulsively she stepped forward and took his hand. Her skin was unnaturally cold. "Thank you."

"Katie, listen to me," he said gently. "It's daytime. You need to go home. Do you know your address?"

She nodded her head.

He pointed to one of the desks, where a pad and paper lay. "I want you to go there before you head home and write it down; your address, and your full name. I promise you I will visit you later. I just need to do some work first."

She held onto his hand a little longer, then reluctantly let go. Alan watched as Katie walked to the desk and scribbled something down.

"Good girl," he said. "I will see you later."

"Okay," Katie replied as she put down the pencil. She faced him briefly. "Thank you, mister."

"Just remember that if the Red Lady comes after you, you come here and call for me as loud as you can. I'll be here as soon as I'm able, and my...my friends will protect you until I get here."

He glanced around at his tenants. He could feel them give their silent assent.

She nodded once more. Alan noticed how her tears had dried. "I'm glad I came here," she told him and walked off. He watched her melt away into the murk of the far corners of his sanctuary.

"So am I," he replied to no one and everyone as he slipped from his interior world to the real one. And as he got up from his bed, one question dominated his thoughts.

How did a still living person find her way to his inner thoughts?

•••

The Red Lady meant one thing to Ferryman.

Rose Red.

A flame haired beauty with a penchant for crimson ball gowns and bloody murder, Rose Red was a monster in a woman's skin. It was she who was indirectly responsible for a gun going off inches from Alan's eyes, permanently snuffing out his sight. It was she who utilized her weird mystical talent to absorb the remaining life of her victims to goad the denizens of Lincoln into a race war just so she could seize control of the Underworld. It was her blood he spilled to prevent that plan's success with her own blades.

The general consensus was that Ferryman killed Rose Red, thus releasing the multitude of men and women she murdered from this material plan. When she was committed to the ground, The City That Lived By Night breathed a sigh of relief and moved on.

Except.

As Alan became more and more familiar with his condition, as he learned more about the ghosts that wandered through his mind looking for retribution, he had the nagging feeling that Edwina Laurence survived. There was no concrete proof, but the suspicion perpetually hovered in the back of his mind.

The presence of Katie and her story of being pursued by this 'Red Lady' was potentially the most concrete evidence his suspicions were true. And he knew what he needed to do to find if this evidence was valid.

Wally's Way Far looked like any other honky-tonk in the Lincoln section of Nocturne. It smelled of cigarettes and musk, its crooked widow sills painted shut. An astute person would notice that unlike the other dives in this dangerous part of time, Wally's was relatively quiet. The reason for that was simple.

Wally's was a front, a facade to conceal its true purpose, namely to serve as the headquarters of Tyson Becker.

Becker had been at Rose Red's right hand, serving as her aide throughout her insane plan to tear Nocturne apart. And when she had disappeared, Becker had been co-opted into Johnny Seven's gang and given Lincoln as his territory. If anyone knew if his old boss was amongst the living, it was Tyson Becker.

Alan sat in the shadows between two ramshackle homes opposite the club. He bid his tenants outwards to give his blind eyes sight and something more. Once more the spirits of the newly dead who, in exchange for revenge, put themselves at his service and flowed forward across the street, finding cracks and gaps to slip into the club.

Alan had become used to receiving so much extra visual stimulus than he did when he was normally sighted. His brain had learned how to put together the different angles and approaches to create a coherent map; a map that was better than any accurately marked up piece of paper. Before he even entered, before Alan Dennings gave way to the fearsome blindfolded persona of Ferryman, the three-dimensional view of the room he was about to enter made a plan of attack clear.

He strode forward, a subtle change in his pace taking effect. A certain determination grew with each footfall, a lengthening of his stride as a dark confidence welled up deep within. In one uncannily smooth motion, Alan reached down for the two Colt Hammerless pistols strapped to each hip.

Ferryman pulled them up, priming them for the battle ahead.

The strange figure in the tattered cloak did not miss a beat as he came up to the club door and kicked it open. The spirits in his service seemed to howl as Ferryman stepped inside. He flung his arms outwards, guided by those who were wronged by the guards on either side of him. The guns barked, brief flashes turning the murky darkness into day for a split second. Two sacks of meat that were once men fell to the polished floor as Ferryman seemed to drift forward in the semi-darkness, guns at the ready for the next foolish assailant to charge him.

Another gunsel in slacks, tank top and suspenders ran at Ferryman, raising his machine gun to fire. Ferryman noticed the youth of this criminal; his stubbly chin had the telltale patchiness of a teenager trying to grow his first beard. He hesitated but the roaring in his ear from a shade that claimed this boy had beaten him to death prompted him to aim and fire. Ferryman was not looking as the bullet reached its mark in the boy's throat; he did not have to when his spirits could do it for him.

"Becker!" he called out as he continued walking toward the back of the main room. Another attacker, waist going soft with flab, sweat staining his pale blue shirt, rushed to Ferryman's left. He listened to the spirits rustling in his head.

None claimed this one. So when the corpulent goon came within range, Ferryman turned one of his Colts over in his right hand. He dodged the man's first feint nimbly then brought the butt of the pistol down hard on the crown of his head.

"I can do this for hours, Becker!" Ferryman proclaimed, blocking the blow from another attacker before thrusting hard with his pistol into the man's windpipe. The gunsel's eyes bulged before falling to his knees, struggling for breath. "I'd hate to see what would happen if I slaughtered most of your little honor guard and one of your enemies found out."

It looked like a number of Becker's men were about to continue the assault when a single handclap rent the air. Slowly, the men about to engage Ferryman drifted backwards into the darkest corners of the bar. Ferryman lowered his guns. He was still coiled for action but willing to stand down.

A door opened to the left in the back of the bar. Two familiar faces, the same face in duplicate, stepped forward and moved to either side. The men were silent and poised, and Ferryman did not doubt that the grip on their guns was firm. He had become extremely familiar with these identical twins over the years. A howl went up in the back of his head, a howl made up of the outrage of the spirits dwelling inside his skull demanding vengeance for the countless wrongs against them leveled by these two.

Alan had long ago learned how to drown out these specific demands. As long as he could use Tyson Becker as a source of information, as long as the young man was his one lead to his nemesis, it was to his benefit to keep the Sweet Brothers alive.

Ferryman stepped closer to the door as the man himself emerged. Even after all these years Tyson looked very young. Alan had to remind himself that this was a man who had been integral to Nocturne's criminal firmament for several years.

"Okay, Spook Man," Tyson sneered as he adjusted the collar of his jacket. "I'm here. Tell me what you want, then get out."

"Where's your boss?" Ferryman sneered in return.

One of the Sweets—Alan found it difficult to tell Rondell and Dontrel apart—stepped forward. "You speak with respect to Mister Tyson!"

The hulking twin was about to raise his machine gun, but Tyson raised a hand. The gunsel stepped down. "I thought you knew. Mr. Seven is at his home. He's not feeling very well these days."

Ferryman turned his head toward the leader of Lincoln's criminal element. "You know who I mean."

Tyson Becker laughed hollowly. His eyes gleamed with amusement. "This again?"

"There's a young girl," Ferryman continued, "who claims she's being pursued by 'The Red Lady.' You understand the conclusions I've jumped to."

Tyson's face grew hard. He looked down at the ground for a moment before locking eyes with Ferryman. "Ghost, I would think, given Mr. Seven's fading health, that you'd want to keep me and mine happy. You skulking around accusing me of hiding a dead woman we both know was bad for business isn't helping our relationship any."

Ferryman took a moment to take in the sights the spirit shared with him. A shiver of anger went through him when the smug look on Tyson's face loomed in front of him. "The only reason I haven't shot you…"

"Is because I have never killed anyone," the leader of the Lincoln branch of the Seven Gang finished. "Go home, Ghost. Go to Bailey Cemetery. I hear those corpses are real talkative."

He tightened his grip on the Colt Hammerless. The urge rose in him to pump ever last bullet into this smug young man and his two gorillas. The wails of his tenants grew in intensity, his skull filled with renewed recriminations against the Sweet Brothers and their long legacy of bloodletting. The tenants he had released from inside him swirled around the three men, focusing on all the kill shots he could make.

He closed his mouth so tightly he could hear the squeak of his teeth grinding together. Reluctantly, Ferryman slid his guns back into their holsters, the action drawing his inky grey, tattered cape around his body.

He turned his back of the three criminals and began walking out. The visions he was receiving indicated that one of the Sweets was chuckling quietly. He stopped.

"I know Rose is out there."

"She is. In lot 347 at Bailey's."

"When I find out, " Ferryman continued, "pray I don't connect her to you. Because, if she's out there, I'll hold you responsible for every murder she committed since her death."

He left before he could hear Tyson Becker's retort.

•••

Once more, Alan Dennings wondered why he hadn't worn a suit and dark glasses in such a long time.

The spirits stared at his reflection in the window. Outside of the glasses, his appearance had not changed from when he was still sighted. Yes, his continuing study of magick in Maybelle Tremems' library had taught him how to slow his aging to a crawl but there was still something different. The ghosts inside his mind whispered jeering comments; somehow Alan recognized that these were the shades he had denied justice to by letting the Sweets live.

He leaned on his cane, another indication of weakness, and rang the bell. For a long moment he worried that the address Katie had given him was wrong. But there was the sound of footsteps, then the sliding of a latch. Alan caught his breath.

The woman who opened the door could have been attractive at one time, when there was still a glow to her cheeks and her auburn hair fell to her shoulders. But her skin was sallow and tightly drawn against her skull, her face lined and haggard, eyes dull and devoid of life. She dressed in a shapeless, faded housedress. The stink of cigarettes, alcohol and sweat came off her so strongly they threatened to overpower Alan's senses.

"Yes?" she asked in a painful sounding whisper.

He took off his hat, nodded in greeting. "Mrs. Yovich?"

She seemed to hesitate for a moment before nodding.

"My name is Alan Dennings. I'm here to see your daughter."

And to his surprise, the woman's eyes came to life with an angry fire. Her worry lined mouth twisted into a grimace of rage. "Can't you ghouls leave us alone?"

She started to close the door. Alan reached out to hold it open. "Wait! Ma'am, I'm not here to feast on your misery. I met your daughter once, and she touched me with her joy. I want to actively help."

"With another one of your pandering articles?"

"No." Alan searched for the words, words he forgot when he was transformed years ago. "I am the owner of WDSK. I genuinely want to help, and put everything I can to make her better. I'm not here to make profit off of her, but to find a solution for her problem."

With reluctance, the haggard woman opened the door. "You'd have to find out what's wrong with my girl first."

Alan followed after the woman slowly, letting her lead him to a small room at the top of a flight of stairs. The lights were off throughout the inside of this home, shrouding the entire place in a gloom that reflected the woman's despair. Every creak seemed to be amplified in the shadowed quiet. Alan wondered how long ago this tragedy had happened: how many days poor Katie had run from the apparition before finding him?

It was a typical little girl's room. In contrast to the other areas of the house Alan had seen, it was bright and airy. There was no dust, no grime. The curtains had been pulled back to bathe the place in sunlight. As Alan stepped inside, he saw the girl who visited his mind earlier that morning. She looked extremely tiny and frail in the big bed, a patchwork comforter pulled up to her chin. Katie looked different than when he had seen her earlier. Her hair matted and darkened by sweat, her features alarmingly pale.

"She had nightmares."

"About The Red Lady," Alan replied as he stepped to the edge of the bed.

"So you already know. Then I won't bore you by repeating it."

The spirits swirled around the fragile figure in the little bed. Alan exerted his influence, prompting some of his tenants to scour the room, soaring over every inch looking for some anomaly, some clue as to what had turned the girl who walked in on his private sanctum into a fragile, broken bird of a thing.

"No, please, go on," Alan muttered. "I want to hear it from you."

There was silence at his back. He saw nothing untoward through the spirits' eyes, just the sort of things one would find in a cheerful little girl's room. He could hear the sound of the mother shifting her weight out of nervousness. "Katherine...she claimed that a door was open...."

He craned his neck so that it appeared as if he were glancing over his shoulder at her. "A door? Here in the house?"

The haggard woman's hand went to her neck. "She claimed it was a door in the sky, one that terrible things stepped through. It got to be that she was afraid to leave the house, for fear of being eaten by the Red Lady, or the Paper Spider or any of these creatures she claimed were going to come through that door."

Briefly, Alan reached out and brushed his hand against Katie's shoulder. "I promised I'd visit," he whispered.

"Pardon?"

He turned. "These creatures; you tried to convince her they were fantasies?"

"Yes! We tried. We sent her to see a psychiatrist. But all it did was make her dig her heels in. The doctor blanched at the pictures she drew and recommended we have her committed. I was resistant, but she got more and more frightened...

"And then," she added with a small sob, "she locked herself in her room, refused to come out. That night, we heard her scream, and when we got up here and my husband broke down the door, she was...she was like this."

Alan moved away from the sleeping child. He turned to face the woman. "I may have some friends who can help you."

"Doctors?"

He paused, tried to hide his hesitation. "Of a sort," he eventually said. Before she could ask what he meant, he added, "Do you have some of those pictures you just mentioned?"

"I...yes."

"Could I have them? So my friends and I know what we're dealing with."

He followed her out of Katie's room and down the hall to a closet. With

"I may have some friends who can help you."

each step, Alan witnessed how this poor woman seemed to sink back down in her own despair, collapsing emotionally in on herself with the thoughts of what brought her daughter to this state. He knew she refused to believe in what he now knew for a fact; there were dark things in the world, even creatures that preyed on humanity.

Even little girls.

He waited patiently while she rummaged through a closet. She emerged after a minute with a couple of sheets of paper. She held them out for him, her arm visibly shaking. "Here."

Alan took the pages and handed her his card. "Thank you. If you remember anything else you think could help me help Katie, call me immediately."

"Yes," she replied. Her voice had lowered in volume. Alan got the sense that she had gone through similar exchanges, had been discouraged when nothing came of these promises for aid.

Alan hesitated. Once more he wondered how far he had wandered away from the humanity he embraced back when he was normally sighted. He struggled to figure out the best words to tell her, the best gesture.

What he did was touch the back of her hand lightly. "I know that this is strange to you, ma'am," he said as quietly and comforting as possible. "I know you're wondering if you're going mad. I have been through a similar experience and I know ways out of these horrific circumstances. You must be patient and you must be strong. But I will be working towards bringing your daughter back to you."

For a split second Alan thought he saw a light of relief, perhaps hope in her eyes. "Thank you."

As he left, he wondered why he hadn't seen that expression for so long given that he was considered a hero.

•••

Alan passed the drawing across the table to the dark haired beauty sitting on the other side. "This is what she made before she slipped into that trance."

The woman sometimes known as Dreamcatcher took the folded pages. Alan and she were sitting in the massive library she maintained at Palmersdale House. It was a veritable storehouse of arcane knowledge and learning filled near to bursting with high bookshelves. This was where the magician studied new spells she could use when she absorbed ambient magical energy. When Alan gained the abilities he had as Ferryman, she opened this room to him so he could better understand what was happening to him.

Alan had yet to tell her what else he had been studying...because he was positive she would not approve.

He had already taken in the pictures himself, the spirits poring over the insane visages Katy produced, images she named with crayon scrawls. There was the strange, multi-limbed thing with eyes and mouths seemingly placed at random all over its thin body, something the girl dubbed 'The Paper Spider.' There was an odd, short, bulky thing with simian arms, a circular mouth like a lamprey's and a ring of teeth circling his angular head like a crown named 'The Gnawer King'.

Then there was the tall and statuesque creature with long red hair dripping with so much blood it stuck to her face, obscuring her features. Her arms were unnaturally long, her hands ending in spindly fingers sporting needle-like nails. It was hard to determine what her legs were like given how the low-cut crimson gown hugged her hips and fell in almost a straight line to the floor. But there was a strange sense in the glimpses between the folds of the skirt that there were more than two limbs underneath it.

Even though it was a child's drawing, the way the spirits in his head grew restless made it clear that this was not some child's fancy. 'The Red Lady' was real, she was about, and she was dangerous.

"The art is primitive," Maybelle Tremens said quietly, "but these may be legitimate demons."

"Or it could be something more familiar," Alan suggested.

Maybelle's eyes seemed to darken. She placed her hands on the collection of drawings and leaned forward. "Alan, I know how you feel. I'd be so resentful if Rose's men did what they did to you. But she's dead. We all saw her die."

"I'm not denying that woman is gone physically," Alan countered. "But both of us know that death is just transitory. Can you truly deny, given the abilities she displayed back in '41, that she hasn't transcended her demise... maybe even become something more than human?"

"And can you truly deny that if she were still alive, or in some state of sentience, she wouldn't be quiet for close to ten years?" Maybelle countered.

"Maybe she hasn't realized what she's become yet."

"Oh, Alan."

"I'm sorry," he said after a moment of silence. "This has proven to be a very strange time for me. I am still trying to understand how a living person entered my head like that."

Maybelle moved towards him. She was close enough that he could smell her perfume, the various scents and smells that mingled together with her pheromones to make something wonderful. The spirits in his head stirred. Some took the opportunity to whisper in his ear, offer a deal Alan had refused some years ago. He ignored the buzzing and pleadings and tried to focus on her words.

"I think you know what happened, Alan. What happened to you opened a door to the other side but an opened door is still opened. At this point, you have grown in power, and that increase has acted to invite others to go through. Maybe that girl is psychically sensitive, or maybe her interaction with this Red Lady has opened her senses the same way that traumatic experience opened yours."

"So now anyone can saunter into my private thoughts?"

"Not anyone," the sorceress replied. She looked as if she was about to continue her thought, but a shift in her position, a pause, indicated this was not to be. "What I think you should do if you're truly serious about helping this girl is look at this development as an opportunity to expand your abilities. You know she found her way to you from somewhere on the ethereal plane; that indicates the door in your head can open up to other places and given the kind of enemies we sometimes face, that's an advantage."

Alan paused. "So you are suggested I go exploring?"

Maybelle Tremens' face brightened. She leaned into him almost conspiratorially, an action Alan found uncomfortably intimate. "I'm suggesting, dear Ferryman, that you go *hunting*."

"I don't know if I'm ready for that."

She rose from the table. "If you can learn to traverse the astral planes," she told him as she moved to one of the bookcases, "it's an advantage. Many demons and other dimensional entities are weakened when they cross dimensional planes. They need to build up their power before fully manifesting. If you can ambush them before they're ready, the Legion can vanquish them before they become a true threat."

The spirits followed her, allowing him to watch the woman sort through one bookshelf. A soft glow was developing around her body, making her simple white linen blouse sparkle; an indication that her excitement was stimulating her mystical mutation. He stood up. "I'm not like you, Maybelle. I'm here to bring humans to justice, not slay monsters."

"Monsters kill normal human beings too, Alan. It's why they're called monsters. There it is!" She pulled a ragged looking book from the shelf, dusted it off with one delicate fingered hand. "You should read this. It should give you a good understanding of the things that dwell outside. I'm positive you can locate all of the creatures the girl drew within here."

When she put it in his hands, he already knew the name. The spirits had raked their eyes over the cover long before. *Monteleone's Demonological Concordance.*

"This is not how I imagined my life would go," he muttered more to himself than to her.

She put a hand on his arm. The nearness of her made his body ache like a broken tooth. The spirits renewed their whispering. When he blinked, he could see that many of them had gained more detail, seemed more active than they were before this situation began.

"I don't know about that," he heard the woman of his dreams, a woman who belonged to his best friend, say. "Colin always said you were devoted to helping people. Now you can help them in a way only you can."

He tucked the tome under his arm. "I wish I had your optimism."

"I'll do some research on my own. Between the two of us, we should be able to find out who this Red Lady really is."

•••

The book was illuminating.

It was not that Alan wasn't aware that there were strange and peculiar creatures dwelling on the edges of his reality; one of his friends and allies flickered back and forth between this world and another as a matter of course. But the sheer breadth of demons, demi-gods and monsters the *Concordance* was revealing to him was intimidating. He had no idea what lay beyond this veil, all the things that lay in wait to prey on this reality.

More importantly, he had no idea how he was going to deal with them.

He was in his own room at Palmersdale House, browsing through the Concordance looking for a creature that resembled what Katie had drawn. He didn't expect to find one; he still believed that what the girl drew was a child's conception of what Rose Red, obviously still alive in some form, looked like. But he valued Maybelle's counsel enough to at least consider that 'The Red Lady' might be something else entirely.

One of the shades inside his head, one of the few who resisted becoming a faceless shape, jeered and mocked him for not appreciating the brunette sorceress' mind. Alan's thoughts turned dark, ideas of figuring out which of his present residents was playing the jester and what he would do to it.

And then he felt a strange sensation in the back of his head; one he had experienced once before. He closed the old book so quickly the sound reverberated off the walls.

"Katie," he murmured before he sank away from this reality into the one he made to house all the ghosts and shades needing satisfaction.

This time he remembered to re-enter his sanctum in his plainclothes and not in the tattered cloak of Ferryman. Eyes that were sighted only in this dream world scanned the cavernous room where he plotted and planned without interference from anyone for the one splash of color amongst the grey.

Alan caught her crouching behind a chair. She was a little paler than she was the first time she arrived, as if she was painted in watercolor. He walked to her carefully, mindful of scaring her further. Her attention slowly turned to him, and Alan swore he saw something in her eyes that wasn't there in his first encounter with her.

Little Katie Yovich was showing signs of hope.

"You came," she said in a quiet little voice.

"Of course I came," he replied, getting down on one knee so he could keep his gaze level with hers. "I promised you, didn't I?"

"You came to my house," she added.

"Yes. I wanted to learn more about your family." He smiled gently. "Your mother misses you."

"I miss her, too," Katie admitted. "But I don't wanna bring the Red Lady back to hurt her."

"Was she chasing you now?"

Katie nodded her head. Around them, the tenants in his head hovered. "Katie, can you tell me why The Red Lady wants you?"

The little girl seemed to shudder. "She said she wants to make me her picture."

It took a moment for him to realize what she was saying. "She wants to make you in her own image?"

Once more, she nodded. Brief flashes of the kind of woman Rose Red was played behind his mind. He put a comforting hand on her shoulder; she felt fragile as if her bones were hollow like a bird's. "I wouldn't allow that to happen."

Alan was so focused on the girl he was unaware of the agitation amongst his spectral tenants. He swept the room to see the grey shapes milling about, a low thrumming moan of despair rising in the room. He strained to hear what these ghosts were saying amongst themselves and could only discern one thing.

They were scared.

Alan rose. His suit ran like melting wax, threads joining and reforming and darkening like his mood to become the raiment of the Ferryman. He flexed his fingers, and smoke gathered and formed to become his Colt Hammerlesses, the pistols gleaming with an unnatural newness in the realm of his mind.

"She's here!" the girl shrieked.

"Get behind me, and stay close, Katie." Ferryman held the pistols at the ready, a mixture of anticipation and apprehension running along his every nerve like wires. The grey shades around him swirled, getting more and more agitated. Those words spoken from dead lips became a little bit clearer, discernable in snatches. Words like 'demon' and 'evil' and 'Babylon' surfaced in his head.

And then the ground shook. Alan struggled to keep on his feet. There was a scream, a collected outburst of terror that came from everywhere at once.

"Mister!" Katie cried as she fell to the floor. Ferryman stepped backwards towards her, mindful of keeping her protected from whatever it was outside his sanctum.

There was another impact, one that cracked the outer wall of this sanctuary. A sharp pain exploded behind Alan's useless physical eyes, one worse than the worst headaches he had ever experienced. For a moment his mind's vision went dark and he was overwhelmed with the fear that the spirits would leave him blind both outward and inwards.

He felt the little girl's arms around his right leg. She clutched at him desperately, and he could almost feel the hope seeping out of her. Ferryman faced the crack, tried to re-exert his control over this sanctum of his mind. The crack struggled to close, even as one unnaturally long arm slid its way through, long black nails clicking together in a strange rhythm like the cackling of crows. He tried to focus past the thundering pain in his head, tried to block the sight of that painfully thin arm with its unnaturally grey skin dotted with crimson gaining purchase on the wall and pulling through the abomination it was connected to. That crack filled his view as it struggled to close only for the seams to burst again, a cycle of closing and opening, closing and opening.

Katie screamed.

There were now glimpses of what lay beyond, something that looked like that child's drawing he examined earlier only much, much worse. There was a strange, sickly light that seemed to emanate from behind the veil of stringy hair slick with blood, a dreadful white radiance that slashed through the semi-darkness of his sanctum like razor blades. It appeared to be wearing a strapless gown of sorts, but its clothing was in tatters, and dripped with a reddish-black ichor. The creature seemed emaciated, portions of its skeletal structure appearing underneath its pearly sallow skin.

Alan aimed for the creature's head and fired. He heard the sound of impact but there was no evidence of any damage. The spirits around him shrieked in horror, all voices intermingling into one overpowering shrill sound.

The intruder raised its head as it pulled itself further into the room. The gore-soaked hair swung in the air as it moved its around looking for its prey.

"*You have something of mine,*" the creature said as it focused on Ferryman.

He was aware of Katie's grip on his leg tightening. The urgency of repelling this monstrosity overwhelmed him. He automatically fired again as the creature freed one leg, the movement of the limb underneath its skirt smearing a swath of crimson on the cool grey floor. The size of the being knocked over nearby tables and weapons racks as it moved.

In the back of his head, rising from the increasing feeling he was out of his depth, was the confusion over what he was facing, and whether it could possibly have been Rose Red at one time. And elsewhere in his mind, he felt something slipping away.

Alan felt the overwhelming need to scream, to release whatever control he had left on his sanctum. The copper-sweet scent of blood was so heavy in his nostrils and in the back of his throat he feared he would suffocate. And there was this urge, this belief that what little sanity he had left was going to disappear the closer the intruder got.

But instead of going mad, he focused past his fear, his loosened grip on normalcy. He reminded himself that he had pledged to protect this little girl, and forced his memories of her mother to the surface. The wish he had to reunite this family came to the forefront of his thoughts.

And he focused past everything that told him to flee. He turned his attention to the shades. "*Push that...thing out of our home!*" he roared.

He could feel the hesitation of some of the ghosts around him. He exerted greater force on them, something he had learned from the study of Maybelle's library over so many years. His imperative increased in power, smacking into his tenants like waves. He felt an undercurrent of fear, another undercurrent of sadness. There was sense of many of these spirits casting their spectral gaze upon him in accusatory resignation.

But he could feel them moving forward with increasing speed, charging the thing that violated his mind. Alan watched, focused on the sight of these grey-ash ghosts smashing into the blood soaked thing. Initially, the spirits shattered upon hitting the Red Lady. With each of the ghosts that broke like glass against her crimson slick skin, a pain shot through his entire body. He found his legs buckling.

"Mister!" Katie's small hands were on one of his arms. He could hear her breathing as she struggled to prop him up. Before him, the Red Lady was slowing down, but still moving toward him. Some of the shades were now sticking against it, pushing it backwards, obscuring its features. He glanced over his shoulder and whispered, "Stay here. If the Red Lady comes too close, run."

Ferryman stepped forward, focusing on the weapons in his hands. His entire body was screaming in agony, and he struggled to grab hold of the overpowering pain and focus it through the guns he used to deliver justice for over a decade.

It was hard to see clearly through all the pinpoints of black that kept crawling through his vision. Through the haze, he thought he could perceive the black metal of the pistols grow and transform into something seemingly of flesh and bone. There was the strange impression of the handle becoming soft and actually pushing back at his grip.

The intruder, this Red Lady, was still advancing on him. Even as more and more of his ghostly tenants piled on top of her, it still moved, its skirts continuing to leave a dark crimson, copper scented trail behind it. Alan swung these new weapons toward the monster's face. There was this strange, subtle sound as they moved, a noise that he swore was growling.

He fired.

There was an explosion of ghostly, luminous white. Alan could barely perceive the spirits that had covered the creature flying away as strangely transformed bullets rocketed toward the female beast.

Upon impact, the Red Lady flew back against the wall from which she had emerged. The creature's greyish, decayed lips pulled back as it struggled back to its feet. Through crooked, needle-like teeth a hiss emerged that sounded more like steam escaping from broken pipes than anything human.

Ferryman rushed forward. He found himself struggling to keep his grip on the things his guns had become; it seemed as if they were striving to escape from his grasp. Not even bothering to look, he fired again. Once more the room was briefly bathed in a whitish light. He concentrated, focused on the wall behind the creature, willing it to flicker out of existence for the moments just after impact. The Red Lady flew backwards through his own personal sanctuary and Alan reconstituted the wall, envisioning it as thicker, made of steel and rivets. The spirits that remained gathered around him as the creature beyond the strengthened wall pounded against it; first as a relentless tattoos, then lessening before stopping.

For what seemed like an eternity, he stood, listening to his own breathing. He could feel his Ferryman outfit melting away; feel the things in his hands once more reverting to his trusty Colt Hammerless pistols. His heart beat against his ribcage madly.

He looked back at Katie. His body swayed unsteadily as his heartbeat slowed. "You should stay."

And that's when everything went black.

•••

When Alan emerged back into reality with a start, his breath stuck in his lungs. The image of The Red Lady was tattooed behind his eyes, so vivid that he feared she was still present somewhere, ready to chase him back into this world.

He sat absolutely still in his chair until he was breathing normally. Even after his heart rate slowed, Alan remained still, struggling to comprehend what he had just experienced. Only when he was comfortable that he was again in the real world did he rise from his seat. He stepped away on legs still unsteady, tamping down the urge to look over his shoulder.

He returned to the books with a renewed interest. He called out for the spirits to help him see the words within and was met with hollow spaces in his head, emptiness left there by the Red Lady's attack. There was a strange pain that throbbed in the back of his skull, a pulsing soreness that represented each ghost torn apart by the crimson monstrosity.

But slowly, amidst whispered accusations, some of his spectral residents moved outwards from his body, letting their sight be his. The book came into sharp focus. He riffled through the yellowed pages with a renewed desperation. The image of the abomination still vivid in his head, Alan scanned each illustration.

It was there in the middle. The resemblance was eerie, albeit exaggerated. The creature stood in the middle of carnage, but what struck him was the small circle of women and young girls in various states of undress dancing around, with faces and bosoms smeared with blood and waving body parts.

He scanned the prose surrounding the illustration. With each new bit of

He called out for the spirits to help him see the words.

information, he felt an increasing chill going through his body. All Alan's suspicions about the true nature of Katie's stalker did one thing.

It prevented him from discovering the true horror coming after the girl.

"La Domona Sangui," he murmured. He continued to read, learning of the nature of the evil he faced.

"I am not ready for this."

•••

"La Domona....I'm surprised," Maybelle said, arms folded. "I imagined whatever was plaguing your little friend had a pedigree that stretched back further."

"I don't think we should be joking."

The spirits lingered on the expression on the sorceress' beautiful face. There was a downturn of her lips, a slight softening of her gaze. He could feel the resentment in the remaining shades' voice when they told him they thought it was pity.

"Why are you torturing me," he whispered under his breath.

"*Why did you send our fellows into oblivion?*" the ghosts shot back sharply.

"Alan!"

He brought his full attention on Maybelle. "Yes?"

"You need to internalize any conversation you have with your tenants. I understand what's going on but if you ever want to regain a normal life, you have to manage your interactions with them better."

"Of course. You're right," Alan replied. "Why did you say that?"

She walked toward one of the many bookshelves in her study. "Anthropologists have found evidence of pre-civilization nastiness in the swamplands around Nocturne; probably explains why magick so infuses the city and why so many of the threats we're encountering are supernatural in nature. La Domona is a Dark Saint, a creature born out of Christian belief. I always suspected they'd be drawn more to European areas than this one. But there is a bright side to all this."

"I'm not so sure about that."

Maybelle ran her fingers along the spines of the books. The spirits followed along with her, giving Alan a close eye view. "Dark Saints are just like regular saints. They begin as ordinary people and then their actions attract the favor of some demonic personage and they transubstantiate into a demonic form themselves. An understanding of the woman who ascended to La Domona, her commendable qualities and her faults—"

"Can that give us insight into how we can defeat her?" Alan finished.

"Although you can take advantage of what we've learned about your abilities as well," she admonished, finally pulling a small, thin tome from the shelf. "Here we are!"

She walked over to the table they were sitting at. "The Concordance is very well written, but general. This book should give you a better grasp of Dark Saints in general, and La Domona in specific."

He picked up the book. It was cooler to the touch then expected, and made of knobble leather. "Thank you. What do you mean, taking advantage?"

She smiled secretly. Her head tilted to one side, and once more Alan ached at the sight of her beauty. "Well, how did you repel La Domona?"

"I was so frightened."

"Being frightened is a good thing," Maybelle admitted, moving closer to him. "Being frightened is natural, Alan."

"I ordered my tenants to attack that thing," he continued. "Some of them I can't feel them in my head any more. She destroyed them utterly, and I found it hard to concentrate through all the panic. I drew my pistols, and they changed in my hands and they were powerful enough to drive her away."

Her smile grew wider. "Of course you built that mental refuge by yourself after we dealt with Rose Red, right?"

Alan nodded.

"The mind is a powerful tool. You can create anything within its confines and because of the way you were affected by the events that made you Ferryman, it's given you such a degree of control that objects you create can affect certain tangible creatures on some psychic planes. Because La Domona was in your domain, you were able to use your imaginary weapons as if they were real weapons. You can use this to your advantage; work on fashioning something even more powerful, something that could repel her, even kill her."

"I don't know."

"You *can* do it. Not right now, but once you learn more about La Donoma, you can gear your creation to her weaknesses." She thought for a moment. "I may know someone you can talk to who can give you more insight on her. Let me call him and set up an appointment."

"I would appreciate that," Alan admitted, rubbing his temples for a moment. He worked to gather his thoughts before adding, "You seem to be, God help me, enjoying this."

"Well, this is my calling, what the Tremens women have been charged with for generations. I can't help but be a little excited by helping you deal with legitimate threats like this." She started heading out of the room. "I'll let you know when I make the arrangements for you to talk to my friend."

"Thank you for your help."

"You're welcome—and Alan?"

"Yes?"

"When you talk to Father Cranullo…be respectful."

Alan wondered what she meant.

•••

Alan wandered into what appeared to be a large Quonset hut tentatively. At the edge of the empty, garbage-strewn lot in St. Carruthers, a sign announced the place as the future site of St. George's Non-Denominational Christian Church. There was a definite scent of rot in the filthy ground surrounding the pre-fabricated building. As the spirits swirled around the area, Alan caught sight of clouds of grayish smoke rising and dissipating into the clear blue skies. It was a strange place for a church to be, hidden amongst the factories, warehouses and garbage dumps of the northernmost point in Nocturne.

The only evidence that this was an operating church, outside of the sign, was over the door; a simple cross seemingly made of steel and wood. Alan contemplated it for a moment before going through.

His footsteps echoed off the tin walls as he wandered through the rows of makeshift pews. There was an eerie silence to the place, a silence that allowed the remaining spirits to share mockeries of him amongst themselves.

"Hello?" Alan called out. "Father Cranullo?"

Alan heard a noise from the direction of the baptismal font. He sent out spirits just as a tall man rose from behind it. Alan got a sense of the man from all angles as the spirits begrudgingly granted him sight and, save for the shock of graying red hair, everything about the man was done in tones of black and white, from the skin that was so pale as to be translucent to the vividly grey eyes that seemed to shift their colors like clouds to the black of his own priestly garb. He held a wrench, and there were dark smears of dirt and grime on his hands and face. "I'm Father Cranullo. Can I help you?"

Alan stepped forward and offered his hand. "May Tremens called you about me. I'm Alan Dennings."

"Ah, yes. She did at that." He put down the wrench. "I have an office in the back. Why don't you make yourself comfortable there and I'll wash up.

I don't want to shake while I'm still messy from trying to fix up this font."

The priest gestured to a simple door to the left of the altar. As Alan walked towards it, he commented, "I would think there are plenty of handymen who could do that for you."

The pale, pale man laughed. "You don't know St. Carruthers. Between the smoke and the chemical stink, it's not conducive to people wanting to work or live here."

Beyond the door was a very simple space with two folding chairs, a desk, a standing closet and books—lots of books—some of them on the chairs.

Alan watched Father Cranullo take a pile of leather-bound tomes holding badly yellowed pages from one of the seats and reassign them to a pile near the closet. For a moment, the pile, now as high as the priest's chin, listed slightly to the left, and he spent what seemed like a long time adjusting the top items to correct this. Only when he was satisfied that the stack would not fall over did he motion Alan to sit and joined him on the seat next to the desk.

"Ms. Tremens told me you may have had a visitation from a Dark Saint?"

Behind his dark glasses, Alan raised an eyebrow. "She was that descriptive?"

The priest nodded. "She and this odd colorless fellow came to my aid once when I was in a parish up in Allyn. A possession case. We saved the child's life and it opened my eyes up to those darker edges of our reality. My willingness to talk about these edges has made me less than a darling with the Church which is why I'm here, ministering to the warehouses, contractors and ruins of this town."

"The creature I saw in my dreams matched the illustrations of La Domona Sangui."

It was now the priest's turn to raise his eyebrows. "La Domona? You may be out of your depth."

"I assure you, Father, that I am not some yokel who has stumbled into a mystical mystery. I am capable of extraordinary things."

The priest raised a hand. "Oh, please, I am not doubting your abilities. If Maybelle Tremens sent you here, I assume you have either skills or supernatural abilities that will make your struggle much more even than the average man on the street. I am just surprised she's exerting herself on the narrow world. "

The spirits swirled around Father Cranullo as he rose from his chair and snatched a book off the small shelf above the desk. "La Domona was a girl in the 15th century."

"Not a good time to be a young girl, I'd imagine."

"Especially not one as poor as she was," the priest responded as he rifled through the pages. "She was horribly abused by her father, physically and sexually. Her mother, not wishing to acknowledge the child's pleas for help, sold her to a local ne'er do well, who by turns raped and pimped her out to others. She eventually was beaten by a client and left for dead in the woods." As the story unfolded, Alan began to worry that this was a mistake; whether inadvertently or not, Father Cranullo was actually humanizing the monster he encountered in his sanctuary and made him wonder if the woman who destroyed his old life, Rose Red, was similarly human. He was aware of his hands, hands that had killed many men; if he knew what every one of the men was like, would he be able to do the job demanded of him by the specters in his head?

Father Cranullo held out the book. It was open to a page about La Domona, complete with another woodcut. "According to legends, as she lay dying, the devil came across her. Impressed that this frail little thing was holding on not because of love or fear or anything positive but because of rage at her life, he restored her to health and whispered in her ear what her purpose was. The girl wandered into town and sought out the daughters of its denizens. She whispered what she had learned from the devil in the ear of every girl child."

"I think I've seen depictions of what happened afterwards."

"Every male in the town, and every woman who had reached adulthood, were slaughtered, torn apart by the preternatural strength of La Domona and her band. Some of the men were partially eaten when the girls became hungry. The next day, they ventured to the next township, but were met by a special contingent of knights. Their weapons had been blessed by the Pope himself, and even though there were heavy losses, the knights did triumph. The few girls who survived were tortured and burnt at the stake for consorting with 'dark forces.'"

"Happy ending," Alan drawled.

"Not quite," the priest countered. For decades, reports of young girls in the immediate area were plagued by nightmares of a beautiful, blood soaked woman whispering to them, enticing them to kill their parents. Some of them succumbed ultimately, the Holy Church had the birthplace of La Domona burned to the ground, the land salted, and her body dug up and destroyed."

Alan took in this information. "Why would she want to re-enter our reality now?"

"I'm more interested in knowing why she's appeared to you. Are you a father?"

"No, I'm..."

"*Mister Alan!*"

Katie's voice was different in his head this time; it was more forceful, more frenzied.

"Are you alright, Mr. Dennings?"

"*Mister Alan!, PLEASE!*"

Alan tried to murmur something to excuse himself, but his mind was already retreating from the reality of the makeshift room, going down towards his own mindscape.

•••

Alan did not bother changing once he entered his mental sanctuary, preferring to be fully equipped as Ferryman. He glanced around the sparse war room. The colorful little girl was nowhere to be seen. Around him, the tenants who relied on him for vengeance glared silently. The anger, the recriminations were palatable. He stepped forward, calling out, "I'm here, Katie, where are you?"

The answer came from beyond the far wall. "She's chasing me, Mister Alan! Help!"

Alan stared at the solid wall. The words of Maybelle Tremens came to him, words about being able to exert his influence on his interior landscape. He drew his Colt Hammerless and stalked forward, an image forming inside his head.

In front of him, the wall bubbled and boiled. A shape roughly the size of a door grew liquid and slid aside, providing a hole for him to venture through.

There was a small touch of fear as he stepped outside of his sanctuary. He never wondered what lay beyond his secret place, and the uncertainty was threatening to overwhelm him. He silently bid his tenants to move before him, searching for Katie and her pursuer.

What met him were corridors sheathed in darkness. A light wind ran through the seemingly endless halls, caressing his form with alternating waves of cold and heat. On either side of him were irregularly shaped windows like open wounds, each one displaying hazy images of jet and grey that shifted like water with each footstep.

"Katie!" he called out. His vision was a jumble of different angles as his tenants swooped through the different corridors, the walls seeming to expand and contract in time with the wind that swept past him.

And there she was running down one of these weirdly pulsating halls, La Domona a dark shape that seemed huge in contrast to the surroundings a ways behind her, skeletal elbows actually distending the material on either side of her.

He gripped his pistols tighter, struggled to keep fear from rising up inside him. "*Guide her back to her sanctum. Quickly!*" he commanded the tenant who spotted the young girl.

There was a sense of resistance but only for a moment and then he saw through the shade's eyes how it interposed itself between the Katie and the Dark Saint and propelled the young girl forward towards their home.

Ferryman charged toward La Domona. He focused on the Colts, tried to reach out and reshape them as he subconsciously did before. The guns softened in his hands, started to transform. He did his best to recall the way the weapons reconfigured in that last confrontation, worked to imagine further growth to make these two pistols even more effective, his head filled with ways to harm a Dark Saint.

Up ahead, he saw the smudgy gray shape of the spirit, Katie in its arms. He had the strange sensation of seeing himself and the spirit passing each other, the weird nature of his ghostly vision giving him both angles. "*Keep her safe,*" he barked as his tenant sped her to the questionable safety of his mental room.

La Domona approached, her form radiating with a dark light. The coppery tang of blood was heavy on his tongue and in his nostrils. Even in the shadow, her eyes were like pinpricks of flame.

In his hands, his weapons seemed to struggle, as these guns wanted to retreat from this female horror's advances. Ferryman exerted further mental pressure on the two items, trying to shape them into weapons antithetical to La Domona's very existence. He saw them start to transmogrify, but then the change would stop, the alterations sink back under the handgun's surface.

"*You keep me from what is mine.*" The voice of La Domona Sangui came from nowhere and everywhere, a liquid tone that sounded like a slowly melting bell. A gash seemed to tear open on her heart shaped face, revealing a mass of crooked, yellow needles that Alan knew were her teeth.

"*She does not belong to you,*" he said in his best Ferryman voice, "*She belongs to her family!*"

"*Are you part of her family?*" The Dark Saint asked as the burning pits that were her eyes flared and flickered. "*Have you begun showing her the back of your hand? Have you pinned her down yet and exerted your dominance over her?"*

He extended his arm and fired instinctively, each bullet setting off a flash of light that illuminated the Dark Saint's true nature. She moved forward slowly, barely acknowledging the presence of these super-heated projectiles digging themselves into her unholy flesh. His remaining tenants retreated, memories of what happened to their fellows still fresh. Alan struggled against the dimming of his supernatural vision, fear rising in the pit of his soul. He kept trying to impose his will on his mental reality, but the increasing dread dominated his thoughts. He found his conceptions dissolving the moment he grasped hold of them.

"I have known what families do to little girls," La Domona continued. He perceived in the landscape of shadows and light that was all that left of his vision that she was reaching out with her talon-tipped hands. *"I know the tender mercies they will receive from them. I will make her stronger, make her powerful. I will help her and her sisters lead an army to raze this patriarchal world."*

Alan could feel her hand brush against him. It radiated an impossible cold. Through his impaired vision, he perceived La Domona's mouth opening and closing. His terror was overwhelming, amplified by his feeling of abandonment. He searched for his tenants and could only catch glimpses of them, hiding in the corners of his sanctum, all surrounding little Katie, a splash of color in an ever-shifting field of desperate grey.

At first he was going to compel the spirits to come to his aid, to give their shred of existence to protect him. His guns barked again wildly, stopping La Domona's advance but not pushing her back.

He stopped. Briefly he thought of Mrs. Yovich, of the sadness in her eyes, of the desperation in her face.

The gun in his right hand changed.

He took the gun in his left and aimed for the jagged yellow field in the darkness. He fired once, then twice.

To his satisfaction, the infernal woman's head snapped back. Without even thinking, he swung what had once been a pistol towards her and fired.

La Domona was hit with a blast of holy water. She shrieked with the sound of a thousand out of tune violins. He fired again and again, each blast driving her away. Fear began to bleed away, replaced by exultation as the creature actively retreated.

He kept Katie's mother foremost in his mind as he watched her leave. For a long moment, he was alone with his own breathing.

When he was sure La Domona was not returning right away, he said, *"I need one of you to be my eyes. Everyone else, stay with Katie. Protect her. And I promise this threat to all of us will be over."*

And then he returned to the reality of Nocturne.

•••

When he found himself back in Father Cranullo's, the priest asked, "Are you all right?"

"A little shaken," Alan admitted. "But I think I have a solution."

•••

"Are you sure you want to do this?" Maybelle Tremens asked.

Alan struggled to perceive his gorgeous friend. Although he could feel his tenants' reluctance, they agreed to allow one of their kind to provide his sight but it was the sight he had experienced before he became the Ferryman. After being able to see things from all different angles, to swoop and pry into what happened beyond walls, the ability to just see as anyone one else could was disappointing.

But this is for Katie, he reminded himself.

He nodded. "This is her weakness. This is what will drive her back through the door."

He reached out and rang the bell. Alan was wearing the gray suit and black turtleneck he wore as Ferryman, choosing only to forgo the cloak he usually wore in favor of a black topcoat. The blindfold pressed against the ruined sockets of his skull. Maybelle was dressed plainly in a white linen blouse and skirt; only her jacket with the elaborate symbol on the back hinted at her heroic identity.

When Mrs. Yovich answered the door, her haggard face grew confused. "Mr...Mr. Dennings?"

"Do not be alarmed, Mrs. Yovich," he said calmly. "I have a way to bring your daughter to you. Ms. Tremens is here to aid me. Is your husband here?"

He could hear footsteps. A tall, slight man, bald on top save for some wisps of hair, came up behind the woman. "Who the hell?"

"Mr. Yovich, this is my work outfit."

"What do you work as," the man shot back, "a circus freak?"

Maybelle put a hand on Alan's shoulder. "We help people with unusual

"Who the hell?"

problems, and your daughter's spirit seems to have been dislocated from her body. We can bring her back, unite body and soul but we need your help."

"Who are these charlatans, Margaret?"

He focused on the mother. "Mrs. Yovich, I told you when we last met that there were strange things in this world, and I have encountered them in the past. This is my guise when I enter these weird edges of this reality. Just as I promised, I have located the part of Katie that is missing, I am keeping her safe and if you and your husband aid me in driving the thing that wants to hurt her away, you will have Katie back."

"This is insane!"

She stared at him for a long time, then glanced over at Maybelle. There was a moment when Alan feared she would bow to her husband's request. "You kept your promise?"

"I did."

"Then please come in."

•••

The four of them sat by Katie's bedside. Alan had feared that the husband's belligerence would cow Mrs. Yovich but as with their meeting several days before, her hope seemed palpable. Her desire to hold her living daughter again overruled his suspicions, which led to them being here.

The sun was setting, casting reddish light on the quartet. Alan outlined what he needed them to do carefully, making sure they understood the risk.

"You are not serious!" Mr. Yovich exclaimed at one time, then turned to his wife. "Margaret, you can't believe this?"

"Of all the people who offered help, Mr. Dennings is the only one who's come back, who's given me answers."

"The ravings of a lunatic! Surely you can't believe this mumbo jumbo?"

"Do you want your daughter back?" Alan snapped. His mouth compressed into a tight, thin line. "I know this is hard to believe, Mr. Yovich, but there *are* things out there in the shadows, things that wish all of us, man, woman, child, dead or worse. I've faced these things down. I've *fought* one of them, barely survived, simply to keep your daughter's soul safe enough that you and she can be reunited. We can bring her back, but your participation is essential if we are to save her from the monstrosity that's pursuing her."

"She's in danger?" Mrs. Yovich asked.

"She was in danger," Alan assured her, placing a comforting hand on hers. "I have placed her somewhere safe for now. If you and your husband cooperate, we can whisk her away before that place becomes unsafe. Time is of the essence."

Mr. Yovich shook his head. He scowled. "This can't be real."

"If it isn't real," Maybelle suggested calmly, "then you have nothing to lose in humoring us and you can bring us up on charges as confidence men afterwards."

Mrs. Yovich glanced over at her husband with pleading eyes. Alan couldn't help but notice that this woman seemed to be sitting straighter, more confidence since his last visit. "Donald, please."

Alan saw Mr. Yovich's eyes flash. He feared that the man's stubbornness would continue but then his shoulders fell, his expression softened. "Fine," he mumbled, "but if you're lying…"

"We know," Alan said.

"Before we begin," Maybelle said. The smile had fled from her face, the perpetual sparkle in her eyes that Alan found so beautiful dimmed. "Please understand that when Katie comes back, she will be different. She's sensitive to things that belong in the other planes like the one that seeks to possess her, and that sensitivity needs to be acknowledged, not ignored. You will need to help her come to grips with the gift that she's been given. I will work with you if you want, but you have to accept the girl you're getting back is not the girl who left you."

The parents of Katie Yovich simply nodded, their hands clasped. Maybelle placed her left hand on top of the couple's, and her right on Alan's shoulder. The telltale sparking glow that indicated that Maybelle Tremens was dipping into the reservoir of mystical energy she constantly absorbed flitted across the surface of her body, rapidly expanding to envelope all of them.

"Go," the woman who went under the codename Dreamcatcher said.

•••

Alan descended down into himself, transitioning himself from his state in reality to Ferryman. Unlike other times, however, he was aware of Margaret and Donald Yovich's psychic energy following behind him like two glowing ribbons. He held onto them, knowing that they were his secret weapons in this fight.

Then all three of them alighted on the floor of his mental sanctum. Like him, like Katie, the Yoviches were in color; although now they seemed younger, less beaten down by the experiences they endured in the last few weeks. Ferryman could imagine that this was what this family was like before Katie began receiving these visions from the other side.

Donald, no longer needing glasses, fully shaved, his face no longer marred by anger or hurt, looked around, mouth agape. "Where are we?"

"Daddy!"

Both Yoviches' attentions were drawn to a corner of the sanctum, where the shades had moved aside to allow Katie to greet her parents. Mrs. Yovich stood frozen as her young girl ran towards her, then collapsed to her knees. Tears started flowing down her face as the mother held her arms open for the daughter to leap into. Ferryman felt some twinge of pleasure at watching the two reunited.

Donald Yovich watched his family. His question seemed forgotten.

"You should be safe in here," Ferryman told the three. "My associates will help protect you if anything goes wrong, and Ms. Tremens has connected all of us, so if I fail, she will pull all three of you back to our reality."

He turned away from mother, father and child, his mind already focused on re-opening the door he had made the last time he was here. The wall had already begun bubbling and boiling to produce the opening.

"Where are you going?" Donald Yovich asked.

Ferryman did not stop moving towards the doorway he made. "The creature stalking your daughter is outside, most likely very nearby. I am going to drive it away permanently so she never has to fear it again."

He heard footsteps behind him. "I'm going with you."

Ferryman turned to face Yovich. "This is very, very dangerous, Mr. Yovich. Ms. Tremens has us all connected, and I can use that connection to empower me. You are better served by staying here, where you're protected."

"This is my daughter!" Yovich declared. "I won't let some stranger risk his life to save her while I sit idly by!"

Ferryman stared at him. "You stay behind me. You do not endanger yourself. Your first, your *only* task is to stay alive so Katie has a complete family. Understood?"

Donald Yovich nodded.

"Good. Come with me then."

•••

The two men stepped out into the plane outside Ferryman's secret sanctum. The endless corridors undulated before them, breathing as if they were living things.

Behind him, Yovich muttered, "What the hell?"

"Shhh," Ferryman said. The wind from the hallways plucked at his tattered cloak. In amongst all the warm winds sliding around him was one that was hot, fetid and tasting faintly of copper.

He unholstered his Colt Hammerless. "I know you are here," he called out in defiance. "Show yourself."

The sole spirit who provided him with sight scanned for the presence of La Domona. He exerted his influence on his weapons, and felt them soften and flow around his hands.

And then that one wind was at his back. Ferryman spun around, the two pistols in his hands growing and shifting, taking on a golden patina, a soft light emanating from their surface. His body tensed, and in the back of his head he wondered if he had made a mistake in putting this mad scheme in motion.

She melted out of the darkness, peeling herself off one of the furthest walls of the furthest corridor. Her dress trailed blood across the floor, each footstep accompanied by the whisper-quiet *shurring* of fabric on stone. The strange pinpricks of light regarded Ferryman malevolently, before her needle-toothed grin burst open.

"You brought the parents to me. It will make it easier to show the child the truth when I split them apart in front of her."

"You do not belong here!" Ferryman proclaimed, the pistols now a strange amalgam of Christian symbols and parochial weaponry. Both were surprisingly light in his hand. "You had your time on Earth, and now you need to go back where you came from!"

La Domona stood up, a dark and ominous rumbling coming from her that Ferryman knew was laughter. *"Have you looked around these days, little man? My sex is brutalized, raped, murdered—used as slaves under the context of 'marriage'—played with as toys in the worst way by their fathers—girls like the one you think you are protecting? They need me now more than ever..."*

"You focus on the smallest tree," Ferryman shot back as he raised one of his weapons, "And do not look at the mighty oaks all around it."

He fired. There was a sound of chimes so loud that they seemed to make the walls around him shake. A bright white light exploded from the multitude of openings in the weapon, throwing the creature back into the far wall. La Domona slid to the ground, her skin smoking, and Ferryman advanced, raising the other gun. "There is something stronger than you, foul thing; the love of parents for their child."

As he moved closer to the creature, Ferryman fired the other gun. This one thrummed like the loudest bass drum in the world, and a column of smoke barreled from the weapon. A hole opened up in La Domona's chest, releasing a strange mist of crimson.

The Dark Saint shifted on the floor, got up on one knee. The crimson that flowed from her wound drifted upwards improbably. Ferryman was now close enough to place the barrel of both guns on the monstrosity's forehead. That dark laughter started again, and a weird sense of unease came over him.

Before he could react, La Domona struck out with one long, nailed hand. Ferryman fell backwards. He could see his weapons falling and skidding across the floor. He scrabbled to his feet, and was met with another blow from the unholy thing that drove him into a nearby wall with the force that made stars explode across his vision.

"*You are pathetic*," it told him as he felt its blackened nails slash his clothes and open up his flesh. Ferryman tried to twist away from La Domona, and was smacked in the side of his head. "*I will show the girl what your true intentions are...and she will kill her parents and lead my new army. You cannot stop her. You cannot stop me.*"

A clacking filled his ears as her hand closed around his head. He felt himself being lifted up. A horrific stench of decay and corruption filled his mouth and nostrils suffocating him as he rose higher and higher in the air.

"You never let me finish," Ferryman gasped. He sought out the spiritual link Maybelle had forged, seized it in his mind.

The monster stopped. Ferryman remained suspended, not sure how far down solid ground was. "*There is nothing you can say to stop me.*"

"You're wrong," he called out as he embraced the energies of that link, accepted it into himself. "I have a parent's love and a parent's love can create miracles!"

And the Ferryman grew. In a matter of seconds, he had burst out of La Domona's grasp and towered over her. She stood up, that needle-filled mouth curled into a snarl. With one enlarged hand, he slapped the creature down the long corridor.

"You made the mistake of coming into my domain!" he roared as she managed to stop herself. "And I'm going to send you back whence you came."

From behind that veil of bloody hair came an inarticulate yowl of rage. It came at him, the tatters of its clothing whipping around its body. Ferryman braced himself and made to scoop the abomination in his hand but it ducked under his oversized fingers and wove around his legs.

A white hot, unbearable pain burst across the back of his ankle, and Ferryman fell.

The dark, rumbling laughter filled the landscape. *"How long have you been on Earth, pathetic little fool? Twenty years? Thirty?"*

He tried to roll over on his back. There was a wetness spreading from his ankle, soaking his shoes. He could feel himself shrinking, the link receding in his mind. La Domona stood over him, one hand stained a bright scarlet. *"I have had influence on this world for centuries, little fool. I know how to bring giants down, even false giants like yourself and I know what you need."*

She reached out for his chest, her nails glittering in the air. The pain in his ankle throbbed.

And then her head exploded in a mass of red mist.

Ferryman craned his head upwards to see Mr. Yovich cradling one of the pistols with both hands. "I won't let you get my daughter!"

As the creature's body shuddered into a mist floating upwards like smoke, the two men locked eyes. An understanding passed between them, and Ferryman glanced around to locate the other weapon. Finding it on the ground roughly ten feet from him, he turned on his stomach and tried to pull himself towards the pistol that, in his own reality, was a Colt Hammerless. The pain stung him like a hornet with each inch he moved.

Ferryman glanced back at La Domona. The crimson smoke had stopped its ascent. It seemed to hang in the air, frozen like a photograph, before the mass contracted in on itself, wisps reforming to restore the malevolent thing's head.

Ferryman's hand reached for the other gun. He propped himself up with one elbow and swung the bizarre pistol in the Dark Saint's direction. "Mr. Yovich, fire!"

Ferryman pulled the trigger just as that thrumming noise reverberated off the walls. The light from his pistol was overpowering as it hit La Domona, pushing her backwards against the column of smoke that tore apart the creature's head and shoulders. More and more of La Domona's body was ravaged as the light and dark pistols tore her apart.

Silently, Ferryman mentally reached for the link that had been severed by La Domona's attack. The moment he had contact with that font of energy, he willed himself once more to grow. As he gained mass, he grasped the unholy thing in his right hand and held what remained up to his face.

"As I said before," Ferryman told the Dark Saint, "you do not belong here."

It was reforming itself at an alarming rate. *In a few seconds, she'll be whole,* he realized.

La Domona twisted in his grasp. Her claws bit into the flesh of his hand, but Ferryman was already pulling his arm back. *"Do you truly think you will be rid of me, pathetic meat? Who do you think you are?"*

"I am the Ferryman, profane thing. I patrol the edge of this reality," he answered. "And you are being denied passage."

He mustered all his strength as he reached the same height he had achieved before and tossed her into the air as hard and far as he could. He watched La Domona turn end over end, pieces of her damaged form breaking apart and scattering.

He continued watching long after the monstrous creature disappeared from the horizon. Slowly, his form returned to its normal size. The pain in his ankle intensified as he shrunk down. The guise of the Ferryman melted away as the dark hero gave way to plain Alan Dennings. Alan struggled to pull himself up, wincing at the sharp pain that the simplest movement brought him, when he felt arms reaching out to pull him up gently.

"I have you," Donald Yovich told him. He placed one arm over the man's shoulders and kept his injured ankle elevated.

"Thank you," Alan said.

"You fought for my daughter," Katie's father replied. "This is the least I can do."

"We still have a way to go."

•••

They gathered in his sanctum. Katie ran forward to hug the both of them. Alan felt a strange wash of gratefulness as the little girl embraced him, and realized that this was a feeling he needed that was sorely missing.

Mrs. Yovich came up behind her daughter. She looked from Alan to her husband then back. Mr. Yovich nodded. "He did it. Whatever that was that was after our girl is gone."

"I don't know if we actually killed it," Alan said. Katie moved away to her mother's side. Around them, the spirits hovered, moving forward but keeping their distance. "She, *it*, was not of this plane. But I tried to fling her as far as I could. Who knows where she landed; if that thing is still capable of reforming, she may takes years or decades to find her way back; at which point we can make sure your daughter is ready."

He looked towards Mr. Yovich. "Right now we need to get all of you into our normal plane of existence. Hold onto me."

As the Yovich family clung to his form, he caught sight of some of his tenants staring at him, their intentions clear. He nodded to them, letting them know he would return to his mission of avenging them shortly.

He reached out to the Maybelle's link. He visualized himself grasping it, riding it upwards and slowly, in the secret mental sanctum of Ferryman, a quartet of people faded away.

•••

Alan emerged into his reality at the edge of Katie's bed. Maybelle moved forward, her expression changing from concern to relief. The pain in his ankle was still very present, throbbing rhythmically. To either side of him, he was aware of the Yovich parents coming to consciousness as if from a deep sleep.

Maybelle's hands glowed as she slid them over Alan's body lightly. He felt his pain lessen. "Thank you," he said.

Margaret Yovich went from her chair to Katie's bed. She clasped the little girl's wrist with one hand, the other going to her forehead. Alan and Katie's father watched anxiously as the girl seemed to stay very still. Alan's heartbeat quickened, and he feared his efforts were for nothing.

But then a moan escaped the little girl's lips. Her eyes fluttered as she shifted position. Donald Yovich practically launched himself from his chair to join his wife in embracing little Katie.

And Alan's heartbeat quickened for another reason entirely.

•••

As they walked away from the Yovich residence, Maybelle said, "I'm glad you did this."

Alan looked at the beautiful mystic. Once more he felt the pang of desire. "I was just doing what I always do: helping people."

"But this is different," Maybelle replied. "I worry about you sometimes. Ever since that party that changed you, you seem to spend your life stuck with one foot in the afterlife. I worry you're losing track of your real life. Alan, when you're not off on one mission or another avenging some ghost trapped in your head, you're in my library. You need to restart your life again; not this life, but the life you had before you gained your power."

"But there are so many of them. New ones every day, demanding satisfaction, needing resolution so they can move on."

"But they *are* dead, and you're alive. You need to take care of yourself to take care of them."

Alan felt himself flush. "But they're so insistent."

"And they've got eternity ahead of them. They can wait." Maybelle sighed. "Alan, you've gained a better understanding of your abilities. There are new things you can learn but only if you live your life for *you*. You discovered these things because you weren't obsessed with vengeance, but with salvation. And you saved that girl's life, and most likely the life of her parents. I'm proud of you."

Alan paused. "I will think about it."

"See that you do."

•••

Alan Dennings adjusted his jacket and stepped into the wooded area. His heart raced, unsure of what the hours ahead of him would bring. He felt strange being dressed so casually, and wondered for the fifth time if this was a bad idea.

Bird songs filled the air. There was a strong scent of grass and flowers, and a light breeze rustled his hair. The spirits swirled around the place, giving him a multi-angled view of the beauty surrounding him.

He was about to turn around, when a familiar joyous noise stopped him. "Uncle Alan! Uncle Alan!"

The spirits focused in on little Katie Yovich, her angelic face smiling widely as she rushed towards him. Margaret Yovich rose from one of the far lawns to follow after her daughter.

Alan hesitated, then got down on one knee and accepted Katie's hug with open arms. The little girl giggled as she hugged him back.

As Margaret came up to him, Alan realized what a beautiful woman she really was. No longer marred by sadness and distress, she was full of life. "Thank you for coming."

"Thank you for inviting me," he answered.

As he felt the affection coming off of both mother and daughter, Alan realized one thing. Maybelle Tremens was right; he needed to start living a life of his own.

And here was the best place to start.

The End

NOTES ON THE FERRYMAN

While I was working on *New Roads To Hell,* the first Shadow Legion novel (available from the same place you got this book), I decided to write a novella for each of the four heroes introduced therein. Since there are twenty-five year gaps between the first three novels of the series, I thought it would be good to fill in readers on what happened to these heroes and the world during those periods. It also allowed me to explore some of the characters more deeply—as I've mentioned elsewhere, if you look at the novels as a graphic novel collecting a single story line of the Shadow Legion comic, each of these novellas represent a single story from the comic book following that hero's solo adventures.

Which leads us to 'A Waltz In Scarlet.' Even though Ferryman is one of the two heroes whose origin story is one of the main narrative threads of *New Roads,* there was still work to be done with him. To be precise, I leave Alan Dennings' in a place where, due to his powers and what they give him, he is pretty isolated. He's got a version of his sight back but only at the expense of being the social worker for the unjustly dead. He's had his life's work taken away from him and he has serious unrequited lust for his best friend's girl. If you look at him at the end of the novel, there's no reason for him to continue interacting with the real world.

So with 'Waltz,' I endeavored to give The Ferryman some new connections to humanity. Since Alan's condition has let the newly dead sit in his head until justice is done, I posited that the door to his head is open...and anything can walk through. I had the visitor who wanders in unexpectedly in mind right away and little Katie shaped up to be another bit of connective tissue between the first and second novel, as you'll see in due time. I figured having this special little girl in peril might also give me a chance to put Alan in close proximity with his personal obsession, the sexy sorceress called Dreamcatcher, and confront his feelings about what happened in his first adventure.

The other thing I'm trying to do with this, and the other three novellas that will make up *The Shape of Fears to Come,* is expand upon the mythology behind the Chimera Falls Universe. Given Ferryman's status as a mystic avenger, it allowed me to expand upon the pantheon of demons that plague the city of Nocturne.

But then, I think most of you might be intrigued by the concept of Dark Saints. I'm sure I'm not the first person to reason that there can be malevolent Saints like the one we meet herein. Any creative person who, like me, were raised Catholic must have wondered why Hell didn't have its own cadre of men and women who are elevated due to their devotion to the realm's tenants. I think La Domona Sangui makes a unique villain much as the other villains in these novellas are—that gave Ferryman a different challenge from the one he encountered in *New Roads,* much as I hope the menace in the next novel will be unique from the first novel's delicious devious dish, Rose Red.

My close friend Derrick 'Dillon' Ferguson pointed out that each of the novellas I've been writing reflect different genres that were popular in the history of comics. In the case of The Ferryman, I like to think this story is a callback to the pre-Vertigo horror comics of the 80's, especially given the way those prototypical heroes dwelled on the edge of the DC Universe. I like to also think that I put Alan in a better place emotionally and power-wise, but only you can tell me that. Thank you for reading.

•••

THOMAS DEJA - has been writing professionally for almost twenty-five years. Starting with a column and random horror serials in the seminal Brooklyn 'zine *Inside Joke,* Thomas began placing stories in such independent magazines as *After Hours* and *Not One of Us* before becoming one of the contributing book reviewers and feature writers for *Fangoria* magazine, a position he kept for over fifteen years. He wrote stories featuring classic Marvel Super-heroes for such anthologies as *The Ultimate Hulk* and *Five Decades of The X-Men.* Recently, he had become known for writing stories in what he calls "The Chimera Falls Universe," including tales in both editions of *How The West Was Weird,* and the Shadow Legion series, starting with *New Roads To Hell.* Along with his best friend Derrick Ferguson, Thomas co-hosts *Better In The Dark,* a (more or less) bi-weekly movie podcast. Thomas' passion for film has extended to maintaining *Damn Your Ears! Damn Your Eyes!,* a blog where he publishes his notorious '10 Statements About' kinda, sorta movie reviews. A lifelong Jets fan, he also writes and podcasts about football for Tricycleoffense.com. Thomas lives in New York City, something he hopes to rectify soon.

People who are interested in learning more about the Chimera Falls Universe are invited to visit The Nocturne Travel Agency at http://welcometonocturne.blogspot.com/

THE ADDER, THE EEL, & THE BOMBER IN:
"CULT OF THE STRANGLER"

By Joel Jenkins

It was midday and the sun rested briefly at its apex shedding its unforgiving rays upon the Manhattan city streets, when a battered yellow cab pulled up in front of the First Manhattan bank, right onto the sidewalk amidst a gaggle of dismayed pedestrians. Cabby Donald Defrenzio gripped the steering wheel with sausage-like fingers and ignored the angry jeers of the displaced pedestrians. He wiped away a bead of sweat from his forehead and glanced into the back seat where a man dressed entirely in black, including a low slung fedora checked a brace of .38 revolvers to make sure that they were fully loaded.

"This good, boss?" asked Donald.

Vincent Spinelli, known to the criminals of New York as only The Eel, preferred to do his work in the dead of the night where he could operate in obscurity and shadow; however sometimes necessity dictated otherwise. He scowled from beneath his handlebar mustache. "This will have to do. Thanks for the lift, Donald and thanks for the tip."

Donald gave a tense shrug that threatened to split the seams of his jacket. "Sometimes a cabby hears things. I thought news of an attempted robbery might be something you'd be interested in."

Satisfied that both revolvers were fully loaded, the Eel shoved one back into its holster, but retained the other in hand as he eased open the back door. "You overheard who talking about it?"

"Two turbaned East Indian chaps said it was going down today at noon. They spoke quietly, but I have sharp ears."

The Eel smiled. Besides fingers thick as sausage links, Donald had large ears that protruded from either side of his cabby's cap. "Pull around back of the bank. If I'm not out in fifteen minutes, or if the police show, make yourself scarce."

"Got it," nodded Donald.

"Say hi to Teresa and the kids for me." Then the Eel was out onto the street, his dark jacket flapping around his knees as even the jaded residents of Manhattan cleared the way for the dark clad man with the brim of his hat pulled low to conceal his features. In a few moments the Eel was up the concrete steps and through the front door of the First Manhattan Bank and into the tiled and spacious lobby that was flanked by fluted granite pillars.

Corpses lay strewn wherever the Eel cast his eyes, their eyes glazed. There was no sign of life within the lobby. The counters and desks were empty, papers scattered across the floor and chairs upended. Cash draw-ers were opened and emptied with just a few stray bills that lay upon the floor. As the Eel drew nearer to a high society woman who lay ashen faced, carefully coiffed hair splayed upon the floor, he noticed the bulging eyes and the marks of a strangler's cord upon her neck. With his left hand, the Eel checked for a pulse and found no sign of life. He moved onto the next body, a uniformed bank security officer. His holster was empty; there was a bruise upon his forehead and marks around his neck. There was no whis-per of breath or tremor of heartbeat in his chest. It was the same for each of the patrons and bank employees. All of them had been strangled to death.

Apparently he had been far too late to prevent both the robbery and the deaths of everyone who had been in the bank, but who would be so ruth-less to slay everyone within the bank, and the victims of these murderers had been dead for at least half an hour. With an unlocked bank door, why hadn't other patrons of the bank entered and stumbled upon the crime be-fore the Eel had arrived. Surely, a busy bank like this would have enough customers that these bodies would have been discovered between the time of the murders and the time that the Eel had arrived.

These thoughts were swept away when a muffled scream reverberated from the rear of the bank. The Eel leaped to his feet and ran for the open vault that was imbedded in concrete walls behind the tellers' counters and desks. The thick door was open and at the rear of the pillaged vault was a teller that was bound hand to foot and a gag tied between her teeth. Her auburn hair spilled about her shoulders and she trembled in fear as a taran-tula the size of a rat crawled up her stockinged shin.

The Eel was a handy enough aim to hit such a target, but the slightest flinch from the teller might move her into the bullet's path, so rather than risk a shot with his revolver he flicked out with the tip of his boot and send the spider flailing across the vault, to strike at the corner of the far wall. Stunned, the spider began to scuttle back in the direction of the teller and that was when the Eel put a bullet through its fat body, spattering its bilious innards across the floor.

With a flourish, the Eel spun his revolver back into its holster and drew a narrow blade which he always kept secreted on his person. He reached into the auburn tresses of the teller and carefully cut away the gag. "They're back!" she shrieked. "They're back!"

The Eel heard the creek of the vault door's great hinges and he whirled, pistol leaping back into his hand. For a moment he caught a glimpse of two turbaned figures who drew the vault door closed. They were moving quickly and the door would fast be beyond stopping. The Eel was too far away to reach the vault door and stop it, but he knew a bullet could travel faster than he could. He snapped off a shot at the closest Punjabi who had hold of the great wheel at the front of the vault door and was hauling it closed. The bullet struck in the center of the Punjabi's forehead and he pitched backward, his body falling between the door and the jamb of the vault, keeping it from closing and locking The Eel and his captive companion inside.

Now, the Eel sprinted toward the vault door firing his pistol as he ran, but these remaining bullets were not so accurately aimed as the other, and though some slipped through the narrow gap, another ricocheted from the edge of the vault door, and none connected with the sliver of the other turbaned figure that seized the feet of his fallen brother and was drawing him out of the vault. The Punjabi must have had some help because this was accomplished faster than the Eel thought possible and the body disappeared, trailing only the scarf worn by the dead man. The Eel stomped a boot down on the scarf and reached for his second pistol, hoping to fire through the narrowing gap and kill the other Punjabi or Punjabis that were pulling the vault door closed.

Instead of his boot stopping the body from being withdrawn from the vault, the scarf unraveled from the corpse and the vault door closed, the lock clicking into place, and the Eel still standing on the scarf. He eased off the trigger, since firing now, against the vault door, would only result in ricocheting bullets that might kill or injure himself and the auburn-haired teller, which were now trapped inside. Ruefully he knelt down, gathered up the scarf, wrapped it and pushed it into one of the many pockets inside his vest.

"Who are you?" asked the teller.

Spinelli rose to his feet and approached the captive woman, kneeling beside her. "People call me the Eel. Now turn to the side so I can cut your bonds."

She rolled on to her side so that the Eel could cut the ropes that tied her wrists to her ankles. Her voice trembled. "I don't know why they let me live. There were seven or eight of them, and they strangled everyone else in the bank. I expected them to do the same to me, but they tied me up and brought me in the vault."

"Don't try to stand up right away. Wait for your circulation to recover." The Eel finished cutting her bonds. "Did they want you to open the safety deposit boxes?"

She shook her head. "These can't be opened without two keys, one of them that only the customer possesses. At least that's what I thought. One of the Punjabis was able to pick the locks quite easily, but besides the cash they were only interested in certain boxes. They seemed to know what they were looking for. I'm not sure what they needed me alive for."

An alarm began to wail outside the vault and the Eel frowned. "They needed you alive to serve as bait. It was your scream that drew me deep into the vault."

She brushed at her stockings. "When they were done stealing what they wanted from the vault a tall, hideous man with scarred face and turban entered the vault. He sprayed me with something from a bottle and then laughed like a crazy man. Then they set the tarantula loose. I might have died if it had bit me!"

"It might have made you sick," said the Eel, "but they're not poisonous enough to kill a full grown adult. They just wanted you to scream so that I would come running. They must have sprayed you with something that would attract the spider."

The teller rubbed at her wrists and she seemed to have regained some of her composure, and she examined the Eel with interest. "Now that the alarm has finally gone off the police should be here soon to rescue us. I've read about you in the papers, don't you know? You're quite the mysterious man, you and the others: the Adder, and the Bomber. How did you all meet?"

"I've never met the Bomber," said the Eel, "and the Adder I met one night while I was trying to stop the Nazis from dropping a poisonous powder over Manhattan."

The redhead looked at him with an inscrutable expression. "Is it you that has been killing all those Mafia mobsters that they've been reporting in the newspapers lately?"

"Only a handful of them, though whoever is doing the killing seems to be employing a similar style."

She offered him her hand. "I'm neglecting my manners. My name is Talia McCormac."

The Eel took her hand and helped her to her feet. "A pleasure to meet you. However, the circumstances are somewhat less than desirable. I'm afraid that the alarm is not a fortuitous event for me. The Punjabis that robbed your bank delayed the alarm until I was trapped inside the vault. They've cleared out and I will be blamed for the robbery and the murders."

"But I will witness that you were not involved!" protested Talia.

"I appreciate that, but I'm wanted for other murders, also."

"But you're innocent, of course..." said Talia.

"The police sometimes take a very dim view of freelancers attending to what they think is solely their business," said the Eel. "That any one of those men would have slit my throat, given the chance, doesn't mean much to most of the police."

"But the dead Nazis that they found in the dockside warehouse. You had something to do with that, didn't you?"

"I might have," said the Eel, but his mind was clearly elsewhere. He examined every corner of the vault looking for some sort of weakness.

"You're a hero!" insisted Talia. "They should be thanking you for your help."

The Eel climbed the trays of several open lock boxes and begin unscrewing the grating of a small air vent. "Perhaps, but until that day I'm going to make myself scarce."

"How are you going to make yourself scarce?" asked Talia. "You're trapped in here with me until the police open the vault."

"I'm going to climb through this vent," said the Eel.

"You're not going to fit into that," said Talia.

"I'm double-jointed," replied the Eel, "and a trained contortionist as well."

"You're apparently a man of many talents, but I don't want to be left alone in the vault. What if another spider is lurking about?"

The Eel set aside the grating and examined the impossibly narrow shaft inside. "There's no more spiders, and besides, now that your arms and legs are free, a capable woman like yourself is perfectly equipped to dispose of a spider by herself."

"So you think I'm perfectly equipped, do you, Mr. Eel? Tell me, what is your real name?"

When there was no response, Talia McCormack turned and saw that there was no sign of her erstwhile companion, except for a bundle of clothing at the base of the vent. To this bundle was tied the scarf the Eel had torn loose from the Punjabi he had shot. In a few moments, as the Eel worked his way up the narrow ventilation shaft, he drew up the bundle of clothing behind him.

• • •

Jean Belanger climbed the stairs of the Manhattan's Palladium Theater with the aid of a straight cane that was capped with a silver head inscribed with the sigil of a snake. He scarcely put any weight upon the cane, but something besides his leg seemed to be distressing him, for a frown marred his handsome features, which, upon close inspection, seemed to have taken on a waxy pallor.

The beautiful blonde accompanying him leaned close to Belanger, the masses of her curly hair falling across her shoulders. "Are you well, Jean?"

"I once felt more at home in the theater than anywhere else," admitted Belanger, "but since the fire theaters make me most apprehensive."

Though Belanger was reticent about revealing the details of his past, through the months of their association Emma Goodbody had been able to glean a few details of Belanger's history. Once he had been a lauded French stage actor, lauded for his ability to completely immerse himself in his roles so that he appeared to be entirely different people, honing his craft in various Shakespearian productions, but it was one night performing a theatrical adaption of Baudelaire's *Fleurs du Malthat* an arsonist set fire to the theater. Many died that night and though Belanger escaped with his life, he was permanently scarred, both body and soul. Beneath the putty and stage makeup that formed a replica of his formerly handsome visage, was a tableau of burled and scarred flesh.

"I'm sure that the drama will contain itself on the stage this evening," Goodbody said, and then to distract Belanger she changed the subject. "Where did you find this lovely gown I'm wearing? Surely, this cost a fortune!"

"It once belonged to an actress associate of mine. Unfortunately I lost contact with her after my accident."

Goodbody found this curious. "Surely, she was more than just an associate, Jean."

Belanger cast a sidelong glance at his associate. "That was to be her wedding dress."

No more details seemed forthcoming, so Emma chose to pry. "Wedding to whom? To you?"

"Unfortunately, after the accident I lost both my mind and my fiancee. *C'est la vie. Mais oui, ma chère?*"

"Such is life," agreed Goodbody with a sigh, and with the mention of marriage her mind turned inevitably to a certain Italian. "Where is Vincent?"

Belanger mounted the top step and they proceeded, together, to a private box on the balcony of the theater which provided an excellent view of the stage. "Indeed, if it were not for his invitation to see this parlour magician, Viswanathan, I wouldn't have been inclined to set foot inside a theater for anything less than life or death."

"Well, Vincent assured me that there would be plenty of death defying spectacle on display this evening." Goodbody smoothed her gown and sat. "He says that short of Houdini, Viswanathan is the preeminent magician and escape artist of our day."

"I prefer carefully crafted and emoted dialog in my stage presentations," grumbled Belanger, "but I do suppose that such sort of displays do provide for a sort of visceral reaction that may appeal to those of more plebeian nature."

"As opposed to the visceral thrill of fighting crime on the streets?" teased Goodbody.

"That, *ma chère* , is done purely for a higher purpose, and in the defense of the innocent citizens of Gotham." Then his lips betrayed the slightest of smiles. "And any visceral thrill is merely a secondary benefit."

Goodbody raised an eyebrow. "I see."

"But we're speaking of art," said Belanger, "and I contend that thespianism is the truest art form. Magic is simply deception and spectacle and the study of which cannot be undertaken with same seriousness as thespianism."

Emma watched the crowd below flow to their seats and listened to their excited murmurs of anticipation. "I'm sure that, were Vincent on time and here with us that he would most strenuously disagree."

"I'm sure he would," nodded Belanger in the most affable of manners. "We do have the most lively of conversations, sometimes. It's no wonder that we keep our relation to mostly professional pursuits."

"Do you have the time?" asked Goodbody.

Belanger pulled out an engraved *L'alloutte* pocket watch and consulted the hands. "Five minutes to curtain."

Goodbody bit at her lower lip. "I'm starting to get worried."

"Nonsense," said Belanger. "Vincent is never the most timeliest of individuals. I'm sure that this is just another case of his perpetual tardiness."

"Perhaps," said Emma, but her tone of voice suggested that she was not convinced. "But he's been talking of this for weeks. I can't imagine him being late unless he's involved in some serious trouble of some sort."

"Vincent in trouble?" scoffed Belanger. "Why, he's the model of caution and propriety."

"I do believe that was sarcasm," said Emma

"Did you hear that an attempt was made to rob the First Manhattan Bank this afternoon?" asked Belanger.

"Do you have a contact in the police department?"

"No," said Belanger, "but I do have a radio that is tuned to police frequencies. Apparently, the thief became caught in the vault with the teller and they are still endeavoring to get the vault open. By the time anyone thought to locate the off duty bank manager the police had already ruined the locking mechanism."

A sudden expression of shock crossed Goodbody's attractive features. "You don't think that Vincent..."

"Of course not. He's left that life behind, and even if he had reverted to his old ways he wouldn't be so careless as to let himself be caught in the vault."

"Of course not," repeated Goodbody.

The house lights dimmed and the last few stragglers quickly found their seats. The orchestra in the pit beneath the proscenium began a wild selection of screeching violins underscored by the deep hum of the oboe. Spotlights swept the stage and fog began to creep from beneath the curtains.

Both Goodbody and Belanger turned their attention to the stage as the curtains swept open, sending coils of fog swirling across the audience as if they were skittering phantoms that coruscated then dissolved in the intensity of the sweeping spotlight. Though Goodbody's concern about the possibilities of Spinelli being caught in the bank vault had been mollified, she still felt uneasy and unable to completely immerse herself in the unfolding spectacle of the show.

As if appearing from the thin air, suddenly a tall and skeletally thin man stood at center stage, amid the churning fog. His complexion and features marked him as East Indian and he wore gold rings in his ears, a crimson turban upon his head, his sharp nose underlined by a thick black mustache. When he spoke, his deep voice rolled like thunder through the auditorium. "All ye who enter here abandon all hope."

"Great projection," critiqued Belanger, "though it sounds as though his voice has been amplified."

"I am Vasras Viswanathan, and I bring from the Far East the secrets of swamis and gurus. I bring the secrets of life and death. I bring the knowledge of mysteries and magics, the likes of which your finite and feeble minds have not the capacities to fathom."

The crowd murmured, suspecting they had been belittled.

"Insulting your audience," murmured Belanger. "That's always good for a reaction, if your patrons have the vocabulary to comprehend it."

Viswanathan swept his right arm forward, the wide-hanging sleeve cracking like a whip. "And from the Far East I bring exotic beauties to titillate and tempt you masculine libidos and to assist me as I delve into the darkest of arts."

From stage left and from stage right came two pairs of East Indian beauties, wearing ornate lehengas and adorned with gems draped over their foreheads and golden rings dangling heavily from the lobes of their ears. For those members of the audience that did understand Viswanathan's prior insult, these beauties served to distract them from their anger.

Even Belanger ceased his running commentary about the stagecraft of the production. "It can't be," he murmured. "She would still not be that young."

Goodbody eased forward so that she could see what Belanger was looking at. "What are you talking about?"

"That assistant on the left of Viswanathan."

"She is very beautiful," observed Goodbody.

"She is the spitting image of someone that I knew, many years ago," said Belanger.

Now stagehands dressed in black from their shoes to their turbans rolled forward a coffin-shaped box.

"Interesting," murmured Belanger.

"Are you still referring to the woman?" asked Goodbody, with the slightest of smiles upon her full lips.

"In this case, no," said Belanger. "Do you see the pendant that has escaped the collar of the closest stage hand?"

Goodbody hesitated, then nodded. "Yes?"

"That is the symbol of the pickaxe."

Goodbody shrugged. "Why would someone wear a symbol that stands for a pickaxe?"

Belanger rubbed his chin, but only lightly for fear that the grease paint might smear. "There is only one reason that I know of."

Goodbody gave a wry smile. "He belongs to a guild of ditch diggers?"

"Grave diggers is closer to the fact of the matter," said Belanger, and he returned his attention to the center of the stage, where Viswanathan was assisting the young woman up a set of stairs so that she could climb into the coffin. Once she was sitting upright in the coffin, Viswanathan lifted a veil, and from behind it he produced a saw. "The teeth of this blade have been honed to exquisite sharpness, so that the merest touch will draw blood. "I will now saw the lovely Jaya asunder. The fairer sex, or those who are squeamish, may want to avert their eyes."

There was a thunder of kettle drums and the spotlights flickered lurid light as Jaya settled inside the coffin and with great theatrical movements, the magician latched the lid closed. "These are hasps of the strongest steel which are used on elephant cages in India. Not even a bull elephant could burst this coffin!"

Then, at the center of the coffin, Viswanathan inserted the saw into a precut notch and began to worry the blade back and forth in great motions that brought beads of sweat to his forehead. A terrible shriek resonated from within the coffin and the audience gasped, then there were more shrieks but this time from the women in the audience who had not looked away from the spectacle. For blood gushed forth from the cuts in the coffin, pooling crimson upon the planks of the stage. Several women in the audience fainted dead away in their seats.

Goodbody had seen plenty of blood since casting her lot in with the Eel. She came to her feet, gripping the rail in front of her. "Belanger, perhaps you should do something?"

"Not me," came the reply.

For a moment Goodbody thought that Belanger was being coy, for he often insisted that his alter ego, the Nazi hunter and crime fighter known only as the Adder, was a completely different person. She turned on him, blue eyes fierce. "No not you, but perhaps someone that you know."

Belanger did not rise from his seat, but his eyes were still fixed upon the stage. "We've come to see a show of spectacle and illusion. I am no expert in magic, but I do know a thing or two about illusion. Perhaps we should let this scene play out before we act hastily."

Goodbody was unsure, but she lowered herself back into her seat, still gripping the rail in front of her.

Viswanathan turned to the audience, his features placid beneath his turban. He flicked blood from the tips of his fingers. "Gentlemen and gentlewomen do not be alarmed, for I am versed in the dark magicks and I possess the power over life and over death."

His three remaining assistants came forth with censers that billowed flame and black smoke depending upon golden chains. They waved these around the coffin in wild patterns that conformed to the erratic rhythm of the orchestra within the pit. Viswanathan chanted strange dirges in the language of his homeland and then he rapped upon the lid of the coffin eleven times. "Join your sundered body together and come forth!"

He unlatched the lid and threw it open. For long moments there was no movement in the audience or upon the stage.

"I say, come forth Jaya," cried Viswanathan.

Still, there was no movement from within the coffin.

Viswanathan's lower lip began to tremble and the audience could detect a tremor within his formerly assured voice. "One last time, Jaya. I say come forth."

Still, there was no stirring inside the sawed and blood-spattered coffin. Hollers of anguish and fear came from the audience.

"You've killed her!" shouted one of the male audience members. "You've gone and killed her!"

Then, as if a phoenix from the ashes, Jaya rose up from the coffin in her blood-stained lehengas at her torso and showed a scandalous amount of flesh, but though it was smeared red with blood, there was no mark tearing the skin. The lethal wound had been healed, as if by magic.

"She is alive and well," shouted Viswanathan. "My powers have brought her back from the gates of hell."

The crowd was so relieved that it cheered, the roar of the audience only dying down when Viswanathan proceeded with his next magical trick, while Jaya disappeared back stage. Only to return later in the show, wearing a fresh outfit which was dripping with gaudy gemstones and designed to distract.

Goodbody became so enthralled in the stage show that it was forty-five minutes before she realized that her date, Vincent Spinelli, had yet to make an appearance. "At this rate he'll miss the entire show."

Belanger, however, was entirely in a world of his own musings. "There is something familiar about that woman."

As the show reached its concluding acts and Viswanathan performed death-defying escapes that the Eel would have been most interested in, including being dunked into a tank of sharks while being bound hand and foot, an usher crept into the box. Belanger's first reaction was to reach for the pistol hidden inside his smoking jacket, but when he realized that it was only an envelope that the usher held, he refrained from resorting to deadly force.

"Sir," whispered the usher. "One of the performers has seen you in the box, and asked that a message be relayed to you."

Belanger accepted the envelope and handed the usher a quarter as a tip. He ripped open the envelope and unfolded the piece of stationery inside.

Of Goodbody's many admirable characteristics incuriosity was not one of them, and many times her inquisitiveness had come close to killing her. "What does the message say?"

"My powers have brought her back from the gates of hell."

"Apparently, a Miss Jaya Sampath would like to personally relay a message to me."

"Is this a message of a romantic sort?"

Belanger chuckled. "You flatter me, Miss Goodbody, but I doubt that this message is anything of the sort."

"Why do you think that she looks so familiar to you? Obviously, she must know you somehow, too."

"My guess is she's related to a Miss Kirti Patil, an Indian actress I once worked with in the Shakespearian production of Macbeth."

"So this Kirti Patil, she was merely an associate?"

"You won't give up until I divulge every last detail, will you, Miss Goodbody?"

Once again fog rolled across the stage and the spotlights strobed like lightning. Vasras Viswanathan disappeared as abruptly as he had come, accompanied by the shrieking wail of the violin and the ominous rumble of drums. His four lovely assistants swept away through the mists and the curtains fell.

"Well?" insisted Goodbody. "I'm waiting for you to answer the question."

"And most impatiently, I might add."

"We were once engaged to be married," said Belanger.

"And why weren't you married?" asked Goodbody.

"The fire," said Belanger, and without further explanation. "The fire destroyed everything."

Fighting against the crowds they headed to the backstage where one turbaned man was turning away a number of well-wishers who wanted to congratulate the performers on their show.

"Guru Viswanathan finds that performing such feats of magic drain his energies and he cannot be bothered while he recoups his strength," said the door guard. Even the young women were turned away in this manner, and all that sought to meet the mysterious magician went away disappointed.

When Belanger and Goodbody presented themselves at the door they were greeted with a similar rebuffing. "Guru Viswnathan had given orders that he should not be disturbed."

"It is not Mr. Viswanathan that I wish to speak to," explained Belanger, his cane firmly in hand. "It is a Miss Jaya Sampath."

"Guru Viswanathan has left me strict instructions that his assistants remain untainted from the presence of unbelievers."

Belanger frowned and handed the door guard the letter he had received. "As you can see, it was Miss Sampath that requested my presence."

The turbaned guard glanced at the missive and grunted. "Very well. You should be able to find Miss Sampath at the back of the stage. Please do not bother any of the other stage hands or performers, especially Guru Viswanathan."

"I have no desire to bother Guru Viswanathan," replied Belanger.

The turbaned guard opened the door to the stage's stairs. "See that you don't."

Belanger passed onto the stairwell, but when Goodbody tried to enter the guard outstretched his arm, blocking her path.

"The invitation was for him only," said the guard. "You'll have to wait here."

Belanger was about to protest, but Goodbody spoke first. "No need to make a fuss, Jean. I should call Vincent and see if I can get a hold of him. I'll meet you in the lobby when you're through."

"Well enough," agreed Belanger and he made a show of leaning on his cane as he climbed the stairs and crossed the worn and battered planks of the stage. Through the lingering wisps of fog he saw a slender figure in the glittering lehengas Jaya Sampath had worn on stage earlier. A number of black-turbaned stage hands worked around the perimeter packing up the magician's equipment, and these Belanger eyed warily for the amulet that he had seen escape the collar of one of the stagehands was not merely symbolic of the pickaxe, it was the insignia of a cult of thieves and stranglers that were thought to be long extinguished. Naturally, there would be imitators who would adopt the secret symbols and combinations of the cult, but Belanger found it disturbing that even the semblance of the worship of the dark goddess Kali would find its way from the depths of India to the modern melting pot of New York City.

"Miss Sampath, I received your message."

She turned, wiping at the corners of her almond-shaped eyes, and she was even more lovely without the harsh stage lights upon her features. "I'm sorry to have disrupted your plans this evening, Mr. Belanger, but I have an urgent message from Kirti Patil."

Belanger stopped short. "Are you her daughter, because you bear a remarkable resemblance to her."

"I am Kirti's niece," replied Miss Sampath. "Kirti never married after you disappeared."

"How did you know I was here?" asked Belanger.

Sampath's voice tremored and she whispered, drawing Belanger closer so that he could hear her words. "I didn't know you were here ... HE knew you were here."

Her lower lip quavered. "No one knows his true name, but he is called many things: The Left Hand of Kali-Ma, the P'hansigar Guru, the Tiger King, or the Tarantula!"

Belanger glanced at the black-clad stage hands to make sure that they were not being overheard. "What does this man with no name have to do with Kirti? I thought you had a message from her."

"Don't you see?" she pleaded. "My Aunt has been kidnapped by the Tarantula. He threatened to kill her unless I spoke with you."

"How do you know that this Tarantula even exists, let alone has kidnapped Kirti?"

"Oh, the Tarantula exists! Everywhere I hear whispers of his evil doings, and anyone who dares raise their voice to speak against him disappears, and is never seen again unless they are made an example of. In that case they are found strangled and dangling like a chicken in the butcher's shop."

"And how do you know that this man has Kirti, and what does he want with her?"

"He knows who you are. He wants to get to you," said Sampath. "I am so sorry!"

She backed a step away and then Belanger felt a quick procession of stings on his neck and face. He slapped his hand upward and found small darts protruding from his skin. Before he could pull more than one loose his footing tumbled from beneath him. Jaya Sampath had lured him into standing atop of concealed trap door, and he had been so concerned with the possibility of the stagehands being hostile that he did not notice. The trap door fell away, and he tumbled into the great glass tank full of sharks, which Vasras Viswanathan had used in his show.

Belanger felt a tingling numbness spread through his body. Even his brain seemed to be thinking in slow motion. The darts must have been tipped with curare. He reached for the .45 pistol that he kept hidden beneath his jacket, but his numbed fingers couldn't seem to grasp the butt of the gun. If only he could reach the pistol, he could fire it and shatter the glass walls of the aquarium. Through the haze of turbulent water he could see Jaya Sampath stumbling away, her hand thrown across her face, and then he saw one of the turbaned stage hands climbing a ladder next to the tank. He dumped a bucket of bloody chum into the water and the circling sharks scented it, as the crimson tendrils sank through the waters, driving them into a teeth gnashing feeding frenzy.

• • •

The Eel's slow, painstaking progress came to a halt at the top of the ventilation shaft where further movement was blocked by a cap on the rooftop of the First Manhattan Bank. It was much easier to gain access to a ventilation shaft from the outside of the shaft, then to leave a closed shaft once inside of it, but crawling back down the shaft and returning to the vault was not an option. He could hear Talia's voice below, calling through the vault to the policeman who had arrived. They had not yet figured out how they were going to open the bank vault, but to go back to the vault was to ensure capture by a constabulary who had no love for him. If the papers were any indication, they considered the efforts of the Eel and his sometimes partner in adventure, the Adder, to put the New York Police Department in a bad light as though they were not capable of handling the criminal element by themselves.

In a former life, Vincent Spinelli, had been an escape artist with a renown second only to the great Harry Houdini, himself. Though escape artists often relied upon prearranged tricks and deceptions, there were a number of qualities that marked the best escapists: one was an unassailable calm during life threatening situations, and second was the ability to contort one's body into all sorts of implausible configurations. Even now, the Eel's ribs were compressed so much that he was forced to take in tiny breaths, for his lungs could expand no further, and each movement that he made forced him to exhale in order to give him enough room to wriggle just a bit higher.

His vest dangled by the Punjabi's scarf, which he had tied to his ankle. In one of the pockets was a miniature propane torch with a flint. The Eel was confident that if he could somehow get to this torch he could use it to heat the thick tar that sealed the vent cap to the roof of the bank building, and loosen it enough that he could push his way out to freedom. However, the shaft was so tight that he was not sure that he could retrieve it from his vest and get it past his half-naked body.

Still, he had spent many hours training himself to accomplish the seemingly impossible, and now he drew up his bundle of clothing after him, by wrapping the scarf around his foot. Once the bundle was close to his foot he drew it up and clamped it between his ankles. Now, he blew out his breath and bent one double-jointed arm and began to work it downward, until the fingers of that hand could touch the packet. Even for a contortionist the position was incredibly awkward, and the nerves in his joints and sinews sang in agony as he explored the pouches and pockets of his vest. Finally he felt the shape of the miniature propane torch, drew the torch from the pocket, and painstakingly pulled it past his body and back into the position with his arms raised above his head.

Below, he could hear the muffled shouts of the police as they called to Talia McCormack, warning her to stand back as they began to drill the safe. The Eel could hear the whine of the drill and the reverberations that followed. It took two tries to fire his torch and he squinted against the stinging miasma and ignored the hot spatters of burning tar that fell against his cheeks, and his bare shoulders and arms. He wanted to rush through the job, but there was no quickening the pace. As soon as he softened the tar at one corner he would push it up before moving on to the next corner. The tar cooled quickly enough that one corner would harden by the time the next was softened. The Eel had only a limited amount of propane in the small torch, and he was concerned that his flame would run out before he had managed to extricate himself from the shaft.

He had lifted three corners and was softening the fourth when torch sputtered and died. Quickly, the Eel pushed against the fourth corner and managed to lift it a couple of inches from its moorings, but still it stubbornly clung to the roof of the bank building. The Eel shoved the empty torch through a gap on the opposite side and onto the roof. Now, he found the slender knife that he had used to cut Talia McCormack's bonds, and by cocking his shoulder and elbow at a painful angle was able to slowly slice through layers of gooey tar paper. Unfortunately, the soft tar quickly gummed the edge of the blade, dulling it so that much laborious effort to finally slice the cap of the vent free.

With the cap shoved aside, inch by inch the Eel wriggled out of the tight confines of the vent. When finally he was free he lay bare-chested upon the rooftop and waited for the excruciating pain in his joints and limbs to pass. He breathed in the chill air, thankful to be released from the confinement of the shaft and grateful that he could fully expand his lungs. The wind brisk, so once the majority of the pain passed he drew up the bundle of his clothing and pulled on his shirt over his tar-spattered chest. In two minutes he was completely attired. He replaced the cap over the vent and crept to the edge of the bank building, peering over the raised wall that ran the perimeter.

Black and white police cars formed a perimeter around the bank. Even the narrow back alley contained a police car, an officer sitting nonchalantly on the hood, worrying at an apple. Across the alley was a large warehouse that was about a story lower than the bank. With a running start he might be able to clear the alley and hit the roof of the warehouse, but if the jump went awry he might not make the leap. Even the drop of one story was enough to do some serious damage if he landed badly. However, the Eel was used to making such calculated risks. It was the police presence below that deterred him from making the leap. Even if the officer's attention was not focused upward, he would doubtlessly hear the weight of a body landing on top of the warehouse.

So the Eel waited, listening at the vent from which he had crawled occasionally overhearing Talia McCormack as she shouted communications to the police officers who were drilling at the lock of the safe. Darkness began to fall and finally he could hear the police officers as they breached the door and entered the vault. McCormack would be forced to tell the police about his presence in order to explain the dead body of the East Indian or, perhaps if the body had been removed, to explain the bullet holes, when every death had been performed by strangulation.

He heard a motor fire in the alley and when he checked he found that the police car was moving out of the alley. The Eel carefully paced himself backward and then began a run toward the edge of the building. He measured his paces so to leap to the surrounding lip of the wall and then launch himself with his forward momentum, across the gaping alley. He hurtled over the cracked pavement and then came down on the roof of the warehouse. Instead of allowing his knees to take the brunt of the shock, he bent them and rolled forward on his right shoulder, going head over heels twice before coming to his feet.

Scarcely had he accomplished this when he heard a door slam open on top of the bank building. Glancing over his shoulder, he could see a half-dozen policemen emerge onto the roof with drawn guns. The Eel moved quickly through the dusk and then one of the police officers spotted him.

"Hey, you! Halt or we'll fire!"

The Eel had no intention of halting and in the time it took for the police officer to call out the warning, he reached the edge of the warehouse and flung himself over the lip of the roof, hanging onto the eaves for dear life. The crack of gunshots sounded in the night air and the Eel could hear bullets whine past. Another bullet picked up a scrap of shingle and flung it past his head, spraying sand into his eyes.

Blinking, the Eel surveyed his surroundings. Below him was a flatbed truck filled with coal and tarped over to protect against the rains. He dropped the intervening twelve feet and landed awkwardly, pitching down the mountainous slope of the coal and landing ignominiously in a puddle at the tail of the truck. His ankle stung, but he lurched to his feet and staggered for a back alley, anxious to put as much distance between himself and the constabulary as he possibly could. He had instructed his cab driver, Donald DeFrenzio, to wait around for only fifteen minutes. It had been closer to six hours since the Eel had entered the bank. Donald would be long gone, or so the Eel thought, so he was surprised to see a yellow-painted cab parked in the shadows of the alley ahead. The Eel recognized the lettering on the cab and as he drew nearer he could make out the licence plate that confirmed that this was indeed Donald's cab. Why Defrenzio had stuck around for this long, the Eel had no idea, but he was thankful for the presence of the cab all the same.

He limped up alongside the cab and found that the front passenger door was ajar. He opened it up and climbed in. Defenzio was, indeed, inside the cab, but his head rested back upon the seat as though he were sleeping. However, there was something odd about the angle of his head, and when the Eel called out to him, there was no response. The bitter scent of death hung in the air, and the Eel could see the abrasions of strangler's rope upon Defrenzio's neck.

There was no life left in him. He had been dead since shortly after he had dropped the Eel off. After waiting for fifteen minutes he had taken on a fare who had climbed into the backseat of the cab and slipped a strangler's cord around his neck, and finished Defrenzio's life. Sorrow and anguish welled up inside the Eel, but he knew that now was not the time to mourn the death of his loyal friend. He pulled Defrenzio's body into the passenger's seat and then crossed around to the driver's seat. The keys of the automobile were still in the ignition and the engine fired easily.

The klaxons of the police cars sounded as word of the Eel's escape was passed back to the street level. The Eel wasted no time threading through the Manhattan back alleys and losing the pursuing police officers in the encroaching night.

• • •

Emma picked up the phone in the lobby and dialed the operator. The crowds of theater goers were thinning as they filed out into the cold night, the men buttoning their coats and the women drawing their furred collars more tightly around their necks. Emma relayed the phone number to the operator who made the connection with Vincent Spinelli's home phone, which rang and rang. She shifted the strap of her heavy purse on her shoulder and continued to let the phone ring, but no answer ever came. Finally, she gave up and hung the receiver in its cradle.

The crowd had emptied out onto the street now, and the lobby was curiously quiet. Two turbaned men stepped onto the broad front steps and drew the large double doors closed, shutting out the chill wind. Completely alone now, Goodbody sighed and crossed to a cushioned bench, where she planned to wait for Belanger to be finished with his private meeting. However, a soft rustling in the nap of the carpet caused her to turn, even while her hand dipped inside her purse.

At that very moment a braided loop descended over her head. Each end of the loop was attached to a grooved stick, and holding this strangulation stick was a turbaned man completely dressed in black. Once the loop had passed to Goodbody's neck, her assailant violently twisted the strangulation stick, tightening the cord around her pale throat so that she gasped and choked. In such instances, it was instinctual for someone to reach for their throat and attempt to pry loose the tightening cord, but Goodbody realized that attempting to loosen the cord now would be an effort in futility. The rope was being drawn quickly into her flesh and trachea with each successive, brutal turn. Black spots swam before her eyes as she writhed and struggled. The strangler, though not much taller than her, picked her up off the ground, and with one flailing heel Goodbody managed to strike her assailant's knee cap.

Though the strangler did not relinquish his grip upon the strangling stick, he did drop Goodbody back to the floor and at this point she twisted slightly, letting her purse fall away and revealing the antique Gasser Montenegro revolver that her Hungarian grandfather had bequeathed her brother, and which had been passed to her after he had died fighting the Nazi's in France. She cocked back the hammer and pulled the trigger, the first .42 caliber bullet punching through the strangler's side and between his ribs.

Now, her assailant abandoned the strangling stick and Goodbody fell to her knees, prying away the coils with one hand and gasping for breath. The strangler staggered away, clutching at his side, trying vainly to stem the crimson flow. However, he was not finished with Goodbody yet. He produced a rod about two feet in length from inside his pant let. This was spiked at the center, and that spike was meant to puncture the larnyx, keeping a victim from crying out, while the strangler put his knee in the small of his victim's back and pulled on both ends of the rod. This technique had gone out the window now, and the strangler intended to use the rod as a simple bludgeon, instead. He raised the rod above his head, with the intent of cracking open Goodbody's skull.

Goodbody thumbed back the hammer of her Montenegro and fired. Still struggling for breath, Goodbody did not take the time to aim, but rather pointed it in the general direction of the strangler and prayed for the best. The bullet hammered into the strangler's chest, and his body crumpled, the rod falling harmlessly against Goodbody's shoulder.

Pushing herself into a sitting position against the padded bench, Goodbody pulled the loop of the strangulation rod from her neck and massaged the abrasions on her neck. The strength in her limbs was slowly returning, and she climbed onto the bench, and then, a moment later, forced herself to stand. If a strangler had come after her in the lobby, just because of her connections with Belanger or the Eel, what were they doing to Belanger backstage? Her first few strides toward the stage were reeling and unsteady, but as she progressed her gait become more steady and assured. She clutched the narrow butt of the Montenegro pistol with white-knuckled fervency, wishing that she had brought an extra handful of the rare .42 caliber rounds along with her. The revolver held just five cartridges, and now she had just three rounds left.

When she reached the side door of the stage she no longer saw the burly guard that had blocked her way before so she pulled the door open and climbed into the inky tenebre that filled the stairwell. She saw furtive shadows fleeing to the edge of the stage, but Jaya Sampath had crept to the edge of an open trap door, and she was stifling a scream as she looked at the horrific tableau that lay beneath. Goodbody reached the opposite side and saw a turbaned man balanced upon a ladder and dumping bloody chum into a tank of water, and within that water she saw Belanger, the putty and greasepaint that had formed the handsome features of his face, peeling away in the salt water as sharks on the edge of a feeding frenzy hungrily circled.

Without much thinking through the repercussions, Goodbody fired her Montenegro through the back of the man dumping the chum, and he tumbled inside the tank, alongside of his empty bucket. Then she leaped through the hatch and into the briny and bloodied waters. Immediately the skirts of her gown billowed up around her head, blinding her so that she could not see the vicious sharks that circled. This actually worked to her advantage, because a shark darted forward, teeth snapping, but the voluminous layers of skirt and slips confused the shark, and all that he got was a mouthful of dress. He veered away, trailing torn cloth, and jerking Goodbody behind.

Another of the three sharks lunged toward the turbaned man that Goodbody had shot and tore a chunk of flesh out of his side, further clouding the waters with crimson. The third shark had been eyeing Belanger with great interest, but the scent of fresh blood caused it to veer away and tear loose another chunk of flesh and sinew from the unfortunate fellow that Goodbody had shot.

With the shark tugging down her skirts, with stinging eyes Goodbody was able to see again. She still held the Montenegro pistol firmly in hand, and she figured she had two choices: she could attempt to shoot the shark that was dragging her around the tank at increasing speed or she could shoot the plate glass of the tank's wall and try to take the sharks out of their element. There was really no option, in Goodbody's mind. The shark was a difficult shot and it was nearly impossible to miss the glass wall.

Fortunately, the cartridges in her pistol had not been in the water so long as to ruin the primer and she fired her last three shots. The first two rounds, their velocity slowed by the water, cracked the wall of the tank, webbing it so that it bulged outward from the pressures of the seawater. The third shot pushed through the glass, so that water spurted through the hole, then the wall of the tank gave way, unleashing a deluge of water, shattered glass, sharks and humans beneath the stage. A number of the black-clad East Indian thugs had been watching the horrifying tableau with great interest, and now they were swept from their feet.

The shark that had been dragging Goodbody through the water relinquished its grip and clamped down on the arm of one of the thugs, who gave out a shriek. The other sharks flopped and leaped like a drop of oil on a hot skillet, coming dangerously close to Goodbody and Belanger. Goodbody pried loose the .45 semi-automatic pistol from Belanger, shook the water out of the barrel and turned it on the nearest shark. Before she had come to New York to seek work at Standard Mechanics she had been a Kansas farm girl and she had learned to shoot along with her brothers. She sighted down the barrel and put three rounds into the head of the nearest shark. It continued to flop and writhe for a few moments, and gradually its death throes became less agitated and it went still.

There were three of the turbaned thugs left uninjured and they recovered their feet, drawing forth their blow guns with curare-topped darts. Goodbody turned Belanger's pistol on the nearest, sighted for the chest and pulled the trigger. The hammer fell upon the cartridge and nothing happened. The cartridge had been spoiled by its descent into the shark tank. As soon as Goodbody realized what had happened she pulled back the slide of the pistol to clear the dud round and sent it splashing to the water-covered planks. This lost moment gave the thugs enough time to load their blowdarts and their cheeks puffed out as they prepared to fire upon her.

Before they could finish their attack there was a low laugh which was punctuated by the rapid fire of a pistol. Two of the thugs fell immediately, blood spurting from head wounds. The third thug managed to fire his dart and it went awry, catching in the soggy folds of Goodbody's torn dress rather than pierce her flesh. She wheeled and saw a figure emerge from the shadows, dressed in dark clothing with a black fedora pulled low, and a handlebar mustached bristling from beneath. "Oh, Vincent!"

"What did I tell you about getting into trouble?" he said.

She gave him a sheepish smile. "You said that I should save all my getting into trouble for when I was with you."

"And what do you call falling into a shark tank?"

"I didn't fall," protested Goodbody as she plucked out the dart from her skirts. "I leaped in!"

The Eel turned his attention to Belanger, who was also known to the underworld as the scourge called the Adder. Belanger lay upon the floorboards struggling to breath. "What's wrong with Jean?"

Goodbody handed the dart to the Eel by the feathers. "He was shot with some of these and dumped into the shark tank."

The Eel examined the sticky brown paste upon the tip of the dart. "This looks like curare. It's sometimes used by magicians and fakirs in small quantities to reproduce the qualities of death."

Goodbody bent over Belanger who was unable to move his limbs. His lips trembled as he attempted to take in breath. "He was hit more than once. Will the curare kill him?"

The Eel fired a series of bullets which finished the remaining sharks. "It's hard to say. The tribes of the Amazon are rumored to have some antidote, but they are reluctant to reveal just what that antidote is."

A voice came from a ladder that ran to the stage above, and they saw Jaya Sampath descending. "I know how to save him."

"Who are you?" demanded the Eel.

"I am Jaya Sampath," said the woman and she threaded the maze of dead and dying, her sandaled feet sloshing through the salty brine. "It's my fault that your friend is lingering near death. Let me see if I can save him."

Goodbody pointed Belanger's pistol in Jaya's direction. "Why should we trust you, hussy!"

"You have no reason to," admitted Jaya, "but I may be Mr. Belanger's only hope."

"You know the antidote?" asked the Eel.

"Will the curare kill him?"

"Not precisely," said Jaya, "but I have seen this poison in action many times before. The Master had done very much experimentation with it."

"The Master?" questioned Goodbody.

"They call him by many names," said Jaya. "The Master Strangler, the Guru, the Left Hand of Kali-Ma, the Tarantula."

"And just what experiments did the Tarantula perform with curare?" probed the Eel.

"He injected his subjects with various quantities to see if they would die or if they would recover." Jaya leaned close to the Adder, checking the rate of his respiration. "He found that a sufficient dosage would paralyze the lungs, but that the heart would continue to beat until it ran out of oxygen. He used bellows to simulate breathing and found those subjects would recover and live. Those he did not simulate breathing with would die."

"He's still breathing," said Goodbody. "But barely."

"He won't be for long," said Jaya. "He took at least three darts."

"Maybe we can find bellows before he stops breathing," said Goodbody.

"That won't be necessary," said Jaya. "I can do the breathing for him, by blowing into his mouth and lungs; but we can't stay here. The Master will send his hashishin shortly, and they will kill all of us if they find us here."

Goodbody scowled. "Hashishin?"

The Eel crouched down and hoisted the Adder over his shoulder in a fireman's carry. He grunted as he rose. The Adder was a larger man than he. "I've heard of them. They are assassins under the effects of hashish, which makes them calm even in the face of great danger."

Goodbody nodded at Jaya. "But can we trust her? She's the one that lured Jean down here in the first place so that the Master could kill him. Why is she trying to help him now?"

Jaya's lips trembled, her eyelids fluttering rapidly as she tried to blink away the tears. "Because of my fear I've become a slave to the Master, but when I saw you leap into a tank of sharks to rescue Mr. Belanger you showed me that there was another way."

• • •

The four of them holed up in a dingy hotel room less than three blocks away from the theater, for the Eel feared he would not be able to carry Belanger any further. The neon sign glowed outside the dirty window and Goodbody pulled aside the curtain just a crack to peer at the desolate streets below. "It doesn't appear that we were followed."

"That's good," said the Eel. "I don't think I could have carried Jean another step."

"I don't understand why you couldn't have called Donald to pick us up," said Goodbody. "You know that he would do anything for you."

The Eel was silent but his expression betrayed him.

"Oh no!" cried Goodbody. "Don't tell me that he's dead!"

"I'm sorry," said the Eel. "I found Donald strangled in his cab."

Goodbody choked back a sob and fell into the Eel's arms. "Has anybody told Teresa?"

"Once I realized that I had been framed for murder and trapped in the vault at the bank, I was worried that the Adder might be next on the list, so I made my way to the theater as fast as I could. Once we sort this out I'll pay a visit to Teresa."

As Belanger gave out a gasp, Jaya ceased breathing into his mouth; a process that she had been repeating for the last thirty minutes. "He's breathing on his own again. He should recover the use of his limbs in a few minutes."

Goodbody crossed to the bed and looked down at the ragged and peeled scraps of putty that still clung to the hideously scarred visage beneath. "Hang in there, Jean. You'll be through this soon."

Jaya's almond eyes narrowed into slits, her long lashes nearly concealing her pupils. "You do realize that Donald betrayed you, Eel. He was ordered to tell you of overhearing about the planned robbery of the bank."

The Eel frowned. The suspicion of such a thing had been nagging at him, but he didn't want to say it aloud and impugn the memory of his good friend.

Goodbody turned upon Jaya with sudden rage. "How dare you say such a thing! It was you who betrayed a friend of your mother's by using her name to lure Jean into your trap."

Even in the face of Goodbody's ire, Jaya did not raise her voice. "I deserve your distrust and your anger. I did not mean to slight Mr. Defrenzio. I am sure he was a very good man. The Master discovered his connection to the Eel and threatened to kill his family if he did not cooperate ... much like he did with me by telling me that he would kill my mother if he did not cooperate."

Goodbody lowered her voice, but her anger was not yet sated. "So, aren't you risking your mother's life by helping us?"

"Possibly," said Jaya, "but I am gambling on a suspicion that I have been harboring for some time."

Belanger pushed himself up into a sitting position on the bed. "And just what suspicion is that, Jaya?"

"Jean!" exclaimed Goodbody. "How do you feel?"

"Like I've been run over by a truck," said Belanger, "but I'm glad to be in the land of the living thanks to you and Jaya."

"Good to see you moving again," said the Eel. "Jaya was just telling us that ..."

"The curare paralyzed me," interrupted Belanger, "but I was fully aware of everything that happened around me. I just couldn't do a cursed thing about it." He looked about the room. "Do you have my cane?"

Goodbody produced it from behind the chair. "I retrieved it from the tank before we left the theatre. It may be a little water-logged."

"Good girl, I may actually need to lean on this for a little bit." Belanger accepted the cane and checked the sword blade hidden in the hollow sheath, wiping away the rust that was already forming on its surface. "Jaya, please continue to tell us what your suspicion is."

"My suspicion is that my mother may just be the Master's one weakness."

"What do you mean by that?" asked the Eel.

"I know exactly what Jaya means by that," said Belanger. "Because Kirti was my one weakness, also, well, besides my over-inflated ego, but stage actors often suffer from an over-valuation of their own worth."

Goodbody glanced out the curtain once again. "You mean to say, that you think that the Master is in love with your mother, and for that reason, despite his threats to kill her, he won't harm her."

Jaya pressed her lips together. "I'm almost sure of it."

The others in the room realized that Jaya needed to believe that she was sure of it, else she had just condemned her own mother to death.

"We'll do everything we can to rescue her," said The Eel. "But we need to know just who this Master is and where we can find him."

Belanger swung his feet over the side of the bed, tentatively testing the idea of putting some weight on them. "It's plainly obvious who he is or at least who he is pretending to be."

"Vasras Viswnathan," said Goodbody. "He's masterminded this whole thing: the trap for Vincent in the bank and the shark tank for you."

Jaya nodded. "At first I didn't understand why I had received such a lucrative job offer. When I discovered that the stagehands were all Faithful Tigers beholden to someone they called the Master, or the Left Hand of Kali-Ma, I became scared and told Mr. Viswanathan that I was leaving his employ."

"What are Faithful Tigers?" questioned Goodbody.

Jaya shuddered. "They are worshipers of Kali-The Black Mother. They are Thuggees, thieves, stranglers and murderers."

Belanger struggled to his feet and took a few tentative steps while holding to the wall. "The religion is called Kalipuja, and it's a thinly disguised excuse for looting, murder, and wanton temple rites. Kirti told me that contrary to popular belief that the worship of the Black Mother had not been exterminated, but that they had instead been driven underground."

"So what does Kalipuja have to do with us?" asked the Eel. "Why is Viswanathan so anxious to see us dead, when most of us didn't even realize that the cult of Kali even existed?"

Belanger forced himself to take a few more steps. "I suspect that if we let Jaya finish her story, she may be able to shed some light on that question. What happened when you told Viswanathan you were leaving his employ?"

"His demeanor had always been kindly up to that point, but his face became hard and his voice angry. He told me that I was important to his plans and that if I did not continue to work for him that he would kill my mother. That was when I suspected him of being the Master that the stagehands whispered about, and when I accused him of it he did not deny it."

Now Belanger took a few steps with the aid of his cane. "That he used you to bait me backstage, instead of your mother tends to strengthen the argument that the Master is indeed infatuated with Kirti. Otherwise, why not use Kirti to lure me backstage, unless the Master did not wish to risk losing her to me?"

Jaya raised an eyebrow. "Maybe a bit of that inflated ego still exists?"

Belanger laughed at this suggestion and his response was harsh. "Look at this hideous face and tell me that I would have a chance at charming even the cheapest street trollop! No, my days as a lady's man are forever gone."

The Eel thought it wise to move the conversation along, for Belanger could be prone to raging fits of temper when melancholy set its teeth in his soul. "So what brings the Master to New York City?"

"In India his influence is spread far and wide. No criminal act is performed without his authorization, and the guru as well as the beggar on the street is required to give a portion of his gains to the Master's coffers. But no amount of power can be enough for a man with insatiable appetites like the Master. He wants to control crime in the United States of America as well."

"And where better to start than the great City of New York?" finished Belanger.

"He's been killing off the Mafia leadership," said Jaya, "and making it look like the work of you two, and another vigilante named the Bomber. The Master hoped that by killing the three of you that the remaining Mafia foot soldiers would fall into place and let him take over leadership."

"That explains a few things," muttered the Eel. "When we catch the Master I'll have to thank him for taking out so many mobsters; saves the Adder and I quite a bit of dirty work."

Now, Belanger was moving about the room with much greater ease. "The remaining question is where we can find Kirti and the Master."

Again, Goodbody was looking out the window. "I'm afraid that the Master may have found us first. There are dozens of Thuggees coming toward the hotel!"

Belanger turned up the collar of his jacket, concealing his scarred features which still hung with scraps of putty and grease paint. "In that's case, it's time for Jean Paul Belanger to retire and for the Adder to come out of convalescence!"

• • •

"We'd best take our leave of this hotel room," said the Adder.

"I can descend the side of the building," said the Eel, who once, before his reform, worked as a highrise cat burglar. "But I don't know if that will work for the rest of you."

"They've left a pair of men behind to watch the building," reported Goodbody, who could scry them out lurking among the shadows. "Even if the rest of us could manage to scale the walls, they would see us and alert the other long before we reached the street."

"We've got to use misdirection on them." Belanger, who had now taken on the role of the Adder, had his make-up kit in front of him and was peering into a small mirror as stripped away the old putty and worked the new into the scarred crevices of his face. With amazing speed he reformed his features into those of a Hindustani with a thick mustache."

"They are all dressed in black," observed Jaya, "and you have no turban."

"All in good time, my dear," muttered the Adder. "Eel, I'm going to need your shirt. It's the right color for my disguise."

The Eel took off his jacket and unraveled a long scarf from the pocket. "I took this from a strangler at the bank. Would this help complete your disguise?"

The Adder took the scarf. "Most definitely. This peculiar scarf seems to be standard issue for Viswanathan's henchman."

"It is called a rumal," said Jaya. "It's a sacred scarf that the Thuggees use to strangle their victims. For a non-believer to wear it is to mark them for death."

The Adder took off his white shirt and traded it for the Eel's black turtleneck. "Then the rumal will be a perfect addition to my costume."

"But you still lack the turban," said Jaya.

"God will provide," said the Adder. "Now, Miss Goodbody, would you so kind as to open up the window and show yourself to the watcher's on the street?"

Goodbody was perplexed. "What?"

"They need to be sure that we're here."

Goodbody threw open the drapes and then pushed the window up, peering outside as if she was thinking about climbing out onto the narrow ledge. Then she slammed the window shut and closed the drapes, as if she had decided that there was no viable means of escape by that avenue.

"That should be sufficient," said the Adder as he added a few finishing touches of powder to give his skin the proper skin tone. "Now, I believe there is an adjoining room. Eel, would you be so kind as to pick the lock?"

The Eel was already at the adjoining door and he held up a set of lock picks and turned the knob. "Way ahead of you, Adder. Now, let's pray that there are no occupants."

"Send Miss Goodbody in first. A beautiful woman appearing in your chambers is slightly less alarming than seeing the Eel or Adder."

Emma headed for the adjoining chamber. "You are a piece of work, Mr. Belanger."

"I'm no longer Belanger, Miss Goodbody. "Please refer to me as Rakesh. It's a common enough Indian name, correct Miss Sampath?"

Jaya nodded. "I know two or three with the name of Rakesh."

Goodbody wandered into the adjoining room, her torn dress still damp and bedraggled from her dip in the shark tank. She found an open suitcase on the bed which contained some women's clothing, and next to it was a closed suitcase. A copy of the Manhattan Times sat on the bedside table next to a can of toothpowder and a crimson towel was thrown across the back of a chair. Thankfully, the occupants of the room were currently elsewhere. "We're clear!" she called to the others.

The Eel was the first through and he quickly checked the bathroom and closet to ensure that they were, indeed, alone. The Adder was the second through, his sharp eyes sweeping the room for details. Immediately his eyes caught sight of the crimson towel and when he saw the newspaper he quickly rifled through it, finally finding an advertisement for Vasras Viswanathan's stage show, which included a picture of the turbaned magician, a pair of golden earrings dangling from each lobe.

While Jaya shut the adjoining door and locked it tight, the Adder opened up his disguise kit and began to work the features reflected in the mirror as he compared them to those in the photo. "Jaya, may I borrow your earrings?"

Without saying a word, Jaya removed the rings from her lobes and handed them to the Adder. He immediately punched these through the lobes of his ears and wiped away the blood.

"Doesn't that hurt?" asked Goodbody.

"Mon cher, the sensation is trivial compared to the pain of burning alive." When the Adder was satisfied with his sculpting the wrapped the crimson towel around his head and the likeness to Vasras Viswanathan was remarkable. "Jaya, you have been in the presence of Viswanathan more than any here. Do you think the likeness is credible?"

"It's amazing," said Jaya. "If I had not seen you make the transformation, I would not have believed it possible."

"Hopefully it will be enough to throw the Thuggees off balance for long us enough to gain the upper hand," said the Adder.

They fell silent as they heard footsteps sound in the hall. At first they thought it was the Thuggees creeping up to slay them, but the sound of jovial, and somewhat drunken, voices gave the lie to this idea, for the thuggee hashishins were quiet and deliberate when approaching their victims. The voices were male and female, and each of the room's occupants fervently hoped that the couple would stop down the hall and enter their room. However, the voices approached and halted at the door of the room in which the four fugitives were hidden.

"What do we do?" whispered Goodbody.

The Eel turned off the lights. "We let them in, and keep them quiet. Otherwise they'll be the death of us all."

For a long time someone fumbled with the key to the room, until finally managing to insert it in the lock, and then with chortles and giggles a couple spilled drunkenly into the darkness of the room. While the male groped for the light switch, the Eel kicked the door closed and grabbed the woman, holding a hand over her mouth to stifle her scream. The Adder flipped the light switch on, revealing themselves to the startled couple.

The Adder appeared in the guise of Vasras Viswanathan and pointed his .45 at the male. He spoke with a thick accent that approximated the magician's voice. "My name is Vasras Viswanathan. Do not make any sudden moves and do not cry out for help. If you do these things you and your wife will not be harmed."

"She ... she's not my wife," stuttered the man.

The Adder viewed the attractive brunette that had ceased struggling when she saw the gun. "Well, isn't that a shame. Now, we're going to send the two of you back to the bathroom. You may hear gunshots. Stay low. Whatever you do, do not come out and investigate. When it is safe, someone will be in to let you know."

The Eel tentatively loosened his fingers from the woman's mouth and she mumbled a protest. "We can't ... if my husband finds out ..."

The Adder gestured with the snout of his pistol. "Not my problem."

As the couple scurried into the bathroom the straining ears of the oddly-matched quartet picked up the sound of furtive footfalls in the hallway.

"We'll flank them," whispered the Adder, but the Eel already understood the plan.

The Adder held a brace of .45s, and he nodded to Goodbody. "Open the door when I give the word."

The Eel removed a small collapsible tube from one of his vest's interior pocket. It was nothing so much as a miniature periscope and he slid one end of this beneath the adjoining door and peered at the mirror, at first seeing nothing but darkness. He rotated the periscope and saw a sliver of light that grew larger, and then dark-clad figures crept through in a procession. The Eel picked up his twin .38's and began firing through the door. Splinters flew as holes punched through the thin wood panels and he heard groans and gurgles as bullets found their mark.

The Adder nodded at Emma and she threw open the front door of the hotel room, releasing the master of disguise into the dimly lit hallway. He immediately encountered a trio of Thuggees lingering in the hallway, and they were startled to see their master suddenly appear. This unlikely appearance might have been enough to arouse the suspicions of even the most simple-minded of criminals, but the Thuggees followed Viswanathan with a religious fervor, for was he not the Left Hand of Kali, and Viswanathan was a magician, and so they were accustomed to performing unusual and astounding appearances and disappearances.

Taking advantage of this moment of confusion, the Adder pointed out the door of the other hotel room, and performed his uncanny mimicry of Viswanathan's voice. "Quick, they need your help!"

The trio of Thuggees turned and rushed to help their dying companions, and immediately the Adder began firing into their unprotected backs, slaying all three before they could reach the door. The Adder stepped across the blood-spattered carpets and the fallen bodies and began firing at the Thuggees within the room; the Thuggees who were caught between the Eel's guns and his own. To escape the crossfire one thuggee leaped out the window, hurtling to through a haze of broken glass and breaking his neck on the pavement four stories below. By the time the Eel and the Adder had emptied their pistols only one of the Thuggees remained alive. He bolted for the door and bowled the Adder over. He was about to strike him with grooved end of his strangulation rod when he saw the visage of his master. Confused, he turned and fled down the hall, taking the stairs as fast as his legs would carry him.

The Eel took up pursuit. He holstered his empty pistols and leaped down flights of stairs, vaulting over railings in an effort to catch the fleeing thuggee. The door to the street banged shut, and the Eel was only a few moments behind. He burst through the door, staying low in the case that a strangler's loop was awaiting him. As it turned out, he had nothing to fear, for the thuggee was climbing onto the running board of a sedan that was filled with Thuggees that were making their escape. Apparently, when they had seen their compatriot dive out the window in a hail of bullets and break his neck on the pavement they had become spooked enough to rethink their plans.

Though the Eel was already winded from his run down the stairs, he picked up speed, hoping he could leap onto the bumper of the sedan before they made their escape. However, as he began his headlong sprint he saw something arc from the corner of the block, spinning in the air and emitting a trail of sparks. This bundle of sparking sticks flew through the open passenger window of the Sedan. Immediately, the thuggee on the running board let go of his purchase and went tumbling across the concrete. Then the sedan went up in a ball of flame that threw glass, chunks of metal, and flesh in all directions.

The Eel was picked up and hurled in the opposite direction that he was running, and the rear cargo hatch clanked heavily to the concrete a few feet behind him. Still somewhat stunned, the Eel pushed himself to his feet and approached the last living thuggee, who lay groaning on the pavement, both his leg and arm broken.

A man in a stained brown trenchcoat, with an earth-colored fedora pulled low over his face also approached, coming from the corner of the block where the thrown dynamite had originated. He walked with a pronounced limp. "Pardon me, Mister, but that's my prisoner."

The Eel was about to protest that he hadn't chased the man down four flights of stairs just to give him up, but he opted for the most obvious question. "And just who are you?"

"Some people call me the Bomber."

• • •

After dispatching the wounded with a quick thrust through the heart, the Adder cut an 'A' into the forehead of the last of the dead and dying.

"You're laying claim to all those deaths?" asked Goodbody, who couldn't help but feel unnerved by the dispassionate efficiency that the Adder performed his job. "It seems to me that the Eel shot more than a few of those men."

"But it was my plan," said the Adder, a wild gleam in his eye. "And the Eel doesn't much seem to care for marking his victims."

"No," admitted Goodbody. "It seems rather barbaric."

"Don't shed any tears for those p'hansigar," Jaya told Goodbody. "They are cold-blooded murderers who prove their desire to serve Kali-Ma by sneaking into homes after dark and choking an infant in its cradle."

"Marking them instills fear into the hearts of other criminals," said the Adder. "If I can urge them to reconsider their criminal ways then I have done my job."

"What is a p'hansigar?" asked Goodbody.

"It is the third rank of the Thuggee," explained Jaya. "There is only one rank higher, and all these are commanded by the ..."

Jaya was cut off by the sound of an explosion from the street. Jaya and Goodbody went to the window and saw a plume of smoke rising from a destroyed sedan. Debris was scattered across the street and a couple of bodies lay upon the pavement. One was that of a thug, but even from this distance Goodbody could see that the other body was that of the Eel.

"Vincent!" Goodbody said his name, but even in her concern she did not cry it out, for if criminals were to learn his true identity it would put him and every member of his family in grave danger.

"I can see him stirring," said Jaya..

Indeed, the Eel stood up and approached the fallen form of the thug.

"But who is that approaching from the corner?" asked Goodbody as she saw a man in a worn trench coat emerge from the shadows.

"Let me see," growled the Adder and he shouldered his way into the space in front of the room. He took a moment to study the approaching figure. "Why, I do believe that we may be looking at the man the papers have been calling the Bomber."

"What does he want?" asked Goodbody.

"That's a good question, but since the Eel isn't in the habit of carrying dynamite in his hip pocket, I suspect that it was he who was responsible for exploding that automobile."

All around the neighborhood people began to come to their windows to see the cause of the commotion. Perhaps Nazi war planes had made it to the shores of the United States and commenced bombing or perhaps the mobs had decided to hold a gang war on this very street. Whatever conclusions the residents came to, they would soon be on the phones to the police station and squad cars would be dispatched. The Eel could not afford to linger on the streets.

• • •

"He's my prisoner," repeated the Bomber.

"I chased him down four flights of stairs," said the Eel. "If you think I'm giving him up, you've got another thing coming."

The Bomber pulled a bulky semi-automatic pistol from a holster beneath his jacket. He didn't point it at the Eel, but the implications were clear. "I don't believe I said that I was giving you a choice. Mobsters have been ending up dead all over New York and I intend to find out why."

There was a sudden crack of gunfire and a bullet ricocheted from the pavement near the Bomber's feet.

The Eel smiled. "I've got friends that say you should beat your feet, but I'm not an ingrate. I appreciate you taking care of that car full of thugs for me. I can tell you why mob bosses are ending up dead."

Even in the face of taking a bullet from the Adder, who was perched four floors above, The Bomber was stubborn. "I'd prefer to hear it directly from the thug."

The Eel could hear the sirens drawing closer. "What do you intend to do about it, once you know?"

The burly man shrugged. "Maybe nothing. A few dead mobsters doesn't hurt my feeling any. I just want to know what's going on in my town."

In the distance the klaxons of approaching police cars sounded and the Eel made a snap decision. "How about we share the thug? I've got a garage not far from here where we can interrogate our prisoner."

"He's my prisoner."

Beneath the Bomber's battered Fedora a crooked smile spread across his face. "I think you've got yourself a deal."

"I've got a cab parked around the corner. Help me get this thug into the trunk."

The Bomber holstered his pistol, removed a blow gun, knife, and punjab lasso from the stunned thug, then hoisted him onto his shoulders without any help from Eel. "Lead the way."

"You got that, yourself?" questioned the Eel as he started toward the corner.

"Easy as pie," said the Bomber who, despite his limp, carried the stunned man with a surprising ease. "I've carried heavier men out of the trenches in France and for longer distances."

The made their way into the alley, past rows of tin garbage cans where mangy cats prowled for the oversized rats that lurked in the shadows. The Eel found his cab where he had parked it, but there was a bullet-pocked motorcycle leaning on its kickstand which was not there when the Eel had parked the cab.

"I do believe I'm parked right behind you," said the Bomber.

The Eel used a key to open up the boot of the cab, revealing the body of Donald DeFrenzio which he had stowed there for safekeeping.

The Bomber paused before dumping the still-stunned thug into the boot alongside the dead cabby. "Who's that?"

"A friend of mine," said the Eel.

"I'd hate to see how you treat your enemies," said the Bomber, as he divested himself of the slack weight of the thug.

The thug began blinking, his eyes beginning to focus. Suddenly, he realized where he was and he made a flailing attempt to scramble out of the boot. The Eel slammed the trunk, breaking two of the thug's fingers. The thug cried out and withdrew his fingers and the Eel slammed the trunk again. This time there was no body parts in the way and the lock latched.

"He's going to be angry as a treed raccoon, once we get to your garage."

"You aren't from around here," said the Eel. "I thought you said that Manhattan was your town."

"It is at the moment," said the Bomber, "and I never said I was born here."

While the Eel clambered into the driver's seat of the cab, the Bomber kicked his motorcycle to life, so that its throaty roar rebounded from the alley walls and sent stray cats scurrying.

"What about your friends?" called the Bomber.

"Just follow me," replied the Eel, and a plume of exhaust enveloped the

Bomber as he sent the cab barreling down the alley, then took a sharp right that took them along the back side of an office building and then the hotel. As they approached, the back door of the hotel burst open and a blonde and brunette spilled out. The blonde's gown was torn and damp and the brunette still wore the ornate lehenga which she had worn while she assisted Vasras Viswanathan. The Adder swept through the door after, looking for all intents and purposes, like Vasras Viswanathan, except for the pair of Colt .45 automatics that he gripped. He kicked the door shut behind them and then the three of them piled into the cab.

Before the doors of the cab were closed, the Eel hit the gas, his passengers lurching into the seats in a jumble. The Adder thrust a .45 out the side window. "We've got a motorcycle on our tail!"

"Don't shoot!" warned the Eel. "He's with us!"

The Adder reluctantly pulled his pistol back inside the vehicle. "Is that the Bomber?"

The Eel wrestled the wheel of the cab and sent the auto sliding around the corner. "Based on the way he blew up that car full of thugs, I'd say yes."

"Why is he following us?" asked Goodbody.

"I've agreed to share our prisoner with him."

"Just how do you propose to do that?" asked the Adder.

• • •

Two hours later a 1940 Packard turned the corner near the railroad tracks. The back door opened up and a battered and bruised thug spilled out the back, hands and feet bound tightly. His cheek was marked with a blood 'A'. The Packard sped off.

The Adder scowled, his face was still in the disconcerting form of Vasras Viswanathan. "I still think that it was a mistake to let him live. What if he gets word back to Viswanathan that we're onto him?"

The Eel was behind the wheel of the Packard; one of half a dozen vehicles that he owned. "It will be hours before the rail-workers find him, by that time we'll have grabbed Kirti Patil and disposed of Viswanathan."

"Assuming that we were given correct information," said the Adder.

The Bomber sat on the back seat, rolling a stick of dynamite between his palms. The surface of the dynamite showed deep bite marks. "He was a tough nut to crack, but once I shoved a stick of dynamite between his teeth and lit it, he seemed very willing to tell us everything that he knew."

"He even admitted to killing Donald," said the Eel, "but that was after I promised to let him live if he cooperated."

"Where did you park his cab?" the Bomber asked the Eel.

"A couple of blocks away from the police station. Manhattan cab will put the word out to the police that they are missing one of their cabbies and it won't be long before it is discovered."

"And his body?"

The Adder steered the Packard toward the industrial district along the Manhattan shoreline. "Still in the trunk, but I put a scrap of the thug's torn rumalin his hand. The thug's still wearing the rest of the rumal. It shouldn't take any special genius for the detectives to put together the pieces. I may have promised not to kill the thug, but if the police want to hang him I am just fine with that."

They pulled up in front of a molasses factory which had been shut down two years prior, and they looked across the weathered fencing and abandoned courtyard.

"I pray that she's still in there," said the Adder, and the Eel and the Bomber knew that he was referring to his former flame, Kirti Patil.

The Bomber opened the back door. "What are we waiting for? Let's go get her."

"Close the door and we'll formulate a plan," said the Adder. "If we burst in we might get Kirti killed."

The Eel turned and regarded their new companion with great scrutiny. "Tell me, Bomber, just how was it that you got on the track of the Thuggees?"

The Bomber shrugged. "I heard about the bank robbery, and thought I'd see if I could bring the robbers to justice but my police contact was playing it very close to the vest and wouldn't give me any information."

"You have a police contact?" asked the Adder. His expression was such that the Eel couldn't tell if he was expressing disbelief or considering the advantages that such a contact might bring.

"I wasn't getting anywhere until he mentioned that there was a teller who was trapped inside the bank vault with the Eel. I managed to look her up, a very lovely redhead named Talia, who didn't seem to mind answering my questions when I told her what I was up to. But I already told your friend, Emma, all about this."

The Eel groaned. "You didn't happen to mention how lovely Talia was, did you? Because, when I told Emma about being trapped in the vault I chose to downplay Talia's appearance."

"I don't know much about women, but if you don't mind me saying, Mr. Eel, but my mother always told me that honesty was the best policy."

The Eel grimaced. "Yes, well that's always been a struggle of mine."

"After talking to Talia I still didn't have much to go on, but I knew what to look for. So when I was patrolling and saw a group of these thugs hanging around on the street, I took an interest."

"And expressed that interest by blowing up a car full of them?" interjected the Adder.

"Well, after the hail of gunfire I was quite sure they were up to no good. Do you think that I acted improperly?"

"No, no," said the Adder. "A man after my own heart."

The Eel directed their attention to the warehouse. "They've got a man patrolling up top of the factory. He's dressed in black, so he's very hard to spot, but I see movement."

"There's also a pair of men at the gate," said the Adder. "I suggest we take the direct route and drive right up to the gate."

"Are you going to drive yourself?" asked the Eel, "because I thought you didn't know how to drive, and though you may look like Viswanathan, the Bomber and I look nothing like East Indian Thuggees."

"That's why you'll be riding in the trunk," said the Adder.

"I'm not liking this plan," said the Bomber.

A few minutes later the Packard lurched to a grinding stop in front of the gate, the Adder accidentally killing the engine. He left the headlamps on and stepped out of the car, barking an order in Viswanathan's voice and in the dim light where he stood he was the complete likeness of the Master. "Open the gate, immediately. Why the delay?"

Two figures wearing black turbans and rumals melted from the darkness and became visible in the cone of the Packard's headlamps. "But Master," protested the closest in Hindi, of which the Adder only understood a few words.

"Speak English," demanded the Adder. "We must blend in."

That an East Indian in black clothing and turban would blend into the local populace was a dubious proposition at best, but these p'hansigar stranglers were used to obeying the commands of the Left Hand of Kali-Ma with unconditional loyalty. "But Master, we thought you were inside interrogating the woman."

"I slipped out to take care of an important matter," said Viswanathan. "Now, open the gates!"

They obeyed the Adder's command and then he pointed at the closest. "Drive me to the woman!"

"Yes, Master." The strangler climbed into the front seat of the car, carrying the scent of curry with him, and the Adder seated himself on the passenger side. With as little skill as the Adder he got the Packard started and ground the gears into an uneven roll across the courtyard and around to the south side of the factory, past grimy windows and rusting barrels. They jerked to a stop in front of a closed door.

The driver said nothing, so the Adder assumed that this was the building where Viswanathan was keeping Kirti Patil. He couldn't actually inquire without arousing suspicion that he was not the actual Vasras Viswanathan. The Adder reached into the back seat and grabbed hold of his cane.

"Is that not the cane that belongs to our enemy, the Adder?" asked the strangler.

"Yes, indeed." In a quick succession of movements the Adder removed the hollow sheath on the lower end of the cane and thrust the revealed blade through the throat of the strangler, effectively silencing him while he writhed, and then died, blood spilling down his front. When the strangler had finished his death throes, the Adder removed the blade and went around the back to open the boot of the Packard, releasing the Adder and the Bomber from confinement.

The Eel passed around to the front of the Packard and saw the dead strangler in the driver's seat. "Did you have to kill him in the Packard?"

"It seemed expedient," said the Adder.

"Do you know how much one of these things costs?"

"I haven't the faintest," said the Adder.

"It's the 180 series," said the Bomber. "Probably runs five or six thousand dollars."

"The Bomber knows his cars. I've got two of these." The Eel dragged the dead strangler from the passenger seat and disposed of him behind a few rusty barrels.

The Adder checked the door and found that it was not locked. "Yes, but it's no substitute for knowing one's Shakespeare."

They slipped inside the warehouse and even years after shutting down the scent of molasses rolled upon them, for it was steeped into the floorboards, the beams, and the rafters of the building. The interior of the building was pitch black and after they crept inside, the Eel lit his torch to shed some light and to ensure that they didn't break their necks stumbling over something in the darkness.

As soon as he lit up the torch, they heard the door slam shut behind them, and a blazing light went on in the center of the building, beyond the crated equipment and in an area clear of everything except for Vasras Viswanthan, who stood next to a beautiful woman who was bound and gagged in an iron chair.

"Ah," said Viswanathan, his voice booming through the nooks and crannies of the factory, "it's the Eel and the Adder. I see you've finally followed my trail of clues. I've been expecting you ... just a little bit sooner, but I can't really expect everyone to be on the same level of genius as me. Also, I see that you've brought me the Bomber. That is an unexpected bonus. I wasn't planning on disposing of him until much later, if he proved to be an annoyance."

Though they were meant to be distracted by the brilliance and the light at the center of the warehouse, for Viswanathan was a master of deception and illusion, the Bomber noticed dark shapes creeping in around the edges of his vision. They came bearing rumal, punjab lasso, and strangler stick, moving in jagged diagonal motions, creeping low, just below the line of sight, through the thick shadows. The Bomber recalled the night the Nazis had crept upon their trenches and he had nearly lost his leg. He pulled out the gnawed stick of dynamite and struck a match on the metal buttons of his coat.

When the Adder caught sight of his long lost love, Kirti Patil, he lurched forward, sword cane in hand, ready to cut down Viswanathan, but the Eel's hand snaked out and caught him by the jacket. "Wait! It's a trap."

"Of course, it's a trap," snarled the Adder and pulled away, "but I won't let Kirti slip out of my grasp!"

"But she's not there," said the Eel. "It's a projection ... an illusion ..."

The Eel's words were lost on the Adder for he plunged through the dark and toward the flickering image of the beautiful Kirti Patil, whom he had lost so many years ago. The floorboards were uneven beneath his careless tread, but he bridged the gap in but a few moments, and his sword cane whipped out, slitting Viswanathan's throat or the image of Viswanathan's throat, for his sword blade had not cut through flesh, but rather the screen material upon which the likeness of the Master had been projected. The severed screen folded to the floor, and then Viswanathan's mocking image suddenly appeared next to the wall on the far side of the factory.

"You're a fool, Jean Paul Belanger," mocked Viswanathan from across the factory. "Did you think that I would so easily let you steal away my prized possession? You may have had Miss Patil once, but no longer. Now, she belongs to me."

Enraged, the he had fallen for such a deception, the Adder futilely reached out for the bound Kirti Patil, but his hand thrust through the projection, shadowing her features. She blinked out of existence as the projection ceased. The Adder roared out in rage. "Show your true face, Viswanathan! I dare you!"

The flickering projection spoke again. "No one knows my true face, Belanger. I've killed everyone that has seen it. I strangled even my own mother so that she would not be able to betray my true identity. Do you think that I would show you my own face? Vasras Viswanathan is only as real as the face you wear right now, which is as much your true face as it is mine."

"Just come out of hiding!" demanded the Adder.

Viswanathan continued to goad the Adder. "Your true face, however, I have seen; a hideous thing to match your hideous soul."

"Get out of there!" the Eel warned the Adder, but the warning came a moment too late because a half dozen stranglers converged around the Master of Disguise. Two stranglers showed themselves in front of the Adder to distract him, while another dropped a punjab lasso over his head, and with a sudden jerk, tightened it around his neck, twisting the bar to tighten the lasso, even as he lifted the Adder from the ground, so that his own weight would aid in strangling him.

The Eel fired his .38 into the back of two of the stranglers, dropping them to the ground in front of the Adder's flailing feet. He dared not make the shot to kill the strangler who was rapidly choking the Adder to death, for the distance was long and his target would not stay still. The slightest miscalculation would put a bullet through the Adder's skull instead of the skull of his strangler.

The Bomber sent a stick of dynamite arcing into the air, so that it would drop in uncomfortably close proximity. "Hit the deck, Eel. And cover your ears."

Scarcely had the two of them thrown themselves on the molasses-stained floorboards and endeavored to cover their ears, when a great concussion tore at their clothing and a wash of heat passed over them, along with the flailing and sundered bodies of four stranglers who had been creeping upon them from behind. The Bomber had expertly placed the stick of dynamite so that it was just far enough away to not kill or severely injure him and the Eel, but close enough so that it would dispose of the hashishins that were preparing to spring upon them.

They climbed to their feet, hair singed and clothing torn and charred. A still living hashishin lay groaning near the Eel and reached for his strangler's stick, intent upon breaking the Eel's shin. The Eel put the last two bullets of his revolver through the hashishin's heart, holstered the pistol, and drew forth his second revolver. He heard a rush of footsteps behind and whirled, ducking low beneath a punjab noose and firing twice into the body of the strangler, whose dead weight crashed against him and sent him tumbling to the ground.

Even as black spots formed before his eyes, the Adder thrust out with his sword cane and impaled one strangler upon its point. The strangler fell to the ground, tearing the cane from the Adder's grasp, and as consciousness began to slip away the Adder reached for his pistol, his spasming fingers finally touching the butt of the gun. With the semi-automatic still halfway in its holster, he thrust a finger through the trigger guard and rotated the pistol backward, firing through the leather. Bullets splintered the wooden planks, and then one shattered the strangler's knee, and with a cry the strangler pitched backward, bearing the Adder down with him, so that the weight of the master of disguise fell upon the strangler, driving the air out of his lungs.

Still, the strangler clung tenaciously to his punjab lasso, and blackness closed around the Adder's senses. His last conscious act was to continue firing his pistol.

When he awoke the Eel was leaning over him, cutting off the lasso with a stiletto, he lay on top of a motionless strangler who had been perforated three more times by his pistol. When the Adder put his hand down to balance himself, he felt something warm and sticky congealing beneath his fingers, and found that a pool of blood had spread from beneath the strangler. Coughing, he rose to his feet and plucked his sword cane from the body of a thug, he had slain earlier. His breath came in rasps, and a ragged ligature mark had been cut in the putty and grease-paint that concealed the burn scars that extended to his clavicles. However, he looked around and saw that he, the Eel and the Bomber were completely surrounded by black clad Thuggees and realized that he could not afford to take the time to fully recover his breath.

Behind the first ring of stranglers a group of Thuggees loaded their dart guns. The Eel's fingers worked nimbly as he reloaded the cylinders of one of his pistols, but it appeared that he was on the losing end of the race.

The Bomber struck a match and lit the cordite fuse of a stick of dynamite. "Up and at 'em. We've got no time to lose." He tossed the blazing stick, trailing smoke, over the heads of the blowgun-toting Thuggees and they scattered before the hellfire unleashed. It wasn't quick enough for a pair of them, and they tumbled head over heels in opposite directions, their clothing turned to bloody rags.

In front of the Eel a trio of hashishins pitched forward, but though the force of the explosion whipped at him like a hurricane force wind, it did not fell the Eel, the Adder or the Bomber. Again, the Bomber's placing of the dynamite had been impeccable.

The Eel snapped the cylinder shut and fired one shot into each of the hashishins, and then swung around to face the charge of the stranglers as the remainder of the circle closed around them in a ragged wave. With no time to light another stick of TNT, the Bomber resorted to his semi-automatic pistol and blazed away into the encroaching hashishins, felling three before they descended upon him with strangler's rods and rumals, which they wrapped about his limbs as he beat them with his mauling fists.

The Adder sliced to the left and to the right, every time that a target came within distance of the bloody tip of his sword cane. But they were surrounded, and the hashishins came in an unceasing tide, heedless of the wounds they received from the blade of the Adder, and soon the Master of Disguise was subsumed by them. They bound his arms and legs with their nooses and pressed a strangler's stick against his throat.

For a brief moment, the Eel was the only one left standing, darting to the left and right, his stiletto daring in and out, cutting a crimson trail through the stranglers, but even a man as quick as he could not evade the overwhelming numbers of his foes for long, and he found himself buried under an avalanche of bodies, his knife pried away from his fingers. Beneath the pile of bodies, the Eel heard the blasting of a Packard's horn and the roar of an engine, and then he wriggled free long enough to see the loading door burst asunder, and the prominent nose of a silver Packard rammed through in a blaze of headlights.

It wasn't the same Packard that the Eel had driven to the molasses factory, but the Eel recognized it all the same. Emma Goodbody leaned out of the passenger window, curly blonde locks streaming and began firing her Montenegro pistol, even as one laggard strangler was crushed beneath the weight of the vehicle. The horn blared and, thinking that they were under a full scale assault, the Thuggees melted away, fleeing for the shadows in the nether parts of the factory.

Jaya climbed out of the driver's seat and set to cutting free the trio of midnight avengers, while Goodbody spent her efforts firing at any moving shadow, in order to discourage the Thuggees from returning. She quickly emptied the five shots, but unlike her visit to the theatre earlier that evening, she had remembered to fill her pockets with extra ammunition, and she quickly reloaded the pistol with .42 caliber cartridges. She sent one winging into the far corner of the factory, just to let the stranglers know that she was reloaded.

Once released, the Adder stood and brushed the dirt off his suit. His puttied face had been mashed during the altercation so that he resembled a Vasras Viswanathan whose face had been run over by a truck. "I thought I told the two of you to stay safely at home."

"And what would have become of you if we had listened?" asked Good-body. "Viswanathan would have accomplished his aim, and all three of you would be dead by now."

Jaya's face was anxious as she cut the Bomber free from the lassos that constrained his limbs. "Any sign of my mother?"

"We saw a projection of her, like at a movie theater," said the Bomber, "but it flickered out when the Adder approached it."

"I believe that both Kirti and Viswanathan are both still here," said the Adder. He pointed toward a far balcony that contained a dusty hoist. "The angle of projection means that the projector was up there."

The Bomber shone a flashlight up into the balcony and indeed, a projector of curious workmanship still rested upon a table. Before anyone could stop him, the Adder bounded up the stairs to the projector. He followed a thick cable into a back room on the second floor, and there he found an equally curious camera and the same chair to which he had seen Kirti Patil bound. Severed ropes hung from the arms and feet of the chair and the scent of jasmine hung in the air. It was that scent of jasmine that brought a flood of memories rushing back to the Adder, when in a former life he had taken long strolls along the Champs-Élysées in Paris, arm in arm with Kirti, exploring the cinemas and theatres, shops and cafes, and taking respite beneath the clipped chestnut trees. Was it merely another trick of Viswanathan to make him believe that Kirti had indeed been here or had she actually been tied to this very chair?

The Adder put his hand on the seat and could still feel the warmth. Someone had been sitting there, and that someone had been wearing the same jasmine perfume that Kirti had worn all those years ago. The Adder felt a slight breeze on his face, and beyond a curtain that served as a backdrop to the photography studio, he found a door that was slightly ajar. This took him up a flight of stairs and as he climbed the steps he heard the sound of an engine accompanied by great rotors that beat the air. He redoubled his pace and recklessly burst onto the rooftop. At its center, concealed from the road by large smokestacks, was an autogyro that sent a wash of Manhattan dust and grime billowing towards him.

Through slitted eyes the Adder saw Vasras Viswanathan pulling a woman aboard. She turned and through the gritty haze the moonlight shed its wan rays upon her face, and the Adder recognized his long lost love. The Adder cried out and lurched through the wash of the rotor blades as the autogyro climbed into the air and out of his reach. Beneath the sound of the rotors the Adder thought he heard the mocking laugh of Viswanathan, and then the autogryo quickly shrank to the size of a speck in the night sky.

Jaya and the Eel came up alongside of him.

"She was here," choked the Adder. "Kirti was here. Did you see her?"

The Eel didn't know how to console the Adder, and he hadn't seen Kirti Patil, just the disappearing autogyro. "At least we know that she's still alive."

"The Master won't harm her," said Jaya, perhaps in order to convince herself. "He's in love with her."

"I'll find her," said the Adder. "I swear that I'll find her."

"How do you outthink a genius?" asked the Eel. "He had us outsmarted at every turn."

"That's what he would like us to believe," said the Adder. "The reality is that we've dismantled his bid to control the Italian mobs in New York. We may not have captured him or rescued Kirti, but we've set him back years."

The Eel digested this and it was agreeable to him. "You may be right."

An explosion rocked the factory.

The Adder grimaced. "It sounds as though the natives are getting restless."

"Native, nothing," said the Eel. "I'm betting that was the Bomber. We'd better get down there before he brings the whole building down."

The End

ABOUT EEL & ADDER

Though all my work is pulp-inspired (even the nonfiction One Foot in My Grave, to which I tried to bring a fast-paced pulp esthetic) the Eel and the Adder are what I consider pure and unadulterated pulp fiction. What I mean by this, is the stories take place in the classic World War 2 pulp era and the characters take the mold of the classic pulp characters like the Avenger, the Spider, and the Shadow.

Because I was drawing so plainly on these pulp archetypes I hoped to give the Eel and Adder enough spin to differentiate them, and make them characters of their own, rather than pale mimeographs of the original templates. When writing, I like to let characters slowly reveal their secrets to me in a sort of organic fashion where I discover hints and finally uncover what motivates and drives them. Cult of the Strangler is the fifth and longest Eel and Adder story which I have written, and their secrets are starting to come out.

It only makes sense to me that a man who made a living playing other people, and who suffered serious burns in a fire might suffer bouts of mental illness and have spent some time in the asylum. After all, the Shadow and the Spider aren't exactly poster boys for mental sanity.

And that the Eel, who is rival to Houdini in matters of escape, might have once used his skills for ill-gotten gains, gives him a motivation to seek redemption.

My research for this novel led me to books about ancient cults and even a slender tome with explicit instructions for the strangulation of one's enemies. No doubt, Big Brother has been monitoring my purchases and, considering that I believe in Constitutional government and I recently purchased a book on poisons (what self respecting pulp author doesn't need a book on poisons?), I am now certain to be on a terrorist watch list.

JOEL JENKINS - lives in the shade of towering conifers in the recesses of the Great Northwest, where the distant sun and omnipresent clouds paint strange, twisting shadows on the evergreen landscape, and where the dense forests hide the preternatural secrets of lost civilizations. It is here he unearths the skeletons of nearly forgotten myths and composes skeins of pulp yarns in genres from fantasy to weird western. He is best known for his Dire Planet sword and science fiction series about stranded astronaut Garvey Dire and also his trio of Gantlet Brothers guns and guitars novels.

THE BAGMAN IN:
"THE CULT OF KALI KILL"

By B.C. Bell

It was the worst of times. That's why they called it The Depression.

Four years after the crash of Wall Street one in four Americans was unemployed. The dustbowl had begun to spread poverty from the South to the Midwest, and tens of thousands of men traveled road and rail looking for work where there wasn't any. Many came to Chicago and found work of the worst kind: crime.

But sometimes the worst of circumstances brings out the best in people, and Mac McCullough was one of those people. A career criminal, a few months back Mac had been asked by the mob to break his uncle's legs. Instead, Mac broke his partner's nose, put on a mask and took out the man who had given the orders. The newspapers had dubbed him, The Bagman, and turned his alter ego into Chicago's newest masked mystery.

Now he was wanted by both sides of the law.

But a guy like Mac, an ex-grifter, hobo, thief, and hired muscle, didn't mind working both sides of the street; he expected it: even in a city where the streets ran red with blood. Mac had grown up in Chicago. The city was a part of him.

Almost skipping down State Street, he dodged around the late afternoon shoppers, tourists, and occasional horse carts all the while whistling Louis Armstrong's *All of Me*. People turned to look. Mac didn't mind. Nobody was really after him until he put on the mask.

Yup, Mac McCullough was in a good mood. But that was about to change.

He was paying a visit to his old buddy Smitty Klein, a pawnbroker and professional fence. Not that Mac had anything to buy or sell; he just liked to keep his finger on the pulse of his old pals, the Chicago Underworld. And at a place like Smitty's, that pulse pounded pretty fast. Smitty's may have looked like a Pawnbroker's dive at a glance, but a mint in stolen goods and antique rarities made their way through the safe in back every week. Mac knew all he had to do was show up with a pint of corn liquor and, within the course of an hour, he'd know who was moving what stolen goods, where and how many.

While the dilapidated exterior of Smitty's Pawn and Loan might prompt one to believe it had somehow survived the Chicago fire, the windows on both sides of the entrance let you know the place was still in business. On the left side a Philco radio sat on a table, surrounded by hats and boots, with hanging tennis rackets and a banjo above it. On the right sat a display case full of pocket watches and cheap jewelry. The cheap stuff sat in the window. The valuables stayed locked up in back.

Mac pulled on the front door handle. It was locked. The sign hanging in the window said he was "Open," and the "Back in Five Minutes" sign was nowhere in sight. Odd. Smitty sometimes opened late, but he was always open between noon and five, that's when the customers were out.

Mac stepped back out to peek in the display windows. The lights were out. Smitty lived upstairs, so Mac pulled on the handle that rang the bell above. Nobody answered.

Mac thumbed his hat back on his head and glanced up and down the sidewalk. When he turned back around, he had a sly grin on his face and a lock pick in his hand. He was positive Smitty wouldn't mind him plying his burglary skills in order to find out if anything was the matter.

Mac opened the door, and turned the sign around in the window so it said "Closed," then went inside. Locking the door behind him, he flipped on a lamp by the cash register. He could see everything seemed to be in place. The register's cash drawer was still open with about five dollars in it, including all the change. That was a month's rent. If Smitty had been robbed it wouldn't be there.

Mac sighed and realized he'd been holding his breath. Something just didn't feel right. Digging around behind the counter he found a flashlight, made sure it worked and whistling tunelessly now made his way toward the stockroom in back. He told himself it had to be something else, but recognized the smell as soon as he parted the curtains.

The cone of white emitting from his flashlight told him he'd been right. There was blood smeared on the walls. All of them. The light poured over Smitty's iron safe behind a table on the rear wall. The vault door was open, but the drawers full of jewelry were still there.

Mac shined the light on the floors. More blood, puddles of it. He was shining the light in the corners and finding nothing when he decided to simply pull the cord for the fixtureless bulb in the ceiling. He was shining the light on the rear exit as he felt about for the cord in the dark, when something bumped into his forehead and moved. Mac ducked and leapt to the side, switching off the flashlight. He would have dived for the floor, but he had a new suit on and didn't want to get blood all over it.

He drew the revolver from his shoulder holster without so much as a sound and stood still, waiting.

Nothing moved. He stood there a little bit longer and then decided to risk using the flashlight again. Flipping it on, Mac shined it above him where he'd first felt something bump his head.

Above him, hanging in the center of the room from a rope thrown over the rafters, hung two human legs. The rest of the body they had belonged to wasn't there. Mac's stomach turned over but he managed not to throw up.

They were skinny, old legs. Most likely Smitty's.

He pulled the string on the light switch next to them and began to search the rest of the backroom. Mac found of the source of the smell behind the table, in front of the safe. Smitty's disembodied head stared right at him. The rest of his body lay in pieces on the floor. Not just limbs, innards and a head, but some pieces were sliced so tiny it didn't make sense. Mac kneeled to get a look at one of Smitty's arms. There were covered with cigarette burns.

Whoever had killed Smitty had tortured him. The old man had died a slow and painful death. The fingers of one of the dead hands twitched and Mac jumped again. They were covered in blood. Peeling back the fingers of the hand, he discovered a pale sliver of ceramic glass with a piece of string threaded through it. It had taken all his steel reserve to open the hand and take the glass out.

Mac didn't want to hang around and see if it had been the death of a thousand cuts. Instead, he shined the light on the wall above the safe. Strange lettering had been left there, written in blood by someone's fingertips. Probably Smitty's.

Centered above the crimson letters like a logo on hotel stationary was the symbol of a devilish mountain cat, it's ears so long Mac couldn't identify what kind of cat it was supposed to be other than something vile. Its eyes and fangs dripped with the blood it was painted with.

A thump, like something tiny falling over, and a rustling sound eked from the tiny washroom in back. With two strides, Mac bounced around the safe and was at the washroom door; gun in one hand, flashlight in the other.

Nothing moved.

There wasn't much there to move, though. A toilet, a pin-up calendar on the wall and a sink. A sink with a small cabinet under it.

"Ya might as well come on out," Mac said, cocking his revolver. "I'm not going anywhere."

Still nothing moved.

"However, if I were to go somewhere, it might just be this cabinet by the sink. I see old Smitty has some…uh, *had* some magic tricks out front. You think maybe I could do that one where you shove a bunch of swords into a box and somebody disappears?"

After a moment, a whimpering sob escaped from beneath the sink. Only a child could have fit into a cabinet that small.

Mac flipped the cabinet door open with the barrel of his pistol and shined his flashlight into the eyes of a small boy, maybe six years old. He was clutching himself and shaking. Mac took off his jacket, wrapped it around the boy, pulled him out of the cabinet and wrapped an arm around him.

"You okay, kid?"

The boy said nothing, but began to cry.

"That's all right." Mac patted him on the back. "You're going to be okay."

The boy cried and snuffled, wildly and uncontrollably.

"It's okay, kid. It's okay." Mac leaned over the sink, and ran some water over his handkerchief with one hand, the boy's head lying on his shoulder. He wiped off the kid's face, then covered the boy's eyes with his hand as he carried him around Smitty's remains. It wasn't easy; they were all over the place.

He sat the boy down on the front counter, and let him cry for a few minutes before even speaking

"Did you see what happened?"

The boy cried some more. He was a dark haired child with deep black eyes. He had a Tom Mix Ralston Purina badge on his vest. Mac continued to pat him on the back.

"Hey, kid. I see you got a Tom Mix Ralston Rangers badge there. Let me show you something." Mac pulled a copy of the same badge out of his wallet. He'd used it in the past pretending to be a cop. He'd flashed it often and as fast as he could, but he'd never expected it to come in handy in any other fashion.

"Yeah, I've been a fan of Tom and Tony's since I first saw "Riders of the Purple Sage" way back when. So, as one Ralston Ranger to another, kid, I think I know what Tom would do. What's your name?"

"Billy." The boy wiped his nose with his shirtsleeve.

"Well, Billy, first I need you to tell me what you saw."

"Aw, it was horrible, Mister. Two guys came in with turbans on their heads, y'know, like they'd just stepped out of the *Arabian Knights*. They told Smitty they knew he'd bought something from a 'pair of tuna.' Smitty said he'd seen the tuna, but he hadn't done any business with him… Then two more men in turbans came in and then they…then they…" He started crying again and stopped himself. "…they started chopping him up. That's when I hid under the sink."

"Turbans and a pair of tuna? Did they say what kind of business?"

"A jewel. They were looking for a jewel. They kept saying 'blood for the bloodstone,' and Smitty kept screaming, and no matter how hard I closed my eyes and shoved my fingers in my ears…"

Mac pulled a blanket off a shelf and covered the boy with it, afraid the witness might be going into shock. The boy shrugged it off.

"It's okay, mister. I can take it."

"I guess you can." Mac smiled at the kid. "Us Tom Mix Ralston Rangers can't afford to be weaker than the bad guys can we? What would Tom say?"

"I don't know. What?" the boy said.

"He'd say eat a good breakfast and do the right thing."

"Oh, mister, I don't think I'll ever eat again." The boy held one hand on his head and one on his stomach as he groaned.

"Don't you worry about that, kid. Your appetite will come back." Mac pulled a nickel out of his pocket. "Hey, Deputy Billy, how'd you like to be a hero?"

"Me?"

"Yeah, you. In case you hadn't noticed, you're already one. Just surviving something like that back there gets you in the club."

"Really?" The boy still seemed to be catching his breath, his eyes wide.

"Yup, you're definitely in, kid. All you got to do is take this." He handed the boy the coin. "And go call the police. Tell them everything that happened, just like you told it to me, but don't tell them I was here. I have a feeling Tom would want me to work on this case personally, and I may have to go undercover." He slapped the boy on the back. "Go to the soda fountain on the corner, call the police, and get back here. Got it?"

"Yes, sir!" The tiny Ralston Ranger saluted.

As they headed for the door, Mac noticed a tiny ceramic figurine tied to the twine that held Smitty's legs swaying in the air.

The tiny statue stood two inches tall and looked almost alien. Stopping to look at it, Mac couldn't tell if the ceramic sculpture was of a man or a woman. It had blue skin and four arms. One of its hands clutched a blood-dripping dagger, another a curved knife. The two other hands held disembodied heads by the hair, and a necklace of human skulls adorned the thing's neck. The figurine's mouth displayed fangs like a lamprey and a tongue like a knife. They were just as red as the blood dripping from the disembodied heads.

Mac cut the ceramic figurine off the twine. Holding it in his hand, he could see where the chip had broken off the statue and wound up in Smitty's dead hand. On further inspection, Mac noticed the mound the ceramic statue stood upon wasn't the ground, but a body; somebody the evil-looking figure had defeated.

Having read more than his share of Edgar Rice Burroughs' planetary adventures, Mac's first impression was that the tiny figurine was the ugliest Martian he'd ever seen. The little blue creature evoked more terror at first glance than the cat drawn on the wall in Smitty's blood and that was saying something.

Stealing out the door, he locked it behind him and left the key in the lock. He had his gloves on. Even in summertime he kept a pair of deerskins in his pockets.

Great, Saturday night and here he was facing some kind of killer Indian cult after a jewel some fishy guy was carrying around. Then it struck him. These men in the turbans, if they killed Smitty just for talking to the sniveling man, they were definitely going to kill whomever it was that wound up with the jewel they were looking for.

Mac checked his watch, ten minutes to four. The pawn shops would all be open for at least another hour. He could think of three within walking distance. Back when he'd been a crook, Mac had done a lot of business with Tommy The Spoon, just off Wacker Drive at Spooner's Pawn and Loan. There was no way of knowing what the turbaned men would do, but Tommy the Spoon specialized in stolen jewelry.

Mac thought about "The Spoon" getting the knife, slapped himself in the head and spun off the sidewalk, hailing a cab. He hoped he was wrong, but part of him knew he wasn't. He had a murder to stop.

• • •

Mac hopped out of the cab and eyed Spooner's Pawn and Loan across the street. The curtains were drawn, but the lights inside were on, one of them waving back and forth on its cord just beyond the window, like a railroad worker waving his lamp: the signal for a train wreck.

Running through the traffic to cross the street, Mac felt a small man grab his arm in an effort to stop him. He looked right into the eyes of his old pal Wheezy Waldheim.

"Hey, Mac," Wheezy said. "How's business?"

"It's busy, Wheezy!" Mac threw his arm in the air dislodging Wheezy's hand and began to make tracks.

Wheezy followed and grabbed him by the arm again.

Mac shook it off then stopped when he saw the dejected look on Wheezy's face. Wheezy Waldheim had been one of Mac's best informers on the street in the past. A professional gambler who'd lost it all and fallen into drug addiction. Mac had even donated money—money he'd stolen from the mob—to put Waldheim in a sanitarium so he could sober up a few months back.

"You staying clean, Wheeze?" Mac asked, trying to make the ragged little man feel a little better.

"Haven't touched the stuff since I got out, Mac. Listen, about that money I owe you. I should be able to pay it back by the end of the week."

"You don't owe me anything, Wheezy. Forget about it," Mac said, gently pushing him out of the way and climbing the curb in front of the pawnshop.

Wheezy shrugged his shoulders, and then faded into the traffic, headed in the other direction.

Mac decided to use the front door to the pawnshop if he could. He still thought like a crook and his thought was that anybody robbing a joint was going to expect more trouble coming from in back than from in front.

But the door was locked. There was no way he could just pull the bumbling customer routine. Mac's left hand crept toward his jacket pocket as he walked around the outside corner of the store, his fingers caressing the silk lining of a mask.

Five seconds later Mac McCullough was no more. Instead, the Bagman, broad shouldered heir to the Gypsy legend of the King of Thieves, had taken his place in the shadows in the gangway. The eerie masked figure strode down the alley, his revolver hanging from his extended arm at his side as if it belonged there.

He stood in front of the door a moment, breathing.

There's a trick to kicking a door in. It's not like the movies where you just hit it with your shoulder and the door flies off the hinges. Mac had been a professional burglar and knew in some cases knocking down a door was faster than picking a lock. And, if there did happen to be a platoon of angry men waiting to chop his head off on the other side of the door, he wasn't going to be wasting time fiddling with it. Mac planted a foot by the lock, and the bolt broke through the wall on the other side.

The only thing missing inside was wild horses.

Tommy the Spoon hung upside down, swinging from ropes wrapped around the plumbing in the ceiling, his hands tied behind his back and his mouth covered with medical tape. Four tall men in different colored turbans surrounded him with curved swords already drawn. They were dark, bearded, and their eyes were red. The man wearing a white turban standing behind the counter seemed to be giving orders. He yelled something in a language Mac didn't understand, and the swordsmen whirled towards the masked man, blades swinging.

Mac drew his gun, shot the first one somewhere in the chest. The man twisted backward in the air, his hand clutching the wound. Mac was already aiming at the man in the white turban when something whizzed through air and sliced the skin between his thumb and forefinger as it ricocheted off the revolver's barrel. The gun clattered on the floor.

The man who'd thrown the dagger stood just to Mac's right, but the Bagman wasn't looking at him. Because the man in the white turban was coming over the counter with Spooner's sawed off shotgun in his hand. The Bagman charged the man who'd thrown knife.

Bounding behind a display of hanging fishermen's waders to dodge the buckshot, the Man of Steal twisted his left wrist awkwardly and reached up his sleeve freeing the foot-long shaft of iron rebar he'd had taped there then barreled ahead.

The turbaned man with the shotgun fired, and frayed rubber slung in a patch through the air as the waders exploded. The man who'd thrown the dagger held his curved sword's handle with both hands and swung the blade at the Bagman's neck.

Mac's right hand slung out with the rebar in it, slapping the swordsman's blade to the floor. The razor-sharp edge scraped across the concrete, shooting up sparks as the turbaned man holding it fought for control. Mac popped the man's head back with a quick right jab, and grabbed him by the wrist with his left. The Bagman held the swordsman's arm up and twisted beneath it, his hat falling off and blocking his view for a millisecond as the white turbaned man stood over the counter waving the gun barrel around, looking for a shot.

Mac came up behind the swordsman's shoulder, twisting the killer's arm behind his back. The Bagman's hostage dropped the sword, but even as the blade clattered to the floor the swordsman's chest exploded. The man in the white turban had fired the double barrel's second round. He shook the shotgun in front of him, cursing in a foreign language, then looked into the eyes of the man behind the mask. And he froze for a moment.

Those eyes were like ice. Not white, not pure, but the kind of ice that subsists on the street corner in early February. That gray, soot covered, sludge; the kind that sits by a fire hydrant all winter full of ashes and dead wood. The kind of ice you have to break through to find anything clear and pure about inside, and even then it still looks like broken glass. They were the kind of eyes you fell into. The kind that glimmer with wonder, while contemplating the nature of evil at the same time.

The Bagman shoved the dead body off of him, toward the man to his left, and dove over the counter. He smashed into his assailant so fast the turbaned man couldn't even swing the scattergun at him. The two combatants seemed to wad into a ball behind the counter, fists flying. There was a crash and a rattle of chains, and the masked man came up swinging a batch of raccoon traps. They weren't set with the springs to clamp on anybody's head, but they were solid steel with sharp corners.

The Bagman backed toward the wall and swung the batch of traps like a lumberjack at the white turban. The man in the turban tried to say something, but thirty pounds of scrap metal hit him in the side of the head. He went down whimpering.

The Windy City Detective reached in the display case and came up with a hunting knife. His one remaining foe stood armed only a few feet across the counter from him. Mac jumped. The turbaned man ran, and the masked man chased him into the street until he heard the sirens.

Once the police got the story from the Ralston Purina Kid, they'd probably follow Mac's line of thinking and checked up on the other pawn shops in the neighborhood. And in Mac's world, cops were cops, a bagman was a bagman, and never the twain shall meet. It was time to blow.

Abandoning the chase, the masked man trotted back in the pawnshop. Spooner was still hanging upside down from the ceiling. The Bagman grabbed a bucket by the slop sink and slung it into the pawnbroker's face. Spooner's eyes fluttered once, and he woke up sputtering. He waved his arms in front of himself and began rocking back and forth, hanging from the ceiling by his feet. His eyelids fluttered.

The Bagman ripped the tape off Spooner's mouth. The pawnbroker's eyes focused into the eyes of the Criminal Hero and he gasped just a little bit more. The Bagman slapped a hand over Spooner's mouth, more to speed up the process than silence him.

"What happened? Talk fast. It might save your life."

Spooner opened with the official Chicago citizen's credo: "I didn't do nothin'!"

The Bagman slapped him lightly about the head. "What did the men in turbans do?" He tightened his grip on the pawnbroker's hair. Having the wrinkles pulled out of his face made Spooner talk a little faster.

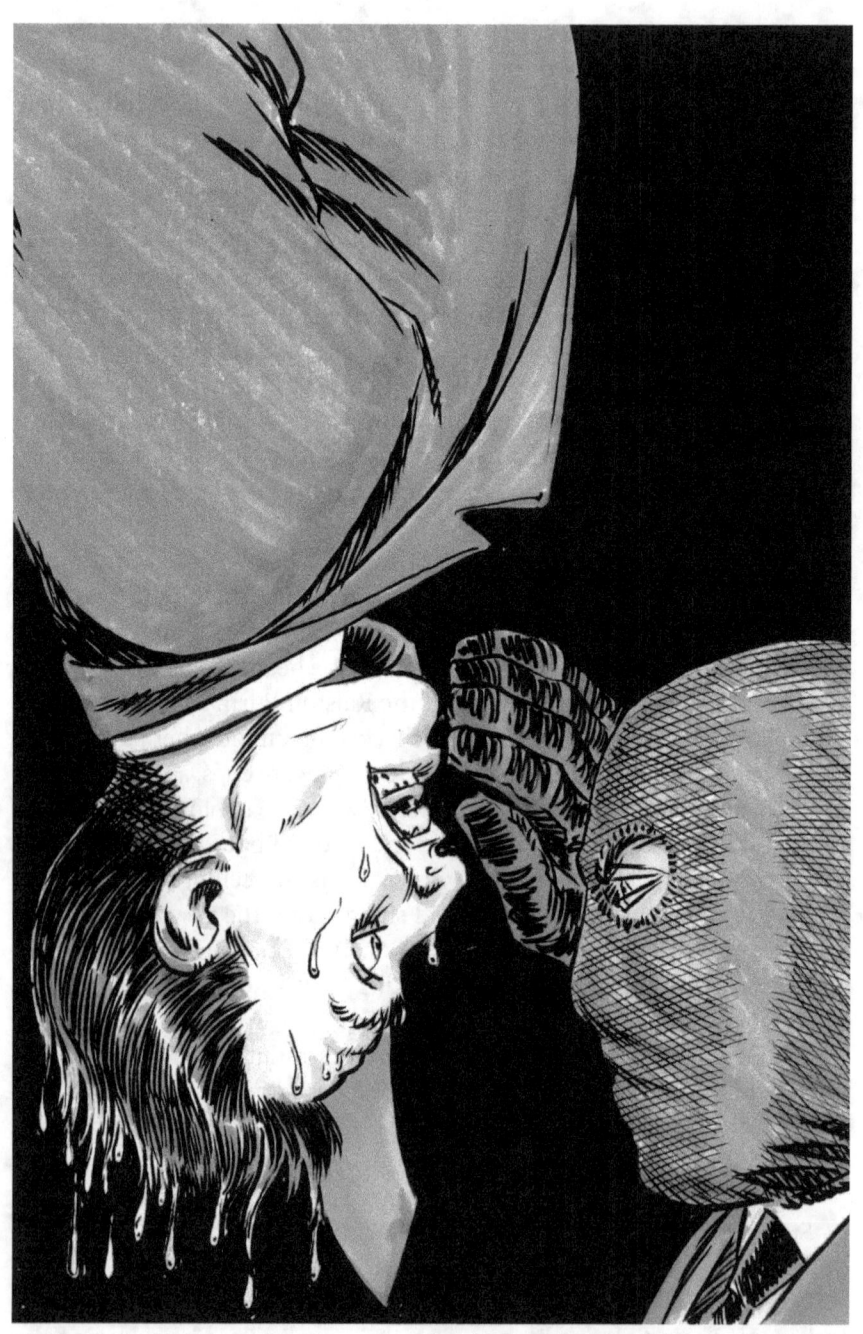

"I didn't do nothin'!"

"They were looking for something called…'The Stone of Shack Tee?'… I think… That's what it was…the Stone of Shakti! Kept asking me if I'd seen 'the Pair o' Tuna.' I didn't know what they were talking about. They were getting ready to chop off my fingers, fer cryin' out loud!"

"So they're looking for the Stone of Shack-tee…?" The Bagman cupped his chin with his hand.

"Duh," Tommy the Spoon said. "Could you get me down from here? My sinuses are all draining into my head!"

"Pair of tuna and the Stone of Shakti," the Bagman said, walking toward the rear exit.

"No, you can't leave me hanging here!" Spooner screamed.

"The cops are on their way, Tommy." The masked man turned as he opened the back door. "Duh."

• • •

Behind a hot dog stand, hidden beneath the shadows of the elevated train tracks on the corner of Addison and Lincoln Avenue, at the end of an anonymous alley sat an almost vacant lot unlike any other in the city. Not because of the amazing amount of scrap metal junk, not because of the cars for sale, and not because the best auto mechanic east of the Mississippi worked there.

A sign above the entrance read "Crankshaft's Auto Repair and Sales." And, while all that alone would have been good reason to recognize this particular place of business, what really made it stand out was the sign hanging above that sign. Sealed like fine print on steel, the silhouette of a dough boy from The Great War could be seen in profile charging up a hill. Below that a banner, painted and immaculately lettered, read "369th Infantry Division, USA, Hellfighters."

Directly in the center of the lot stood a tin shack precariously supported by metal signs and ancient two by fours. It was the headquarters of Mac's friend and aide, Crankshaft Jones, who had not only fought with the Harlem Hellfighters in the Great War, but had also won the *Croix de Guerre,* the French Medal of Honor. He was an old soldier, a coach, and great mechanical mind.

Inside the shack, Mac sat at Crankshaft's desk telling the mechanic about mysterious men in turbans and showing him the ugliest Martian he had ever seen.

Crankshaft laughed and stepped away from the carburetor he'd been toying with. He tore a page off the newspaper on the desk in front of Mac and hung it on a nail over the window to act as a shade, then explained.

"That's not a Martian, kid. It's Kali and that means your Arabian Knights are probably Indian."

"Crank, they're wearing turbans on their head, not feathers."

"Not American Indians, you dope," Crankshaft said. "Indian Indians, you know, from India. Let me see that thing." Crankshaft flipped it around in the palm of his hand. "Yeah, sometimes she's got more arms, but she's always got sharp teeth and a necklace made out of skulls."

"Sounds like a real nice dame." Mac began searching Crankshaft's desk drawers for the bottle of illegal corn liquor he kept there.

"Yes and no. I don't know a lot about it, but religion's always tricky, and Eastern religions are even trickier." Crankshaft slammed the liquor drawer shut, almost on Mac's fingers, and began to pace. "'Kali the Destroyer' they call her. Or him, I don't know. A lot of these Hindu gods are shape shifters."

"And her followers just go around destroying stuff?" Mac pulled the desk drawer open and the bottle out as Crankshaft turned around.

"No, not exactly. See, Kali's a symbol of life; death may be the end of life, but it is part of it. One of the other Hindu gods, Shiva , I think, she's a god of love or something; got in a fight with some sort of demon and Kali was the only one that could kill it." Having known Mac would pull the bottle back out all along; Crankshaft turned around with two cups in his hand and poured two shots. "So, Kali represents one of those Eastern yin and yang things, the circle of life."

"Living with her, I'd want death." Mac sipped the corn liquor and made a face, but it was hard to tell if his expression of disgust was for Kali or the bootleg whiskey.

"Likely, she'd stomp you anyway. Those guys you were fighting, you say they wore turbans?"

"Each one a different color."

"Well, Hindus don't always wear turbans, at least not religiously. But I'm willing to bet these guys are from a different sect, and it's part of some thuggee act."

"You got that right, Crank, straight up thugs. You should've seen what they did to poor Smitty's body."

"You don't even know where the word 'thug' comes from, do you?"

"The South Side?"

"Not quite. East, *way* east. They were a cult of assassins that traveled across India for years, worshippers of Kali. Of course, back then they strangled people. Still, they were really just murdering thieves. Wound up getting outlawed in India seventy or eighty years ago but to this day there's still the occasional rumor of some Killer Cult of Kali roaming the desert."

"Ask Smitty if it's a rumor. These guys are insane, and they don't care who they kill to get this 'Stone of Shack-tee' they're looking for. Their objective seems to be just chopping up anybody who's come into contact with the thing. Problem is, I don't know anything about this jewel, or that ugly looking panther they painted on the wall in Smitty's blood.

"Here's an idea. Try reading part of the newspaper besides the funny page." Crankshaft pointed at the third page of the city section on his desk. A six inch column on the side read:

Indian Princess Honored by Chicago Cultural Society

Princess Abhilash of Kashmir India, "The Princess of the Valley of the Steppes," will address the Chicago Historical Society on the importance of art from foreign cultures and histories to modern nation states. The princess's speech, a comparison of America's Liberty Bell and her own country's Stone of Shakti, will center on the fact that while nations may win great treasures, they create their own by deciding what is culturally important...

The Stone of Shakti, held by her nation for over a thousand years, remains one of the greatest, and greatest guarded, blood jewels in the history of the world...

"So, all we have to do is crash the gate and ask her a couple of questions tomorrow," Crankshaft said.

"Tomorrow might be too late. These wild Indians are good for about two bodies an hour from what I've seen. We've got to find a way to keep them busy and meet with the Princess, *tonight.*"

Mac grabbed a piece of stationary off Crankshaft's desk and began jotting a note down on it. He handed it Crankshaft.

"You mind delivering this to the Queen's hotel room? The article says she's staying at the Drake."

"Great, right next door to Frank Nitti's guys. Yeah, I'll drop it off, but what are you going to be doing?"

"It might keep somebody else alive a while longer if our 'thugs' have a target. So I'm going to hit every speakeasy I can in the next three hours and let it slip that Mac McCullough has The Stone of Shakti for sale."

"Really," Crankshaft said, nodding his head. "That's incredibly noble and incredibly stupid. Sometimes I wonder why I hang out with you."

"It's the incredibly noble part and you know it, Crank. See yah in a few." Mac started to step out the door.

Crankshaft threw his screwdriver at Mac's head. It bounced off the wall and got his attention. Mac counted to ten and cautiously stuck his head back in the door.

"You do realize," the ace mechanic said, "this Princess Abhilash could be the one behind this cult of Kali thing. The killers could be her men."

"Abhilash, corn beef hash, it's all the same. I aim to find out."

"So you just send a note and schedule a shootout? There's a word, I don't know if you've ever heard of it. It's called 'subtlety.'"

"How much muscle do you think you can squeeze into one room at The Drake? And the more tough guys she's got in there, the less room they have to move around."

"You've got a point. Still, you don't expect to just walk in and take her out?"

The door swung shut behind him.

• • •

The Drake Hotel's pink neon sign reflected off the waters of Lake Michigan decorating the skyline between Chicago's fashionable Gold Coast and the new commercial North Michigan Avenue. Designed in an Italian Renaissance style, the Drake boasted over five-hundred rooms, seventy-four suites, two large ballrooms, assorted restaurants, and a palm tree in the lobby.

Unfortunately for Mac's original plan, the Princess was in the Presidential Suite. Five men stood stationed in the living room area. Three of them were dark skinned, mustached and dressed in British Indian Army uniforms. They stood proudly steadfast with red turbans on their heads and medals on their chests. Three more were stationed in the bedroom, and another ten in the next suite. A small army.

Princess Abhilash paced back and forth between her court advisor on one side and her brother, Prince Ahmrit Basir Singh, on the other. She was dressed in Eastern fashion. As the gossamer material wafted on her petite form the flowing silk revealed the curves of her body as much as it hid them. Her green eyes, normally full of light, were dark and surrounded with worry lines that betrayed her perfect image. Her shiny black hair fell across supple lips as she lowered her head and leaned toward her brother.

"Tell me, Ahmrit," the Princess said, almost nibbling one of her pastel-colored nails out of anxiety. "Do you think they hope to ransom the jewel? Or to merely know if it has been stolen?"

"If our visitors wish to ransom the Stone of Shakti our only option is to kill them all, and then leave their leader just alive enough to lead us to it. Should they ask about the jewel's possession…?" He paused and stroked his mustache. "Then of course we must keep maintaining that it is safe at the palace."

"But for how much longer can we continue to lie?" the Court Advisor, Sabat Kirat said. Sabat was the Indian Consulate's representative to the United States. As such, he was dressed in a European-cut, double-breasted suit. The only fashion statement reflecting nationality was the fez he wore on his head. "We have trailed the jewel across continents, and yet with every mile we move to the west our hopes lessen."

"I do not like this…this… espionage. This city with its noises and gambling and strange people."

A knock pounded on the door.

"Room Service," a muffled voice said from the other side.

The Drake Hotel didn't have room service after eleven P.M.

The Princess raised her veil as the two guards stationed by the door turned and opened it.

"Room service," A middle-aged black man, graying at the temples repeated and pushed a covered kitchen cart back and forth in front of the door, giving the guards the chance to make some space.

The Princess looked at her brother. He nodded, and the guards stood back. The bellboy smiled and gently wheeled the cart in.

"How's it going, brothers," he said, eyeing a couple of the guards and waving with his jaw like they were in the same club.

The guards stood unmoving. The Royal staff exchanged curious glances.

Prince Ahmrit Basir Singh, still in tuxedo evening dress but wearing his traditional blue turban, was a commanding presence of a man. He stood easily over six-foot, bearded, broad shouldered and dark. The blood of kings and scimitar-wielding soldiers pulsed in his veins, the blood of the greatest tribes of the Himalayan Steppes. The Prince leaned over the smiling server as if he were about to swat him.

The bellboy raised the cover of the tray, both exposing the food and using it for a shield.

"Well, if there's one thing Chicago has it's food," the black man said, and waved his other hand across the tray. "Brats and German chocolate cake, egg rolls, roasted Greek chicken, Chicago's own Maxwell Street Polish, and strawberry shortcake."

Prince Ahmrit leaned over the server, his eyes bulging with anger. "What sort of fools do you take us for? We know you are not with the hotel."

"True, true," Crankshaft said, "But we wanted to meet you on our own terms, and I don't want this thing getting ugly."

Ahmrit Singh reached across the cart and grabbed the supposed bellboy by the lapels. The bellboy spun, sliding out of his jacket sleeves, and came up across the room with a .38-automatic in each hand. Rifles slung from the guards shoulders, all pointed at the lone black gunman. Every eye in the room was on him when a voice called out from behind the Princess, a voice that couldn't be ignored.

"I wouldn't do that if I was you," the Bagman said. "There's still apple pie out in the hall."

While everyone's attention had been on Crankshaft, the Bagman had slipped from the shelter beneath the serving cart on the other side. He had an arm wrapped around the Princess's neck, a grenade in one hand and the pin in the other, spinning it around on his index finger like he was waiting for a valet to come pick up his keys at some fancy restaurant.

Heads spun. The guards tried to keep their attention on the black gunman, but every eye in the room was drawn toward the masked man like a magnet. His presence was arresting.

Still, out of sheer devotion to the Princess, one of the guards charged. The Bagman locked his left arm around the Princess's head. The guard swayed right, looking for a target in which to plunge his bayonet without hurting her. Mac spun, clubbed him with the grenade in his left hand, pushed the princess away, and a .45 revolver appeared in his right. The gun was aimed directly between Prince Ahmrit Basir Singh's eyes.

A bead of sweat ran down the side of the Indian man's face.

"Now, that you've almost gotten us all killed," the Bagman said, "we can sit down, have a nice little snack and discuss the presence of a certain jewel." He spun the grenade's pin around his finger again. "Or we can all just go *boom*."

They opted for the snack.

Crankshaft sidled over, nudged Mac, and tried to speak under his breath. "You were supposed to set off a smoke bomb!"

"You'd have gotten shot," Mac said.

"*You* would've gotten shot. I, on the other hand, would already be home." He gave Mac a critical look. Crankshaft wasn't fond of Mac's gift for improvisation.

"Never mind that, where's the pie?" Mac put the pin back in the grenade.

The food helped to calm things down a little, just like Mac had planned. The Princess was a vegetarian and couldn't eat the Maxwell Street Polish, but she loved the grilled onions. Mac went so far as to pull his mask above his nose and eat a slice of pie while they talked.

"So, Princess, you wouldn't happen to have a crazed killer cult of Kali working for you, would you?" the Bagman said.

Both the Princess and her brother eyed Crankshaft like they were wondering if they should take the masked man as serious or crazed. Then the Princess giggled.

"Your American lack of tact normally insults me," she said. "But in this case, I can see reason behind your need to 'get down to business,' as you would say. Though first, you must tell me why I should trust a bandit."

"Because it looks like there's nobody else you can trust. That and that World's Fair thing you came to town for? I did manage to save a big part of it a few weeks back."

"I have seen your picture in the newspapers. They say you are not to be trusted. However, I am The Princess of the Valley. There are many I can trust."

"Nah, I don't see it that way." Mac wiped the pie filling off his chin.

"How dare you speak to the Princess that way!" Sabat Kirat, the Court Counselor said, wadding up his napkin and holding his fez atop his head as he stood.

"I dare because I speak the truth, Mr. Foreign Consul. Way I see it is, if the State Department thought you guys had anything to do with those killers you'd already be on a boat back home. Problem is they don't know this whole thing is about a blood ruby that's supposed to be in India. The papers claim the Stone of Shakti is safe back in Kashmir, but if that's the case why is a killer cult looking for it here? You're here for something besides the World's Fair yourself, and I'm guessing it's the same jewel."

The Foreign Consul sat back down.

"Such guesses could get a man killed," the Princess's brother said.

"Wanna bet which one?" Mac held up the grenade again.

Ahmrit Singh seemed to deflate, but his sister pursed her Mona Lisa lips and began to tell a story.

"The Stone of Shakti is rightly Kashmir's and a symbol of faith in every village on the Indus River. Legend has it the ruby was formed from a puddle of the demon Raktabija's blood when he was defeated by Kali. Priceless by modern standards, kingdoms were built and have fallen around it. Until the jewel came into the possession of Kashmir, crops faltered and the river dried.

"The people of Srinigar and Kashmir have thrived for the last fifteen-hundred years, many believe because of the stone. Without it our citizens will lose faith. Others will begin to search for the blood ruby, and great wars will wage. You've seen what those madmen can do. Picture that on a grand scale, nation by nation, as mere rumors spread about the jewel's presence in one village after another. Our entire region would be devastated.

"Are you familiar with the Pakistan National Movement at all?" she said.

"Pack of who?" Mac looked up from his pie.

"The Pakistan National Movement. While India and Britain have established all British possessions in South Asia as Indian, the Pakistani Movement claims the five northern sections are non-Indian nations because they are Muslim, as if there were only one religion in India, where there have always been many." She slowly shook her head, sipped from her tea, and, staring into The Bagman's eyes all the while, continued.

"About a year ago, a man named Bin Ali Khan, the Blood Tiger, and his band arrived in Kashmir, wearing swords where it is against the law for Punjabis to do so. Through wile and guerilla warfare Bin Ali Khan stole the Stone of Shakti while our resources were focused on a battle outside the city."

"This 'Blood Tiger,' does he have a crest that looks something like this?" Mac pulled a tiny notebook out of his pocket and turned to a page where he'd scribbled a version of the blood sketch that left on Smitty's pawnshop wall.

The princess nodded yes and continued to speak.

"As much as he might pretend, Bin Ali Kahn's differences are political, not spiritual, otherwise he already would have announced the Stone of Shakti was in his possession. We believe the PNM will announce it at the Cultural Society's ceremony tomorrow. We have security ready to seize him and the stone, but it will do far worse than simply ruin the event. It will destroy kingdoms." Then deeply, almost as if begging she looked from her brother and into the eyes of the masked intruder.

"Except for one thing," the Bagman said. "If this Bin Ali Kahn guy has the jewel, why's he converting all of Chicago's pawnbrokers into butcher's shops?"

"Our agents believe someone in your city may have stolen the jewel from Bin Ali Kahn."

"That's what I think, too, sis! I mean, Princess." Mac bowed in apology but never stopped talking. "I think Bin rolled into town with rube written all over him, and somebody pulled the pigeon drop on him."

"Rube? Pigeon drop?" The Indian Consul didn't understand.

"It's an old con game, your honor," Mac added. "I mean somebody stole it. And, if you don't have the jewel, and the cult of Kali doesn't have the jewel, then every gang in town's going to be fighting for the thing."

"So we need to find it before the public knows it's missing." Crankshaft made a strange picture still in his bellboy garb, now sitting in an overstuffed chair and swirling cognac around in a glass. "Well, Princess, luckily, you're in good hands."

"I fail to see how one bandit and a black man can succeed where our own national security has failed."

"Lady, we're the guys that steal from the bad guys," Mac said, emphasizing each word as if it were a sentence.

Again the Indian Royalty and government officials exchanged glances.

"Look, if there's somebody trying to sell the jewel in this city, I can find it. If, on the other hand, these 'thugs of Kali' find it first, they've already killed a friend of mine and ruined a kid's childhood. So it's personal."

"How do I know you won't simply steal it for yourself?"

"You don't, but one bandit and a black man are a lot easier to find than the jewel is right now. So, worst-case scenario, you're helping your own odds of finding it. You want a character reference you can walk down the hall and ask Frank Nitti, head of the Chicago outfit, what he thinks. It will not be a glowing review."

Prince Ahmrit and the Indian Consul kept shaking their heads until their eyes met. They looked at each other, almost shrugging for a moment, before finally nodding in agreement.

"I believe you might be of service, Mister Bagman," The Princess said. "But let me warn you, Bin Ali Kahn, the Blood Tiger is no normal man. Should the Stone of Shakti fall into his hands a new age of barbarism would begin."

There was a moment of silence, then Mac slapped himself on the side of the head and said:

"Speaking of pigeons and tigers and everything; one of the witnesses said the Kali Killers were looking for 'a pair of tuna.' He might've been speaking Punjabi. That make sense to any of you?"

"A pair of tuna?" The Princess said.

"Two fish?" asked the consul.

"A pair of tuna," Prince Ahmrit repeated slowly. "Tuna in Eastern languages is usually just plain tuna. What you're saying translates into 'Beyond tuna.'"

"Beyond tuna? What the hell could it mean?" Mac pushed his hat back and scratched his head through the mask.

Crankshaft decided to speak before Mac got too confused and ran off on one of his confounded treasure hunts that made no sense. "You know how if you line up a bunch of people and whisper one sentence, how by the time it reaches the other end of the line it the sentence says something

"Lady, we're the guys that steal from the bad guys."

completely different. It could be they said something else, something similar."

"We'll play with it phonetically and see what we come up with." The
Princess shrugged, but also smiled at Crankshaft. "Meanwhile, what are
you going to do?"

"Friend of mine is making himself a target, saying he stole the jewel," the
Bagman said. "So whatever you do, *DON'T* send your men after a Mister
Mac McCullough."

"We could send men to protect him," the Princess said.

"Nah, Mac likes his privacy a lot. Guy's practically a nut case. Plus, we
got eyes on him; thanks though. No, what you can do is keep your troops
on the lookout, and maybe a team of them on call here, just in case."

• • •

Mac pulled his mask off in the elevator. Crankshaft took off his tie and
shed the waiter's coat. Then they abandoned the serving carts in the center
of the lobby and headed out the door for Oak Street where they'd parked
their car, The Blue Streak.

A month ago, Mac had stolen the new sports car from the local mob.
But the original Graham Blue Streak, while quick, almost flipped over taking tight turns, and, while fast, could be faster. Since then, Crankshaft had
modified it for speed and maneuverability, put reflective windows in, and
a booster tank that could inject alcohol or nitrous oxide into the engine. It
was two cars in one, a performance vehicle that could out-obstacle anything on the course, and a race car that could do over a hundred miles an
hour in the straightaway.

Problem was they had to get to the car.

Before Mac could reach for the door, something grabbed him on the
shoulder. Mac spun with his hand buried beneath his lapel reaching for
his gun.

"Hey, Mac. Funny running into you here."

"Wheezy!" Mac let out a sigh like he'd been holding his breath. "Look,
whatever it is, could you come by and see me tomorrow. I'm really busy
right now."

"Naw," Wheezy said, "it's nothing. Just saying 'hi,' letting you know I'm
good for what I owe you. Not hiding from you or anything. Still, it's kind of
funny you being outside Spooner's…"

"Look, Wheezy, I'm busy." As Mac lifted Wheezy back onto the sidewalk
he sensed something moving in the shadows beyond the cars parked on
the street.

"Pairin turna!" a guttural voice cried. "Saskana!"

Mac ducked as a dagger whizzed through the air and clipped at his brow, pushing Wheezy down in front of him and shoving him under the car. The Bagman turned to face three more men in turbans wielding swords.

The first assassin was already on Mac, the blade striking downward at the back of his neck. Mac rolled toward the swordsman, just under the blow. Sparks shot up from the concrete. Stomping the killer's sword down with one foot, as if it were a step, Mac leaped in the air and kicked the man in the side of the head. The sword fell from the turbaned man's hand as he landed in the middle of the street unconscious.

Mac came up out of a crouch with a revolver in his hand. Aiming to wound the second man, he noticed something about the car parked across the street. There were a row of gun barrels peering across the top of it.

Without time for thought, the Criminal Hero fired at the second bandit then back-dived over the hood of the Blue Streak. Clutching the hood in midair with his empty hand, he levered himself, spinning across the hood, and landed behind the Blue Streak on one knee. The turbaned cult killer screamed and jumped sideways as the battery of firearms across the street exploded, tearing him in half.

"They don't even mind killing their own guys, Crank!" Mac said, as the two adventurers huddled behind the Blue Streak's tires.

Both men fired from under the car, but there was no return fire; for a moment. Then a second volley erupted. Bullet holes and dents stitched their way across the Blue Streak.

Mac and Crankshaft returned fire, then ducked before a third volley.

"They're working military style," Crankshaft said. "Taking orders. Ready, aim, fire; one volley at a time."

Mac stood up and fired even though he knew that's not what Crankshaft meant. He smiled at the ace mechanic, reached for the hand grenade still clipped to his belt.

"You want to play Army in Chicago, we've got a little thing called the Armory."

"I thought that thing was a dud," Crankshaft said.

"At this point, I don't even know anymore." Mac heaved the pineapple like an outfielder trying to catch the runner at the home.

The crowd of men in turbans scattered as the grenade landed behind them. One of the voices shouted orders in a foreign language. Unless the order had been to panic, nobody seemed to notice.

The grenade exploded, and shrapnel perforated the Chrysler the killer cult hid behind. A perfectly good '31 touring sedan blown all to hell.

Screams echoed down the lakeside, but none of them seemed to be from the killer cult of Kali. No, the screams seemed to emanate down the corner from Oak to State Street where the nightclub crowd was. Valets in front of the clubs were suddenly put upon by crowds wanting their cars, while others ran out in the street and down the alleys in search of safety.

Crankshaft was already in the Blue Streak testing the ignition.

Mac jogged across the street to look over the wreckage as quickly as possible. He'd thrown the grenade behind the men, intending to scare them more than blow them up, and in all honesty he hadn't known if it was a dud, a bomb, or a gas grenade, but he'd gotten the response he wanted. The turbaned men were gone.

Glancing down, their weapons caught his eye. There were some military arms, but they didn't look American, not one Colt or Remington among them. He picked up the butt of a broken .30-.06 rifle and noticed Oriental lettering on part of it. Littering the ground next to the .30-.06 rifle lay an assortment of daggers and throwing stars. The writing and the throwing daggers were obviously Oriental, but leaned a lot more toward Chinese than Indian.

Mac picked up one of the daggers and stuck it in his belt on the way back to the car. Sirens wailed in the background. Mac peeked under the car looking for Wheezy, then stood up and shrugged his shoulders when the little guy was nowhere to be seen.

Crankshaft smiled as the Blue Streak's engine turned over. The only part of the car that was bulletproof was the armor around the engine casing. The Blue Streak turned off Oak Street, down an alley and then disappeared headed west.

"Think they were watching the Princess at the Drake, or were they after the blood jewel Mac McCullough's supposed to have?" Crankshaft said, as the Blue Streak sliced through the shadows.

"My guess? They were watching the Drake and they bought some firearms to help themselves with. What was left of their ammo all seems to have Chinese writing on it."

"Really?" Crankshaft sighed.

"Really," Mac answered. "Looks like we're going to Chinatown."

• • •

Back in 1905 Frank (Dong Yee) Moy wrote to eighty-seven of his Chinese friends and relatives, and Chicago's Chinatown was born. Race and real estate being what they are, the city within a city was soon moved from

Chicago's Loop to the corners of Van Buren and Clark Street, where it thrived. Still, after midnight it was not a spot for tourists.

The Blue Streak hummed in the darkness, its lights slashing the Chinatown early morning darkness. Scattered shadows of people still skirted the street. Mac saw where The World's Fair's extension of Cermak Road had cut the little village in half and wondered if some of the midnight lurkers might be looking for a place to stay.

"Let me guess," Crankshaft said. "You're going to be breaking and entering somewhere around here because I don't see anything open."

"You just have to know which doors to knock on, Crank, and which ones not to." Mac fondled the mask in his pocket. He'd be safer asking questions as the Bagman than as Mac McCullough, since the lie that Mac possessed the jewel was out on the street, but The Bagman didn't have any working relationships in Chinatown. He'd have to appear as Mac McCullough. "Pull in here."

The alley was dark and dank, the smell of stagnant summer sewage eking up from the ground mixed with the scent of stale garbage and the ashcans in the corners. A streetlight that looked to be about fifty watts was the only sign of electricity for a block. The rats didn't even bother to scurry away as the two men slammed their car doors. With no idea where they were going, Crankshaft put on his reflective goggles so he couldn't be identified as they approached the back of a black brick building.

The Bagman knocked on the door. Three times, then two, then one…a secret code. A slot opened in the door at eye level.

"Is Phil around?"

"Phil?" Crankshaft muttered in the background as the slot closed and the locks on the door ratcheted themselves open.

"Hong Kong Phil Li," Mac said to Crankshaft from behind the back of his hand. "You didn't think I stole *all* our guns did you?"

Crankshaft remained silent as the door opened.

And with good reason, because as the portal opened a line of scarred and tough-looking Chinese men surrounded them.

"Don't give 'em any lip, Crank. These guys may be small but they know how to fight."

The circle of men closed in on Mac and Crankshaft from behind, forcing them in the door. It was possible they thought Mac McCullough had the jewel. The hired muscle surrounded them, forcing their backs to the wall inside. Crankshaft narrowed one eye. His fist hovered uncomfortably close to the pocket where he kept his Colt Automatic. Mac, on the other hand, acted like he was being welcomed.

"How ya doing, guys? Phil around? I got some business." Mac reached in his coat. The men around him visibly tensed. He pulled out a cigarette and lit it.

"Mac McCullough, good to see you." Hong Kong Phil Li stood off to the side of the crowded room, mostly because he had to. Phil was a butterball of a man, just over five-feet tall, wearing a cheap suit and a beat up camel homburg. The false tone in his voice revealed he thought Mac had the jewel. His eyes were like little black triangles. "I've heard some interesting things about you recently."

The crowd of men tightened around Mac and Crankshaft.

"I don't have the jewel, Phil," Mac said.

"You don't mind. We search you?"

Crankshaft may have been backed into the wall, but he'd made sure he backed toward the light switch. He scratched his right shoulder, then his arm swept down and killed the lights.

In the sudden darkness, the butt of Mac's revolver pounded off two separate heads. The Man of Steal parted the bodies connected to the heads and wound up standing next to Hong Kong Phil Li pressing a revolver against his forehead. The lights came back on.

"I mind." Mac cocked the gun.

The entire room was silent, like the calm before a storm. Crankshaft elbowed a few men away from him as they stood at the ready to spring. His gun hand hung ready.

"Besides, if I had the Stone of Shakti do you think I'd be here? I'm looking for the damned thing."

"You and everybody else," Hong Kong Phil said, as Mac loosened his grip. "Tea, Mr. McCullough?" He turned from the interior of the room as if nothing had happened, and the band of Chinese hoods receded into the shadows.

Hong Kong Phil strolled into the next room lighting a cigarette. Crankshaft and Mac followed him into an office and sat across from Phil at his desk. Two other doors, one on each side, connected to other rooms. The sickly sweet smell of opium drifted through the cracks in one, and the smell of bootleg whiskey and black market tobacco through the other.

"You should know by now, Mac. I got guns and drugs. I don't pass information," Phil said. "Besides, I've got my own men out looking for the thing, supposed to be worth a fortune."

Mac slapped five one-hundred-dollar bills on the desk. Hong Kong Phil started talking.

"All I know is some Indian revolutionary had it on his person and made the mistake of taking a walk on the north side. This afternoon it was in the hands of one Fingers Rollie, a pickpocket."

"I know Rollie," Mac said. Mac knew half the crooks in town, some of them were still his best friends.

"Well, you'll be glad to know he's still alive then. Idiot didn't know what he had and lost it in a poker game, back of Barney's Grill."

"Right in our own back yard." Mac snapped his fingers in disappointment. He and Crankshaft were regulars at the speakeasy. It was right around the corner from the garage. "Who'd he lose it to?"

"Now you're going to laugh. He says he doesn't remember. Says it was a brown-headed guy in a gray suit. Somebody so plain you could barely remember him."

"Was he telling the truth?" Mac lowered one eyebrow.

"I said he was alive." Hong Kong Phil smiled with a gleam in his eye. "I didn't say he didn't have the crap beaten out of him."

The phone on Phil's desk rang. He popped it into one hand, and the earpiece in the other. "Excuse me a moment, gentleman… Yes… Yes, I can do that, but I'll need another five hundred on delivery. Cash on hand. If it's not there when my men show up, I'll have other men, sharpshooters, stationed down the street. Kill you all, you understand?"

A bee buzzed on the other end of the line.

"OK, same as before?" Phil jotted on a pad of paper in front of him. "Different address. What's the address? You got it. Yeah, ask for a kid named Xun Shun, he'll be driving a diaper truck." He slammed the receiver back on the prongs as he slapped the phone on the table. "Anything else, Mac?"

"You sold some guns to some very uncivil men in turbans, any idea where I can reach them?"

"Cost you another two-hundred dollars." The ends of Hong Kong Phil's lips turned up, but you couldn't call it a smile.

Crankshaft grumbled.

"Where are they?" Mac slapped the cash on the table.

"Right here," the Chinese smuggler turned the pad he'd been writing on over and shoved it across the desk. "At least they will be at four this morning. They insisted on delivery."

Mac looked at the pad, tore the page off. "Thanks, Phil, seriously. Really, we should get together sometime."

"Bring cash," the rotund Asian said, and walked them to the door.

Outside the ramshackle building, Mac said: "Crank, that address on the pad? It's mine."

"You don't think they're dumb enough to just unload a bunch of guns in your front yard do you?"

"If you'd seen what I'd seen, Crank, you'd realized they're not stupid. They just don't care. This is way out of my league. International stuff."

"Yeah, but you got a home field advantage, kid. These guys have never been in a Chicago gang fight."

"I got an idea." Mac straightened his hat on his head like his brains were too big.

Crankshaft slowly shook his head. Something bad was going to happen.

"Come with me," Mac said. "I've got to call Hunts."

Hunts Helms was one of Mac's oldest buddies, someone Mac had met on the road in his grifter past. They'd worked a hundred different con jobs as a team and always got along. Hunts was now a press agent for the city, something he called a public relations man. Hunts not only had information on everything "official" going on, but he had access to people, places and things all over Chicago.

• • •

Four AM is a burglar's favorite time of the day. Almost everybody living in the straight world is asleep. Two gaslights played with the dark on both sides of the avenue in front of the modern brownstone where Mac lived. Nobody noticed when one of them went out.

A dozen members of a cult of death stopped at the end of the street where Mac McCullough's apartment sat. Swords and pistols hung from their belts, several carried rifles. The ragged band of Kali wore western pants with some sort of gown hanging low over them. Their turbans were dirty, and their faces unshaven. Two men parted from the others, walked to the opposite end of the alley, and a second dagger shattered the remaining streetlight. The swarm of beards, turbans and swords undulated in the darkness as desert-tempered warriors straggled around the edges of the pack.

"Mac McCullough *akhtyar patthar!*" A bent-backed cleric in back of the swarm said.

"*Pairin tunir! Saskana!*" a broad-shouldered man in an orange turban said, and shoved the cleric away. "*Saskana!*"

The cleric mumbled something else about Mac McCullough and spat back at his orange-garbed tormenter. The men were arguing among themselves.

"Good," Mac thought from the shadows down the street, as he finished wedging the nozzle of a fire hose in the window of Chicago Parks Department truck.

His plan was simple. After the killer cult put out the streetlights, Crankshaft would cut off the arms delivery truck before it could turn down the street, then zip the Blue Streak down the alley in reverse. Going in reverse Crankshaft could use one of his favorite gadgets on the car, rear mounted spotlights.

Normally, Crankshaft used them to blind people chasing the Bagman, but this time he'd be using them to blind Bin Ali Kahn's men. As Kahn's men headed for the other end of the street, Mac would crank the wrench connected to the fire hydrant on the other side of the Parks Department truck. The cult of killers would then be forced back to the middle of the street, where Mac had set up a gun-net; a hunting net that fired out of a mortar apparatus, used to collect wild bird specimens. The Bagman and Crankshaft would bop a few heads beneath the net before the terrorists could cut through the ropes. And they'd live happily ever after.

Mac had been quite happy with the idea of a three-pronged attack when he'd thought it up. Now that he could hear Bin Ali Kahn's men arguing among themselves he was almost beaming beneath the Bagman's mask.

Crankshaft sat on the driver's side of The Blue Streak at the other end of the avenue continuing to shake his head.

As the diaper service delivery truck Hong Kong Phil used to deliver arms approached the corner, The Blue Streak screeched around and in front of it. Even as the van driver slammed on the brakes, The Blue Streak fishtailed, blocking the intersection with its rear end and shifting into reverse. As the rear bumper hit the alley, Crankshaft flipped on the rear-mounted spotlights.

The spotlights hit Wheezy Waldheim like he was about to open a Broadway show. One minute he'd just been strolling home, just crossing the street completely unaware. And then, suddenly, Wheezy Waldheim was walking directly in the path of the Blue Streak. Crankshaft couldn't hammer the throttle down in reverse without running over Wheezy.

"*Saskana! Saskana!*" screamed the Indian in the orange turban. Half the killer cult of Kali raised their weapons and charged at Wheezy.

Mac's plan might have been shot, but he needed to keep the enemy confused. Without time for thought, The Man of Steal cranked the wrench on the fire hydrant open. The nozzle barely held in the window, swishing back and forth to Mac's advantage. The sudden blast of cold water knocked down three of the turbaned men, who tumbled into others.

The Bagman bounded over the hood of the Parks Department van to

The sudden blast of cold water knocked down three of the turbaned men.

help Wheezy. Rushing past the killer cultists who hadn't reacted yet, he knocked down half-a-dozen of them with a body block. Bullets fired and swords swung at his head. The Bagman discharged his revolver into the shoulders of two men, then dislodged the piece of iron rebar taped up his sleeve and deflected another blow.

Wheezy still stood in the middle of the street with his mouth hanging open.

"Mac McCullough *akhtyar patthar!*" the bent-backed cleric said again.

A third of the two dozen men charged Mac's apartment. A third of them charged Wheezy, and a third charged The Bagman.

With tires screeching, Crankshaft backed the Blue Streak around Wheezy and whirled it to a stop between the band of assassins and the frail, little gambler. One of the Indians with a repeating rifle fired nonstop. In the background, Hong Kong Phil Li's diaper truck full of munitions pulled up behind Crankshaft, still trying to figure out what was going on. With hot lead lacing the air around him, Crankshaft stuck an arm out the window and tried to grab Wheezy by the collar, into the car and escape.

That's when one of the stray bullets hit Hong Kong Phil's diaper van. The rear end exploded and the street was engulfed in a ball of flame.

Wheezy dove for the ground, and out of Crankshaft's reach. Bullets and gunpowder continued to blast and pop. The street sounded like World War Two had broken out. Everything was confusion. Crankshaft burned rubber, dodging around the remaining heap of Hong Kong Phil's armament truck. He needed a better view.

When Mac looked up from the small band he'd left lying on the ground around him, he could just make out the silhouette of Wheezy Waldheim next to where the Blue Streak had been.

Six men in front of the down-and-out gambler raised their swords and began to chase after Wheezy.

Zig-zagging up onto one of the lawns as he raced to head Wheezy off, the Bagman set off the gun-net in the middle of the block. Five cultists were captured under it. Mac had to take the time to knock them out, one at a time, as they sawed at the ropes. When he had time to scan around him, he saw Wheezy headed between two of the houses across the street. Between Mac, Crankshaft, and Hong Kong Phil Li's van, there were only about five of the killers left. The Bagman hurtled over the net full of cultists and gave chase.

Straight-arming the bent-backed cleric out his way, Mac was about to knock down the next man in front of him when something hit him from behind. The Bagman turned too late to avoid the second blow. He fell over, tried to get back up and stumbled, only to fall down again. His vision blurred, went from single to double, then dilated into one tiny white dot; all that remained of his consciousness.

The orange-turbaned Indian had been waiting for him.

"Meddlesome American! You are as a flea to Ali Bin Kahn!"

The Bagman's muddled brain only caught the name, and the part of his brain concerned only with self-preservation kicked in.

"Bin, how the hell are ya?" The King of Thieves said, still waving a hand in front of himself trying to feel what he couldn't see. The masked man concentrated on talking fast, anything to slow the rebel leader down.

He didn't get the chance. With only a shadow in a pinpoint of light to go on, Mac could see Bin Ali Kahn's sword glint as it swung in an arc for his head.

• • •

Down the street, Crankshaft had his reflective goggles off and was trying to get a bead on his partner in the smoke, dust and mayhem. It was times like this he realized Mac was in a war for the city. Then, something he hadn't heard in any of Chicago's battles, something he hadn't heard since the War to End All Wars, echoed in the background: the pounding of horse hooves.

Three men in British Indian Army dress rode royal stallions from between the same houses Wheezy had hot-footed through not five seconds ago. The Indian horses leaped hedges and dodged gardens, before they broke into instant gallops across lawns and into the street.

Even as Mac rolled to the side to dodge Ali Bin Kahn's blow it was blocked by the blade of another. Not just any other, but a Royal Indian Scimitar, the blade of Prince Ahmrit Basir Singh, brother to one queen and sworn soldier of another.

Sitting on his white thoroughbred stallion with a sword in one hand and a service revolver in the other, Ahmrit Singh looked like some sort romantic desert sheik from a Valentino film. As Mac's vision began to return, it occurred to him that in real life Valentino would have been the bad guy in all those movies. But Prince Ahmrit looked like a desert-hardened warrior, the kind of Indian regimental man British Generals bragged about and wagered one man against a hundred.

Prince Ahmrit's mount reared, narrowly dodging the stroke of Ali Bin Kahn's blade. The horse's spinning front hooves caught Ali Bin Kahn in the shoulder. He stumbled backward, his left arm swinging limply in the air behind him. Ahmrit Singh urged his mount forward.

But several of the turbaned men had already regained consciousness and escaped from the trappings of Mac's gun-net. Even as Prince Ahmrit's arm rose for the final kill, the upper-half of a net engulfed his body. The three men in faded turbans yanked hard on the net as the spooked horse swept away trying to save itself. Prince Ahmrit slammed sideways onto the concrete, hard.

He'd fallen on his sword. He was not wounded, but the blade was flat beneath him. The Prince could not use its sharp edge to free himself, and his service revolver was tangled in the net.

As his vision cleared, something possessed Mac to pick up one of the swords lying on the ground. These men seemed to be fighting with blades out of some ancient sign of respect. He'd have to try to earn that same respect for himself. Besides, he couldn't find his gun.

Kneeling as he walked, he picked up a fist-sized hunk of concrete that had been blown out of the road by the exploding diaper truck. The three turbaned terrorists stood above Ahmrit Singh, poking the points of their swords through the ropes of the net as the young prince dodged and wriggled to avoid the darting blades.

The Bagman reared back, wound up and hurled the concrete block in his hand like he was standing on a pitcher's mound. The rock bounced off one of the killer cult member's heads and off the curb. One down.

The other two bastards of Kali turned around to face him, and Mac swore he'd never watch another sand and sandals picture again. The men were big. Bigger than Mac, "and uglier," he thought. Their faces were bearded where there weren't scars, and their skin was hardened by the heat, cold, wind and rock of the roughest region in the world. They held wide, bloody swords.

Hired muscle, Mac thought. But it wasn't just Mac the two revolutionaries from the Eastern hill country faced, it was the Bagman. Even Mac's best friends were scared of the man behind the mask. Something about the abrupt change in mood and behavior gave even Crankshaft the willies.

The two killer cultists stood centered only a moment, their swords held vertically in front of them, then charged.

The Bagman held his sword upright, behind his right shoulder with both hands, like a baseball bat, and leaned backward as he saw the red in their eyes. The swordsman on his left began the onslaught, Mac hung his left leg in the air, just like he'd seen Mel Ott, the right fielder for the Giants do it. As he swung, he stomped the man on the left directly in the stomach, then followed through.

The man on the right's torso severed from his left ribcage to the spine. The Bagman's sword was stuck fast. Blood jetted from its edges as Mac wrestled with the handle to pull it free.

The cult killer to Mac's left crawled off the concrete and jumped back to his feet again, his sword centered in front of his body. The Bagman hardly seemed to move as he backhanded his blade back to the left, and slashed across the man's chest. The killer's turban quivered in the summer breeze. His whole body fell to the ground in spasm.

Crankshaft, navigating the Blue Streak out of the smoke like he was part of it, pulled the car up beside Mac, who was busy freeing Prince Ahmrit from the net. All three of them stood up, looked at each other and decided it was time to leave. Prince Ahmrit ordered his men to take the horses back to their stables. Bin Ali Kahn and Wheezy were nowhere to be found.

"You saved my life back there," the Bagman said to Amhrit Singh as they sat in the back of Crankshaft's speeding little juggernaut. "Thanks."

"You are trying to save my country." Ahmrit lit a black-colored cigarette. "It's the least I could do."

"I don't know who gives you your intelligence, Prince, but they're spot on. If you hadn't shown up I'd be ground beef right about now."

"What have you learned?" The Prince leaned back and blew smoke in the air.

"Well, unfortunately, this branch of your intelligence isn't that bright," Crankshaft said, leaning back over the driver's seat as he drove.

Mac made a slapping motion at Crankshaft's head, but the driver's eyes were already back on the road.

"We traced those weapons they're using to a Chinese gun dealer. Evidently they thought my friend Mac McCullough had the jewel in his apartment, the one place I know it's not, and we had to help him out. Seriously, guy needs an apartment; he wouldn't last two weeks in a boarding house."

The Prince gave the Bagman a blank stare.

"What about you?" Mac said pulling his hat low, lighting a Camel and smoking it through the mask.

"Single mercenaries have been tearing up your speakeasies all over town. Two more deaths, but everyone seems to think Mr. McCullough has it," The Prince said. "Perhaps your plan has a flaw when all roads lead to the decoy."

"You got a point." Mac muttered a few obscenities and crossed his arms in front of himself.

"What about the "pair of tuna"? Crankshaft leaned into a turn.

"Funny you should mention that," The Prince answered. "After playing around with phonetics like children, Princess Abhilash and the Consul realized the words are quite similar to the Punjabi phrase "*Pairin Turna*."

"Well, we did get the translation from a scared kid who only speaks Chicago. Not the best source." The Bagman said. "What's it mean?"

"Tramp, or maybe in your vernacular, a hobo." There was a moment of silence, then the Prince asked, almost rhetorically, "What could that mean?"

"It means one of *our* bums has the jewel!" The Bagman snapped his fingers but you couldn't tell with his gloves on. "All we have to do is find the bum!"

"Unfortunately, that's only about half the country right now." Crankshaft drove along in silence once more, the Blue Streak coursing in and out of the back-alley shadows as they loomed closer to Chicago's loop. Nearing North Avenue Crankshaft finally asked: "The Kali killers kept using another word tonight, like they were threatening somebody, 'Saskana'. What's that mean?"

"You'll have to remember Punjabi's not my first language and there are a lot of local versions." The Prince leaned back and his eyes arched to one side as he tried to think. "*Saskana...saskana...,*" he repeated, tapping a finger on the door armrest. He waved his hand beside him as if he were tossing an idea out. "I think it means 'wheezing...to wheeze.'"

"Wheezy!" The Bagman and Crankshaft yelled in unison. The ace mechanic slammed on the brakes and turned the Blue Streak turned around, tires screeching.

"My God," Mac groaned, "who would've thought the guy I couldn't get away from, is the guy I have to find. Where? Wheezy hangs out in half the dives in town. I could find him, but it would take hours. And for all we know Bin Ali Kahn's right on his tail."

"Damnit! We need time to think." Crankshaft hit the steering wheel. "For once," he added, looking at Mac.

"Given Wheezy's background, odds are he's somewhere on the north side," the Bagman said.

"Bums and the north side; that still leaves a fourth of the city," Crankshaft said.

"This 'Wheezy' person, is he stupid or something?" The Prince asked. "Surely, he knows by now someone is trying to kill him."

"It's a long story, Prince," The Bagman said. "Wheezy used to be a professional gambler till the hard times hit, then he got hooked on drugs. I helped him get cleaned up, put him up in a sanitarium. Since then the guy seems to want to report to me every day, like I'm some kind of doctor. They say he ran into some guys in Ohio helped him sober up. Seems to be working. Problem is, I was always so busy I wasn't always listening. I have no idea where he's hangs out these days."

Crankshaft made a sarcastic slapping motion at Mac from the front seat.

"Waitaminute," the Bagman said. "You got a point there, Prince. Wheezy isn't stupid... Assuming Wheezy hasn't wound up back on drugs, I don't think he'd be at the speakeasies. He's got to know somebody's after him, even if he doesn't know he won a world famous blood-jewel in a poker game. I can only think of two places he'd go if he's in trouble. Crankshaft, I need you guys to call every bookie in town."

"Done. What are you going to do?"

"You guys can use the phones at the Woolworth's around the corner from the garage, Crank. I've got one more place to look.

• • •

In an alley just off the train tracks at Addison and Lincoln, hidden behind a hot dog stand and the rail yard, a high wooden fence barricaded the perimeter of a junk-strewn, dusty lot. Inside the lot, a shotgun shack sat behind some used cars. The sign outside said *Crankshaft's Car Repair* and something about the 369th Infantry Division, The Harlem Hellfighters. Wheezy Waldheim knew what the sign said word for word, but that wasn't why he was here. He knew what the sign said because he'd slept here, under the trains, when he'd been down on his luck.

Four years ago he'd been on top of the world, and, much like the rest of the country, he'd been going down in flames ever since. He'd found himself broke, friendless, and homeless. Reduced to selling information, being a rat to survive, he'd lost all ability to cope and turned to drugs. It was the emotional homelessness that killed him. He had nobody, nothing. And now a bunch of crazy Arabs were chasing him all over town trying to chop him up. What had he done? Bet against one of their horses?

At first he didn't realize why he'd come here to sit beneath the tracks to contemplate suicide. Then he remembered, it was the last place anybody on the street had ever been nice to him. That's why he was here.

When he'd hit bottom and couldn't afford the fancy house and the pool, or even something to eat, few people would even stop to recognize him. He'd seen the sneers on people's faces when he made his rounds through the classy joints, the seams of his shiny suit barely holding it together as he eavesdropped in search of information and spare change. He'd become a pariah, and he'd wound up sleeping under the tracks.

But he'd kept running into Mac McCullough here. Mac McCullough, who could've been anything and anybody he wanted to. Almost a big shot if he wanted to be, but he didn't seem to want to. If Mac hadn't donated the money to send Wheezy to a sanitarium, the frail gambler would most likely already be dead. Mac was a busy guy so Wheezy had always thought it kind of odd when he ran into the ex-bagman under these tracks, like lightning striking in the same place twice. But, even when he didn't have time to talk, Mac at least excused himself to Wheezy. He didn't ignore him.

And that meant the world to Wheezy.

If he could just get some money together to bet with. Now that he'd sobered up he knew he could get back on his feet. He'd parlayed a two-dollar bet at the track into a hundred dollar poker game, and thought he'd won. But he still didn't have any money. All he had was this stinking jewel and there wasn't a fence or pawnshop in the world interested. Probably fake anyway.

He once had it all and now had lost it all.

The corner of Addison and Lincoln was an odd one for many reasons. One of them was that it was really a three-way intersection. Ravenswood road ran parallel to the elevated train, creating a dusty, diamond-shaped lot beneath the tracks. The only light sat above the elevated train platform, a world of shadow and chiaroscuro beneath.

Two red eyes glowed in the darkness behind the corner of a dry goods store across Ravenswood. Their centers were pit black with the fire of rage burning in the center. They were the eyes of Bin Ali Kahn, who had sworn to kill any man who had the audacity to touch the Stone of Shakti. The Jewel belonged to him.

Bin Ali Kahn watched as the silhouette of Wheezy Waldheim pulled something out of his pocket. Even in the shadows the blood red ruby reflected. Wheezy turned the fist-sized jewel around in his hand like it was a piece of fruit that had gone bad.

"*Saskana!* The Stone of Shakti is mine!" The voice echoed down the tracks as Bin Ali Kahn loped across the street, his scimitar blade waving.

With the orange-turbaned man still thirty yards away, Wheezy shrugged his shoulders, looked at the jewel and raised his arm to throw it at the madman.

"Don't do it," a voice under the tracks said. The voice didn't echo like the previous one, but spoke in a tone so imperative it couldn't be ignored. It seemed to be part of the darkness itself. A rugged-looking man with a mask that looked like a burlap bag strolled out of the darkness with a .45

revolver hanging from his lowered arm. "Don't let him get near you."

Bin Ali Kahn saw the Bagman and was enraged. All his fury immediately focused on the man in the mask.

"Looks like you brought a knife to a gunfight, Binny!" The Criminal Detective arched his back and raised his head. Two pieces of steel in a polar ice pack stared back at the desert killer. "What you gonna do?"

Kahn could see something in those eyes. Something mischievous. They burned with a cold hatred, but they laughed at him, too. No man could laugh at Ali Bin Kahn and live. Kahn flexed his shoulder and charged the Bagman.

Twenty yards away two shots fired. Both of them hit Kahn's scimitar right above the handle. Kahn still gripped the handle with both hands, but the blade had shattered.

"Peasants," Ali Kahn shouted. "You are a country of peasants!"

As Kahn swung the jagged remains of his sword, Mac stepped inside and pulled an uppercut from the ground and into the madman's jaw. Turning as he punched, he grabbed Kahn's right hand and threw him over his shoulder. Kahn flipped through the air, and his back hit one of the elevated train's upright girders.

The Bagman tossed his gun to Wheezy, said: "Don't let him have the jewel."

Kahn cursed in his native language and climbed back to his feet.

"Well, Binny." The King of Thieves set himself in a boxing pose. "Welcome to Chicago."

The two predators circled each other slowly, their fists testing their opponent's defense and offense. Mac faked a left. Kahn dodged. Mac faked a right.

As Kahn shifted to the Bagman's left to dodge the blow, the Man of Steal jumped in the air and kicked him in the side of the head. Kahn slid across the dusty lot till his head hit concrete. Mac grabbed him by the shirt and stood him up again next to one of the upright girders.

The Bagman punched him in the gut. Kahn folded like a paper doll. The Criminal Hero stood over the cult killer's unconscious body, breathing through the mask and waiting. Kahn tried to raise his head and collapsed again.

"What are you going to do with him?" Wheezy said.

"Oh, I'm going to show him every dirty punch America ever taught me," the voice behind the mask said. "Then he's going to have to deal with the toughest gang in town; the cops."

Ten minutes later the Bagman had tied up Bin Ali Kahn with his own clothes and told Wheezy to wait under the tracks and keep an eye on his unconscious body, help would be on the way. Mac ran around the corner, shed his mask, then threw his coat, tie, and hat in the gutter hoping Wheezy wouldn't see the resemblance between the Bagman and his alter ego.

"Wheezy, you're a hero!" Mac yelled hustling across the lot under the train tracks. "I heard you've got the jewel!"

"Big deal," Wheezy said. "I been trying to unload the damn thing all day. Everybody's scared of it, and now I know why."

"Yeah, but don't you see, Wheezy? You return it to Princess Abhilash and her crew, and you'll probably get a reward!"

Wheezy almost smiled, but he couldn't believe it.

"Look, Wheeze, I heard you parlayed two dollar bet into a hundred dollar poker game yesterday."

"Yeah."

"That's no small feat for a man of no means," Mac slapped him on the back. "You staying off the junk?"

"Hell, yeah, Mac. I don't want to be a slave to that stuff. I'm getting my eye for the horses back. It's just a matter of time." He still didn't sound as if he believed it.

"Good," Mac said, and began to steer the two of them down Lincoln Avenue. "Because the way I see it, with you returning the Stone of Shakti to its rightful owner, the United States might just need a new ambassador to India, or at least one of its smaller provinces."

"Really," Wheezy said, the light of hope desperately trying to crawl into the edges of his eyes. "Me? An ambassador?"

"I'd say it's a cinch. C'mon we'll call the cops from Woolworth's. "Oh! And get this…" an even bigger smile broke across Mac's face.

"What?"

"The Prince likes horses, Wheezy." Mac put his arm around the bedraggled gambler as the first orange light of morning began to pierce the skyline. "The prince likes horses…"

The End

AFTERWORD

I spent a good deal of 2012 reading old stories out of *Adventure* Magazine. Back in the 1920's *Adventure* was THE pulp magazine. Remember, this was still the era of Jack London. The world was a smaller place. Radio was new. Movies had just been introduced, but they still weren't widely distributed, and convenience was far from modern. While today's adventure story seeker simply has to flip a switch to watch an epic, the only entertainment out there for many in the twenties was reading. People read a lot of *Adventure*.

And the reading was good. From the traditional Western to Foreign Legion tales, to lost cities, to Harold Lamb's Cossack fighting beneath the steps of the Himalayas. Needless to say, I was drawn like a magnet. In those old pages rested the kind of excitement that will never be seen again. It was an era of exploration, new science, and a breed of men born for adventure. True wonder lay in those pages.

I'd just finished writing *The Bagman Vs. The World's Fair* and I had a lot of other work to do, but for some reason, I just couldn't get Mac McCullough out of my system. So I gave it some consideration, and thought I'd just sort of sketch a story out on paper when I had the time. But, there was a part of me that wanted to give Mac a dose of that old school, high adventure!

I started with murder. Always a good way to start a story.

But what was the motive? Well, after reading *Adventure* Magazine for a year, that was no problem at all. A stolen jewel. No, not just any stolen jewel, but one stolen from an Indian Princess. Add to that, that having The Bagman meet royalty was like having the Artful Dodger meet Queen Elizabeth and I practically had a story in itself.

But who would the villain be? With no planning I'd already written out this grisly murder scene I really liked, introduced a couple of pawnbrokers and Chicago by the lake, and I still had no idea. Well, the Cult of Kali seemed like the best place to go, BUT, the followers of Kali were famous for being stranglers. I sat on that awhile, while I worked on other stuff. And, that's when I lucked out.

It occurred to me the region between Afghanistan and India had always been an ever-shifting border war from time immemorial to this day. What if our villain was political? So, I'm looking at what happened in history in 1933 and damned if the organization of the Pakistan National Movement wasn't on the top of the list. And all of a sudden, it wasn't just a jewel, but an entire nation being ripped apart. And while our villain may claim to be from the Cult of Kali, he's too ruthless and not nearly devoted enough to just strangle people, especially in Chicago where nobody knew who he was.

Being in high adventure mode, when Mac needed information I could only think of one way for him to get a bit more intercontinental adventure in the city, Chinatown. These days Chinatown is a lot more accepted by the locals than it was back then. While the spirit of adventure always led locals there, back in the day there was still a bit of mystery surrounding the tiny section of the city. And I couldn't help myself, so it's no coincidence Hong Kong Phil Lee sounds a lot like Hong Kong Phooey.

Now, in the scene where Mac first meets the band of killers I used the line "everything but wild horses." So when the opportunity came, I said, "Let there be horses, too!" By this time that little story I was going to "sketch out" had become about thirty pages.

But I needed a happy ending, where Mac wasn't just grinning over the barrel of a gun with his arm around a girl. Let's face it, I'm strong enough to be sentimental, and I'd been using Wheezy Waldheim from the beginning of the story as a comedy relief device. Wheezy's a great character and had appeared in the first *Tales of The Bagman* book, a bit of a tragic figure really. An addict, and back in the thirties that was practically a death sentence. Well, my little Grinch heart grew ten times that day, and I decided to give Wheezy one hell of happy ending. Watching over the Princess' stables seemed like the perfect job for a guy that bet on the horses. I'm sure he's quite happy.

I have to say one of the things I most love about the pulp form is that original novelette length story. For me at least, it's the perfect length for an action-adventure story. Just time enough to introduce the character and somebody walks into the room with a "roscoe," we'll figure out the characterization as we go, through more action, clues, questions and bam! You just missed your bus stop without even thinking about how boring the ride was. That's what I was trying to do.

Writing's a strange thing. It can be terribly frustrating, but ultimately rewarding. I hope you enjoyed this yarn as much as I did.

Oh, and don't ever take anybody's jewelry in a poker game.

• • •

BYRON CHRISTOPHER BELL - is the author and creator of *Tales of The Bagman*, Chicago's very own pulp hero. He has also written Airship 27 Adventures for *Secret Agent X*, *Jim Anthony: Super-Detective*, and both volumes of *Dan Fowler G-Man* adventures. An award-winning short-story writer, Bell is currently working on a tovel length Weird Tale, and is racking up ideas for Tales of the Bagman Volume Four. He is lucky to live with his wife in "the city where the weak are killed and eaten."

Join him on Facebook, or at his weblog: http//chicagobagman.blogspot.com

THE GREY MANTIS IN:
"THE GREY MANTIS STRIKES"

By C. William Russette

Robert Arkwright eased open the door of Maria's Restaurant and his faced hardened into a mask of anger. The waiting area, once populated with olive and nut trees, was a series of broken pots with dirt dashed to the tile floor. It looked like someone had urinated on the wall.

What the hell is going on? Robert wondered.

He bolted into the main dining room. He dimly recalled it being a place of warm atmosphere, filled with rich smells of garlic, spicy meats and red sauce. The sound of silverware clinking, wine and champagne bottles opening mixed with soft, low conversations held between lovers and friends and most importantly, families.

Six men in black trench coats were the only moving bodies in the dining room. Tables were left overturned. Chairs were sitting at off angles after being bounced off walls or the ceiling. One overhead fan spun with limp blades.

"Get lost or get stomped, rich-boy," the bald man in the mirror sunglasses said. He pointed a wooden Louisville slugger at Robert. Six inch nails protruded from the end.

Robert decided to shop for more common clothes for the next time he visited Zeke. The high end silk shirt and slacks were a gift from his parents upon his return. They were just clothes to him.

All six men had a weapon of some kind, Robert noted. Machete, double edged knives, spike-rimmed knuckles and a fire axe. A hulking black man wore what were probably sap gloves. *Those are only the weapons that I can see.*

A moan issued from near the bat-wielder's feet. Zeke lay curled into the fetal position behind the crew. Blood dotted and streaked his white button shirt. Robert couldn't tell how serious the injuries were but none of the weapons looked bloody.

Maybe they only got started and I'm not too late.

"One was all you get, rich boy. Leon, show our guest the door once you get his wallet and watch," Spike-bat said.

The large man with the sap gloves, Leon, strutted up to Robert. He was a head taller and easily outweighed Robert.

"You can gimmie the goods or I can break you down and take 'em. Either way..." Leon looked down at Robert.

Robert pretended to suck something out of his teeth.

Only half of Leon's mouth smiled. He fired a large black-gloved fist at

Robert. He looked surprised to find he missed his rich-boy target. Leon fired a series of jabs and finished with a round-house punch.

"Hold…" Leon started.

Robert's footwork continued to keep him out of reach but close enough to choose his moment to attack. He slapped the roundhouse aside and smashed his shin into the side of Leon's knee then snapped a shot into the larger man's exposed flank. The knee failed to support him. Leon fell with a howl.

He turned to Robert with an expression of rage and confusion as the elbow took him in the temple. Leon's world went black.

The remaining five men bore a stunned expression.

"What the hell? Leon?" Spike Bat said.

"So, guys, all at once, or one at a time, like we were honorable?" Robert asked.

All five approached and surrounded him.

"I thought so," Robert said.

Robert's hands were at his sides when he inched toward Knuckles. With a snarl the thug attacked ahead of the other five. Robert allowed the first punch then stepped inside his guard landing a series of strikes to the tender inside of his attacker's upper arm and armpit. The arm went limp before the man could retract it. Knuckles took a dozen punches to the throat, ear and temple before his remaining arm could be cocked to strike. Knuckles fell hard.

The machete hacked through the air even as Knuckles tried to rise and failed. Again and again the vine cutter swung. Everyone in the room heard the steel whistling through the air but strike nothing. Robert waited; Machete hacked like his life depended on the blow but missed. He had time to lock eyes on Robert's fist as it almost crushed his windpipe then broke his nose. The two blows felt like one in their speed. Weaving an arm around and disarming the man was effortless. Machete almost had time to be impressed when the handle of his machete crashed into his face bringing bright lights and curtain-fall.

"Gore Mongers, kill this fool!" Spiked Bat ordered but did not move.

"Half of you are down. Surrender, now." Robert walked to the approaching duo holding the machete.

The short man with double edged fighting knives slid one blade over the other like he was sharpening them before cutting into the Easter pig. The bald man with one eye carried his fire axe in both hands. It was a strange pairing, these sets of weapons and fighters. Robert doubted they understood the simplest principals of fighting, effective use of their weapons or working together to merge fighters, weapons and range.

A flurry of thrusts like a sewing machine needle came at Robert. The machete worked well deflecting or stopping any steel that came close. The knife fighter grunted then made to come again. A foot struck him in the solar plexus from nowhere and he almost dropped his knives.

The fire axe came down and struck the cement beneath Zeke's dining room carpet. The knife fighter stumbled away for safety's sake.

"Damn it, Little Barry, watch what the hell you're doing!"

"Shut up, Fast Hand." The axe tore through the air again.

Robert deflected the handle with the machete then kicked the axe-head wide. The flat of the machete blade slapped both sides of Little Barry's face. His expression flipped from rage-driven to stunned. Then Fast Hand shot in, one knife thrusting, the other slashing, in alternate rhythms. Robert marked the pattern immediately. The machete handle broke Fast Hand's elbow and Robert easily disarmed the numbed appendage. In agony the knife fighter could do nothing to stop the knee that broke his ribs, the ridge-hand chop to his throat or the flat of the machete that took him at the base of his skull. Fast Hand dropped like a tipped statue to the floor.

The fire axe came down and froze in mid strike. Robert held the machete blade to Little Barry's Adam's apple. Robert shook his head at Little Barry.

"Idiot! Kill him! What are you dummies doing here tonight?" Spike Bat threw his trench coat to the ground.

He was a well-muscled man with many tattoos of barbed wire and swords on his arms. He made a point to stomp as he approached to help his henchman. Robert steered Little Barry with the tip of the machete so the leader could not come up at an undesirable angle.

"Don't let him cut me, Lefty T," Little Barry whined.

"You guys have such colorful names, Lefty T. Do you get to pick them or are they drawn from a hat?" Robert asked.

"Shut up." Lefty T swung his spiked bat at a run.

Robert ducked and brought up the machete with a backhand as a precaution. The machete was almost beaten out of his hand. Lefty T returned to attack immediately. Robert was prepared, planted his lead foot, rotated at the hip then slapped his machete across Lefty T's face. The leader of the pack spit blood and came on again. He shortened his strikes and added thrusts to his attack. The power of the blows kept Robert backing and blocking with the machete. Chips and wedges of the bat came free with each blow blocked.

Lefty T faked a thrust. Robert was not fooled and brought the machete down on the backhand strike Lefty T attempted. The hacking tool cut deep and lodged in the Slugger. Both men struggled but Lefty T quickly won and turned to Robert in time to catch a roundhouse kick in the face. Left T spun in the air and landed in a jumble of limbs and weapons. A heel-palm to the chin took Lefty T's consciousness.

"You, Little Barry of the Gore Mongers," Robert said facing the last thug.

"Hey, man. I've had enough." His face swelled where the machete kissed him.

"What was all this about? Money?" Robert slowly approached the bald criminal.

"Just 'cause I ain't scrappin no more don't mean I'm rattin' out my crew, fool."

Zeke moaned behind Robert.

"See, dude's f…"

Little Barry didn't see the blow that knocked him out.

Robert eased Zeke onto his back. There was no way of knowing what injuries his friend had suffered internally. One eye was swelled shut and his lip was split. Robert was going to get him to a hospital immediately.

"Zeke, don't move, my friend," Robert said.

"Robby? That you?" Zeke squinted his good eye.

"It is."

"You look too skinny, man. Where you been all this time?"

"Zeke, who were the scum that attacked you? You need a doctor."

"No, I need your help, man. I need… I need…"

"Nothing is more important than your health, my friend." Robert drew his cell phone from his pocket.

"My daughter is more important than anything?" A tear ran from the corner of Zeke's good eye.

"You did say that you had a daughter on the phone. Is she here? Can I find her for you?"

"No, no. They have her. They have Sierra. The Gore Mongers."

"Who are the Gore Mongers? Why did they take Sierra?"

Zeke coughed. Blood sprayed. He fell unconscious.

"Zeke!" Robert picked up his friend easily and ran through the front door to his Lexus. Gently, Robert placed his childhood friend into the front seat, eased it back and clasped the seatbelt.

Robert disappeared only to return a few minutes later. Closing the car door jarred Zeke back to consciousness.

"Robby? Where?"

"I'm taking you to the hospital. Now, why would a gang take Sierra, Zeke?"

"Business has been going really good. I was gonna open another restaurant on the other side of town. These Gore Mongers are a gang that's been steadily growing the last few years. I knew they were supposed to be operating in the area but... they're just animals, Robby. They came tonight to tell me that they took Sierra from the sitter and they want two hundred grand or they are going to sell her to the highest bidder! She's eight, for God's sake, Robby." Sobs wracked Zeke.

Zeke ran his fingers through his hair and palmed away the wet from his swollen face.

"Tell me you'll help me, Robby," Zeke looked beyond the windshield.

"What do you want me to do? The hospital will call the police. I guess the FBI will take over? Is that how it works here?"

"Here? Where the hell have you been?"

"China. How can I help?"

"Well... I didn't want to pick up our friendship after fifteen years by begging but there is no way that I can raise the cash they want by dawn. You're still rich, right? Arkwright Inc. is still doing well."

Robert's father's corporation, Arkwright Inc., was doing incredibly well. Robert was heir to billions even after splitting it with his brother should both his parents die unexpectedly. It was his father's money, not Robert's. He was offered the kingdom after his return six months ago but what did he need money for? He borrowed some to get into the university and try to find a career to walk towards.

Much of each day was still wasted remembering the last fifteen years of pain. Robert, known as Jei during his imprisonment, dealt and received more pain than any human should ever have to fighting in the blood circles of Hong Kong.

The rage borne of frustration that helped keep him alive was still strong. Some days it was very difficult to remain calm, to focus his chi and find oneness. He had to keep his experiences secret or it would cause his family, and friends like Zeke, irreparable suffering to know Robert had been kidnapped. He was bound and beaten and forced to fight for food, for his life, for everything. It had been a long fifteen years.

It was over.

Robert brought his mind back into focus. Zeke was crying again. There was a more important kidnapping going on. Eight-year-old Sierra was the victim now.

She's younger than I was when they got me.

I cannot allow her to succumb to a fate like the one forced on me. Robert stopped at the Emergency Room entrance of Pennsylvania Hospital.

"We're at the hospital now, Zeke. I want you to tell the police everything. Leave out no details, my friend."

Attendants were rushing to the car with a wheelchair.

"What about you? Where are you going?"

"I might know someone that can help get your daughter back."

"No, I just want the money! They said they would give her back if I paid them the money. You're putting her in danger!"

"Can we help, sir?" a young blonde man in scrubs asked at the passenger side door.

"This man has suffered a terrible beating. There may be internal bleeding. He has to be seen immediately. Do whatever you have to. Bill everything to Arkwright Inc."

"Robby, no! Please…"

In Zeke's weakened state the attendant had little trouble getting him from the Lexus.

"You will get your daughter back, Zeke. I promise," Robert swore.

Robert heard Zeke bellow at him as he drove away.

• • •

Part of Robert was amused. Another part of him was cold, like a crocodilian easing down the river, seeking prey. Cold like when they knew him as Jei in the fighting circles of Hong Kong under the mask. His keepers hid his identity so there was no way word could leak that the boy Robert Arkwright did not die. He did not become fish-food when the boat he was supposedly being transported on blew up, killing all aboard.

Under new ownership, the boy Robert died, and in his place stood a half-breed called Jei. He was brutal and feared by the end of his tenure, winning death matches in the underground fighting circuits of China.

He had endured many *sifu*: teachers of Kung Fu, in Hong Kong that prepared him for the circle. None spared the cane but that was fine. Robert told himself that the pain made him strong. He used it to feed his hate. The hate fed his fury and that fury let Jei survive long enough for him to escape.

The only friend that seemed genuine after all these years was Zeke and now he needed help. Robert could have bought his daughter's freedom if his father would part with so much money on a moments notice. Which was unlikely. Kidnapping is an art in China. It is a tradition that goes back centuries. This was not China. This was Philadelphia and these Gore Mongers were not adhering to any kind of reasonable timetable. And they lacked manners.

It was Jei that Zeke needed.

It was no problem buying and modifying a simple domino mask and acquiring some clothes from Chinatown. Robert put on the Grey domino mask and a Grey shirt and popped the trunk of his Lexus.

Little Barry, rage purpling his forehead and cheeks, tried his best to hurt Robert with invective. Then he calmed and took in the being standing before him in Grey. Robert took Little Barry by the collar and belt buckle and cast him down into the cement. Little Barry's thumbs were tied together with wire from Zeke's restaurant.

Jei removed the gag.

"Who the hell are you supposed to be, freak show?"

Jei tilted his head. In the Circle he could kill Little Barry with a single strike in a dozen places. He would have made it last thirty minutes if possible so the crowd could get their money's worth. He would not though.

"I'm talkin' t'you mother..."

A front kick and Little Barry was on his knees wishing he could breathe again. Jei freed his prisoner's hands.

"We will do things this way, Little Barry. I need to know where the hideout of the Gore Mongers is. I will get there in time to save Sierra Buckingham's life, and purity, intact. You will also provide details pertaining to the numbers and capabilities of those in residence tonight."

"Really? I will, huh?"

Jei nodded.

"Dude, I know yer that jerk from the restaurant even if you are hiding behind that sissy little mask. I ain't ratting out my crew, man, so you can swing on these." Little Barry grabbed himself inappropriately.

"Option B appeals more to me as well."

Little Barry's brow furrowed.

"A test of will and martial skill." Jei took a Southern Mantis Fist stance and waited.

"Really? Awesome. You got lucky before. Y'know that, right?" Little Barry charged, screaming like a Viking berserker.

Jei crippled his opponent's arms and legs quickly with fast traps and strikes prominent with the Mantis Fist style of Kung Fu. He could have used any number of styles; he had been forced to study under many *sifu*.

The Mantis style had always been a favorite. One should have fun while working, Jei thought.

"My God, let go of me! Yer tearing my arm off!" Little Barry screamed.

"Do you wish to talk now?"

"Christ, yes! I do! Who the hell are you?"

Robert almost answered with his hostage-fighter name but caught himself.

"You will address me as the Grey Mantis."

• • •

The Grey Mantis stared through the irregular, plywood covered chain link fence unsure of whether to smile or scowl. There were at least fifty thugs scattered around the long abandoned train yard tracks. Metal barrels spat yellow flames into the night sky. Men made up the majority but some women were huddled around the barrels for the warmth if not the comradery. The style of dress ranged from threadbare to poorly stitched together cloth fished from the dump. Each and every person carried some kind of melee weapon. Most bore the easily found variety like claw hammers and pick axes. One youth (perhaps eighteen years old) wore a nine iron strapped to his back like a claymore.

Behold the Gore Mongers, the Grey Mantis thought.

"We here, man. Now I can go and you can cut me the hell loose. I can't be no more help," Little Barry rasped.

"Point out the leader?"

"What?"

"Where is the girl being held?"

"I dunno, man, really,"

"How many guard her? Name the leader if you can't point him out. Is it a man or a woman? White? Black? Latino? Asian?" The Grey Mantis drew in, inches from Little Barry's face.

"I... uh..."

"Still you fear reprisals from this nameless leader, Little Barry?"

"Naw, course not…"

The Grey Mantis's gloved hand gripped Little Barry's ribcage under his right arm. The wide-eyed look on Little Barry's face would have convinced most men of his sincerity. The Grey Mantis was born of the sweat and blood of the underground fighting circles of Hong Kong. If you cannot read your opponent perfectly it can cost you more than the match in those secret pits. The Grey Mantis squeezed his fingers together and the ribs they held.

Little Barry tried to howl but The Grey Mantis slapped his hand over the thug's mouth.

"What do I see through the crack in the perimeter wall?"

The Grey Mantis relaxed his grip then slowly uncovered Little Barry's mouth.

"The scum—the nobodies of the gang."

"Shock troops? Fodder?"

"The worthless. Please lemme go, man."

"The train and derelict cars that separate the lower tracks from that building? What will I find there?"

"The boss and the kid yer looking for, man. Now…"

Squeeze.

Muzzle.

Muffled howls.

"What will I find?"

"The Old Heads, man. Damn it. The seasoned dudes. I swear!"

"And beyond the train-wall? The boss?"

The Grey Mantis flexed his grip on the ribs.

"Jersey Sven! He runs the Gore Mongers. It's his gang!"

A gang of this size and style of combat must have a strong leader. He would rule by his fists. He has to have beaten down many comers to keep his throne. To control a gang of this size Jersey Sven must be strong.

"He fights? What is his weapon of choice?"

"Uh… sticks, man. Wooden-bamboo! Bamboo fighting sticks."

"An Escrimador? How many are up there in his castle, Little Barry?"

"Like I know that. I ain't never been up there."

A tightening of the grip and Little Barry tried to roar his pain through the nylon and leather glove clamped firmly over his mouth. The Grey Mantis let him scream for a count of five before deciding he was telling the truth.

"I think the girl is there. Don't you?"

Sweat streamed off Little Barry's face. He nodded.

"I also think that only the strongest of his men are allowed in his presence. Given this riff-raff before us, I say less than five."

He would still have to be able to take down these five if they tried to overthrow him. Jersey Sven is a paranoid man.

"I will allow you to redeem yourself by helping me in my cause," the Grey Mantis said.

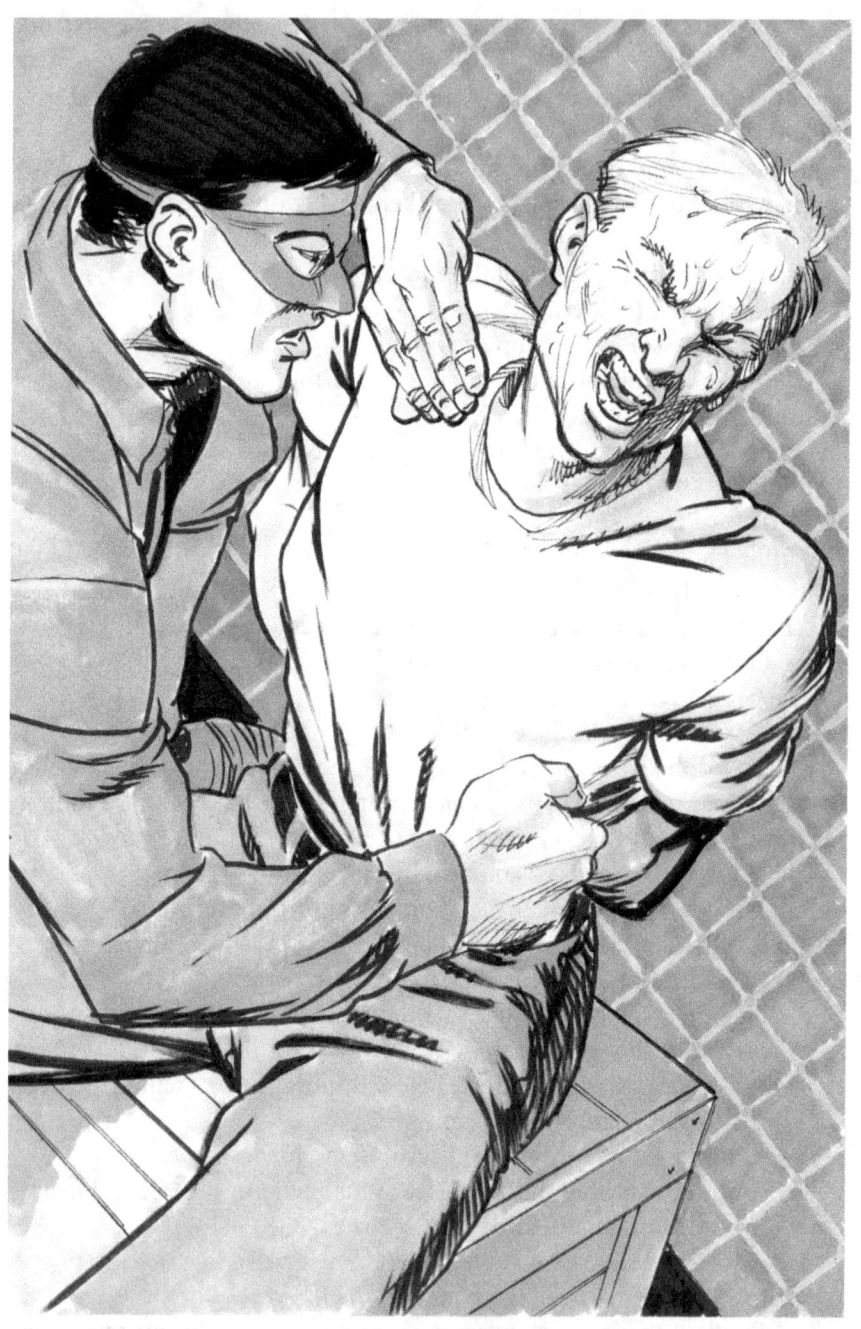

"What will I find?"

"Wait, no, man! Don't…"

The Grey Mantis slapped a vice-like grip on Little Barry's wrist. With a free hand The Grey Mantis thumbed at the top of the fence.

"You decide how you wish to ascend the fence."

Little Barry frowned. He looked like he might cry. No doubt he has committed many offenses in his life. Every man deserves a chance to redeem himself.

In seconds, the Grey Mantis was up and over the fence.

"Who in th' hell is this friggen guy," a young, dark haired man in a leather jacket shouted amidst the mob.

I am going to get to that train no matter how many stand before me.

Predictably, Little Barry ran toward his gang-mates.

The Grey Mantis did not run but maintained a brisk pace. He headed for the only opening on the derelict train cars he could see. The last car was wedged tight against the front end of the semi rig, which in turn connected to more wrecks.

"Little Barry, what the hell, man?" a man in spikes and leather asked. He carried a hatchet.

"That freak over there busted up our crew, man. You guys, take him down!" Little Barry shouted.

The nearest gaggle of lightly-armed thugs drew everything from a pick axe to a pair of flat head screw drivers.

The Grey Mantis did not break pace. Invaluable time crawled by. He knew that the confusion would not last long.

"Dude, Barry. This fool busted up your crew and you lead him here?" Spikes yelled.

"No, well yeah, but I had no choice, man. He moves like…"

Little Barry stopped talking and tried to watch the line of blood run down from his forehead where Spikes had buried his hatchet.

"You betrayed us, *estupido*," Spikes accused. He removed his hatchet as Little Barry fell dead.

Five thugs formed a line in front of The Grey Mantis. Melee weapons were at the ready. There was no theme to the gang. All races were accounted for. The only common thread was their weapon of choice: none of which were projectile.

"You take out his crew, masked man?" Spikes asked.

"I did. No one else needs to be harmed. I want the girl. Then I will go. You have no right to possess her," the Grey Mantis demanded.

He did not stop walking.

"You're killin' me with this. What is your name, man?" Spikes smiled as he glanced at the dozens gathering around them.

"I am the Grey Mantis. It will take more than you have to keep me from what I seek."

Laughter exploded around the lone masked man in Grey. He did not slow his advance.

Spikes charged with a battle cry leading with his hatchet. The Grey Mantis ducked it, stepped forward and threw his enemy over his shoulder and into the crowd. A silence fell on the mass but it was short lived. Spikes had barely been dropped to the ground when the wall of five thugs jumped into motion and attacked.

A man wielding two claw hammers appeared swinging his weapons in a sloppy pattern. From the opposite direction a thug came at him thrusting spikes bound to his wrists. The Grey Mantis slapped the hammers away and dodged before landing two rib-breaking blows. Hammers fell moaning. The poor-man's claws he knocked wide and rapid-fired a dozen jabs to the man's head and neck.

A shovel arced down but The Grey Mantis was faster. One foot trapped the broad blade in the ground; he kicked through the shaft with the other then kicked the wielder in the face while taking the handle from him.

Clubs and fists and cudgels of all sorts shot in and out of the mob of screaming flesh that wanted the Grey Mantis dead for his insult to the collective. The shovel haft took all comers in turn and left none standing who dared test his skill. He knew that he would eventually surrender to the numbers. Eventually he would tire to the point that he would make a mistake. Then he would end and Sierra would be lost to Zeke.

That time is not here yet.

Time raced towards him like a Peregrine Falcon diving at a field mouse. The Grey Mantis simplified his attacks to only to the most crushing and crippling that could be initiated in a single strike. He aimed for specific targeted areas like nerve clusters, major muscle groups and the sense-depriving points.

In just over thirty seconds he had dropped almost thirty into varied forms of consciousness and mobility. Still he was at the eye of the hurricane of violence and malice focused squarely on him.

A side-kick landed on his hip and The Grey Mantis was forced into a roll. He came up in the shadow cast by a giant. A giant with a hammer that had to belong to Lei Gong himself!

The circle of mayhem expanded with The Grey Mantis and the Big Man at the center. The crowd roared its approval. Big Man looked very pleased with himself. He hefted his hammer and swung in a wide arc. The Grey Mantis had little trouble avoiding the slow and heavy weapon. *Were he smarter he would have allowed others to occupy me while he attacked from the side or behind*, The Grey Mantis thought.

Pairings of kicks and punches did little to slow the giant's arc of death.

The Grey Mantis stood in place.

Big Man hiccupped in motion but only for a second before rearing back with the mallet. He left The Grey Mantis a grand opening to attack but The Grey Mantis remained still. The Big Man grimaced under the force he channeled into the coming overhead blow. Until the last possible moment The Grey Mantis remained in place. The sledge hammer was about to hit him then somehow it missed. The Grey Mantis had sidestepped the attack but with no room to spare.

The Big Man was about to raise the weapon again when pain exploded in his head. The Grey Mantis's front-kick left the Big Man with a broken nose. One hand left the hammer reflexively to check his face.

The Grey Mantis went to work on the arm still wielding the sledge hammer with knife-hand strikes and jabs until the thug fell away from the weapon, blind and nursing a crippled arm. The Grey Mantis fired a heel-palm to the chin sending the Big Man staggering backward. The Grey Mantis leapt up and sprung off of the Big Man's chest and over the mob. The Gore Mongers half-heartedly cheered their hammer-wielding champion before noting that the target, the easy kill, was in the air and over the heads of those closest to the action.

Stepping from shoulder to head and even face The Grey Mantis crossed the tightly packed mob before any knew that the fight was no longer taking place. He landed on the rail tracks and sprinted to the end of the line of dead cars and the start of the next obstacle.

A Gore Monger jumped off the train-stairs at The Grey Mantis. The man wielded what might have once been a flagpole. It was a sad attempt at testosterone-fueled bravado. He knew nothing of the way of the staff. The Grey Mantis took him in the air with a side-kick to the trunk then snatched the flag pole from his weakened grip. The Gore Monger landed clawing at the dirt and praying for his breath to return.

Through the window of the first car, The Grey Mantis saw one of the 'old heads' watching him with a pair of sickles, that the Japanese called *kama*, in his hands. The Grey Mantis leaped to the boarding ramp on the rear of the car and slammed the door shut.

The Old Head within shouted obscenities but The Grey Mantis had already scaled the train car to the roof and was sprinting along the top of the train. A well-trod path and remarkable cleanliness identified the exit point on the opposite side of the Old Head car that would lead to the shack Jersey Sven maintained as a headquarters.

The Grey Mantis leaped down from the top of the car, landing without a sound. He slid the large, well-greased, metal car door shut easily. Spying a wooden pallet The Grey Mantis punched through a board then rammed a wedge into the train car's rollers just as one of the Old Heads tried to open it. Cussing exuded from within.

"I am not here to prove that I am the better fighter. I seek only the girl," The Grey Mantis said and jogged up to the hill.

A white man in a sleeveless shirt waited for The Grey Mantis at the door to the iron works warehouse. He twirled a great scimitar easily.

"I am The Grey Mantis. I want the girl you have taken released immediately."

"I'm Buck Fury and I don't think you're goin' no further, masked man."

• • •

The Grey Mantis covered one fist with his hand and bowed his head slightly.

"I seek the girl, not conflict. I ask that you step aside."

"Very formal, man. Old School, but I can't just let you by. You thumped out my guys. Gotta cut you down." Buck Fury advanced.

The Grey Mantis let most of his weight fall onto his rear leg while his hands assumed the traditional Mantis hook-hand form while holding the flagpole-staff. Fury moved in. Jabs followed short-range slashes. It was clear from the beginning that Fury was not trained in the western style of sword-play but rather Eastern, and most likely Middle-Eastern, styles. His right hand held the handle of the sword while the blunt, back-side of the blade received added strength from the left forearm.

The actual exposed length of blade was only twelve inches when used in this manner. The circular fighting style and patterns of the attack were similar to those at the core of Kung Fu. The Grey Mantis side-stepped and spun at the waist to avoid losing a strip of skin. The swordsman continued to advance. The sword was too close to the attacker's body for The Grey Mantis to land a strike or get a grip on an arm.

The Grey Mantis fired a half dozen jabs at Buck Fury's face and trunk.

He quickly found his weapon trimmed by a quarter. Fury was a master with his weapon. The swordsman wasted no time in attacking again. The Grey Mantis retreated. Fury's speed was impressive and he believed that Fury knew it.

When an opening presented itself Fury thrust his scimitar out then cut up severing the flagstaff in two. Fury was not prepared for the shift to the defensive when he found himself facing two whirling sticks, swiping for his face. Fury no sooner got his footing back and gained advantage over the Grey Mantis when agony tore through his leg. He had to drop to one knee as the other could no longer hold his weight.

Fighting through the pain Fury tried to get his scimitar on the defense. The Grey Mantis shattered his thumb with a stick. Before Fury could catch the falling weapon with his free hand The Grey Mantis landed a round-house kick to Fury's temple. The swordsman fell.

The Grey Mantis slid his fighting sticks into his belt at the small of his back.

"There is more to fighting than perfecting a weapon's use. The weapon is an extension of the warrior, Fury." The Grey Mantis saluted again then headed up the steps.

At closer inspection the shack at the top of the cobbled together steps was nothing more than a pair of doublewide trailers slammed together with nails and aluminum. The house of the Gore Mongers was nothing to brag about, the Grey Mantis thought. Perhaps it was with the monies that Zeke was to pay them that they would better cement themselves a respectable location.

Not that it mattered. After tonight, the Gore Mongers were finished.

A Japanese man stood in jeans and a black tee shirt in front of a wall made from cinderblocks and broken drywall. Space on either side of the wall allowed a person to enter whatever lay beyond. The Japanese man had a length of chain wrapped around his right fist.

"I seek the girl, not conflict. I ask that you step aside," The Grey Mantis requested.

The Grey Mantis stepped opposite the Japanese man but remained out of reach of the chain wrapped around his right hand. Once you faced a master and suffered the weighted ends clubbing you in the head, making muscles go numb with each blow landed, you never forget the name of the *manrikigusari*.

Few fighters of any art chose it as their primary weapon. It was difficult and painful to master. The Grey Mantis would need to maintain a high level of alertness if he was to survive. There was still Jersey Sven to deal with.

"Get on your knees, masked man. I'll end you quick," the Japanese man promised.

The Grey Mantis took the wide stance of the Mantis, his hook-hands ready. He swayed subtly, rhythmically and waited for his prey to attack.

The Japanese man spun both ends of the *manrikigusari* performing a shuffle with his footwork. The chain lengths at the end of each arm blurred into discs of potential pain, hungry for blood. While the target reeled from the blow a second would stun him. Once vulnerable, the chain master can break bones or strangle the loser at his whim. The Grey Mantis saw it done many times. *This man was a competition fighter at one point*, Grey Mantis thought. *Very flamboyant. Very precise. He must have many medals and ribbons.*

The discs of pain and breaking drew nearer.

The Grey Mantis swayed.

Under the name Jei, Robert fought to survive. No poor score for imprecision. There was agony and often death. Most opponents would be cowed by the chain master. He expected The Grey Mantis to fall back.

The Grey Mantis reached out into the spinning chain, allowing it to wrap around his arm. He shifted the steel-sheath around his wrist so the weighted end struck only wrapped chain. The Chain Master grinned and caught the free hand of The Grey Mantis as well. He struggled but quickly determined that he could not out-muscle the chain master wrapped in his chains. The Grey Mantis fired a front kick. The Japanese man blocked the kick with the small length of chain he controlled his foe with.

The chain master was still smirking when he was pulled in and head-butted in the face. His nose exploded with blood, his eyes flooded with tears.

The chain master stumbled back one step before The Grey Mantis seized the weapon, wrapped his fists with it and fired jabs loosing teeth and splitting flesh until the Japanese man fell. The Grey Mantis discarded the *manrikigusari* on the felled chain master without so much as a glance.

The Grey Mantis quick stepped around the drywall and cinder block barrier and entered the armory of the Gore Mongers. Standing at the center of the plywood-lined, combination weapon store and throne room was the last man. It could be none other than Jersey Sven. Over seven feet tall and wearing only some well-worn, cracked leather pants, Jersey Sven was riddled with scarred-over injuries incurred during a lifetime of walking the road of the warrior.

His nose looked like it had just been broken but The Grey Mantis knew this was simply the way it was set the last time. There was likely no cartilage left in it. A scar on the corner of his mouth gave him the appearance of forever smirking. The cauliflower ear at the end of the scar was the most grotesque The Grey Mantis had ever seen.

"You must be some kinda fighter making it all the way here," Sven said out the side of his mouth.

"Where is Sierra Buckingham?"

Sven motioned to a steamer trunk behind him, next to his custom-made throne of scrap metal. Swords ranging from sabers to *nimcha, nunchaku* to halberd and knives of every sort were mounted on the walls or stacked military style throughout the iron chamber. The stink was that of the dojo. It was blood and sweat and meat.

"For your sake, I hope she yet lives and is unharmed," The Grey Mantis threatened.

"She's alive. I guess you haven't forced y'self in here just to hand the money over to me personally?" Jersey Sven crossed his well-defined arms.

"I ask that you step aside. The girl comes with me either way."

"I think you're lucky as the day is long. I think you have greatly offended me and my people by bustin' down our door. On another day I might ask you to join my gang 'cause we are only getting bigger. We gonna stomp this city flat. No little girl in silk pajamas and a Halloween mask is breakin' my momentum.

"Chose your weapon, cupcake." Jersey Sven's hand flashed behind his back then a collapsible baton snapped to full length.

Sven started rotating his shoulders and neck to warm up.

He's an **escrimador**. *Primarily a stick fighter but more than adept at knife, sword and open hand fighting. He has chosen to fight using a single baton.* The Grey Mantis eased one of the sticks out from his belt behind his back.

He was already warmed up.

The Grey Mantis advanced. Jersey Sven showed no fear as he stepped forward. As Jei, there had been a number of bouts against stick fighters, some from the Philippines. They were the most difficult. Jersey Sven was decidedly not from the Philippines.

The steel baton cracked against the wooden one again and again in a violent staccato of sound. Each attacker's arms were a blur of speed. The Grey Mantis smelled his baton starting to heat up from the friction. Stories told of traditional bamboo batons smoking during matches.

Sven dashed forward. He worked his empty hand into the striking sequence. The Grey Mantis almost found his pacing in the striking pattern but failed. A backhand rocked The Grey Mantis's face. A blow from the steel baton broke a rib and then he was disarmed. The Grey Mantis dashed backward seeking better footing, a chance to regain his senses. Sven did not allow his enemy that time.

The Gore Monger came on strong, now with two batons: steel and wood. The Grey Mantis had no choice but to shoot in and out of the whip and circle-like movements to block-strike at wrist and forearms. For every blow blocked, a hit landed from a direction The Grey Mantis had not anticipated. His mouth filled with blood. A lucky jab reminded The Grey Mantis of the broken rib.

Jersey Sven saw the flinch and smiled.

"I don't get how you got this far, man." Jersey Sven grinned.

The Grey Mantis shot a heel-palm to block the wooden baton. A wrist-catch took care of a steel strike but not the follow up wrist rotation that brought the baton perfectly into The Grey Mantis's forehead.

Before the flashing blindness settled from the blow The Grey Mantis leaped back while launching a ball kick to the tender inside of Sven's left bicep. The strike interrupted Sven's rhythm and gave The Grey Mantis time to retrieve the second part of the flag pole sheathed behind his back.

Like lightning Sven renewed his striking sequence. The Grey Mantis ground his teeth and he gave ground like he had not in years. The Grey Mantis wasted no time responding in kind. It was precisely what Sven wanted. The *escrimador* trapped The Grey Mantis's arm with the steel baton and hand then drove his forearm into the resulting locked arm, hyperextending, almost breaking, The Grey Mantis's elbow.

Taking a second to admire his work, to perhaps gloat over the easy win, Jersey Sven missed the heel kick to the thigh followed by a front kick to the pelvis.

Both combatants stepped backwards.

The Grey Mantis settled his breathing into an easy rhythm. There was fire in his right arm at the elbow. It could be considered agony to a normal man. To one that was born in the grit and rage of the combat circle it was just a chance to catch his breath. He could still move; he still had three limbs and a mind that could direct them.

Pain is simply weakness leaving the body, one *sifu* had beaten into him.

Jersey Sven limped badly. His breathing was ragged. He continued to smirk.

The Grey Mantis eased to the floor and retrieved his wooden baton. He took a modified Mantis stance and slowly swayed.

"You're crippled! Submit!" Jersey Sven screamed.

The Grey Mantis waited for his prey to come to him.

Snarling, spitting as he swore to himself or whatever god he might worship, Jersey Sven charged in. His batons moved faster than the eye could track. The Grey Mantis did not look at the batons. They were the feint. They could become hypnotic and lure a fighter to his doom. The Grey Mantis watched his foe's shoulders, his eyes and to a lesser degree his footwork. It wasn't a lot but it was enough for The Grey Mantis to predict what the *escrimador* was going to do a moment before execution.

It was clear that Jersey Sven spent a lot of time learning to fight. He might even have survived some death matches. What he did not do was train regularly. The layer of fat around his trunk spoke of a life of giving orders and perhaps instructing. The Grey Mantis didn't think that he trained to fight anymore. Why should he? He was at the top of the city's largest gang.

Jersey Sven was panting. He wasn't angry because of the shots The Grey Mantis landed. He was getting tired and knew that a prolonged fight was going to defeat him. The steel baton caught The Grey Mantis on the nose breaking it. Jersey Sven's eyes gleamed hungrily as he knew victory was near. His scars were flaring purple and red. The Grey Mantis knew he would take the bait.

Coming up from under his peripheral The Grey Mantis drove a shin strike to Sven's lower ribs shattering them. A knee landed to the sternum knocking Sven back. The tall man staggered, unsure of what to favor with a chest full of broken sticks. The Grey Mantis drove hard with his baton. Sven attempted to hold his ground but there was no strength in any of his strikes. Foam flecked the corner of his mouth.

The Grey Mantis broke Sven's right wrist and kicked the wooden baton from the other hand. Temple strikes and an upward hit to the nose knocked the fight from Jersey Sven the Gore Monger and he fell. The Grey Mantis stepped on his neck, forcing strangling sounds from him. There was no resistance when the Grey Mantis took the keys off his belt.

The Grey Mantis walked to the steamer trunk and tapped lightly with his knuckles on the lid.

"Sierra? Your father sent me. Are you alright?"

There was a soft tapping from the trunk. The Grey Mantis found the correct key and opened the lock. He eased the lid open. Squinting in the

The Grey Mantis waited for his prey to come to him.

scant light was a somewhat disheveled, short haired, fair-skinned girl. She was a desert rose mis-planted in the barren wasteland of steel and dust. Besides wearing more dirt than she was used to even in her Levis and Hello Kitty tee shirt, Sierra appeared intact.

She did not look pleased.

"Who are you?"

"I'm...The Grey Mantis. Your father's friend asked me to see if you would like to come home."

"You're named after a bug."

"I am indeed. Are you injured?"

"Nope. Are you? You're bleeding."

"I'll be fine. Your father would very much like to have you in his arms I think. Let's go."

"Okay."

Sierra slowly rose, feeling her stiff muscles try to work out the kinks.

"Are you going to help the others?"

"What others?"

"If Dad didn't pay they were gonna sell me like they did the others. He said I was worth a lot," Sierra clarified.

"We need to get out of here first. I want you to think of everything they told you concerning this sale you were going to be a part of. Places mostly. Can you run?"

"I think so. I was in the box forever. I'll need to stretch."

The Grey Mantis heard others approaching. They must have gotten through the train car. There would be no going out that way. Not with a child in tow.

"Stretch?" Grey Mantis asked.

Sierra took her left foot in hand behind her backside and stretched her quadriceps.

"I always stretch before I run."

"That's smart but..."

She stretched the right leg the same way.

"I'm on the track team at school."

"Of course you are. We really don't have time for a lengthy stretch. The rest of them are coming." The Grey Mantis paced the odd armory and found an exit.

The opening in the wall in the far corner was half the width of a normal sized door. Likely it was only used by Jersey Sven and his inner circle. The Grey Mantis took Sven's collapsible baton and slipped it into his belt.

Sierra jumped up a few times.

"Ready?"

"Yeah," Sierra said.

The Grey Mantis could hear the rumblings, then the shouting, of the Mongers as they entered the building.

"Time to go," Grey Mantis took Sierra by the arm.

They easily slipped through the small exit in the metal shack and hit the ground at a sprint. The wooden planks that were the flooring had been a railed stairway once. One wrong move and either of them could trip— maybe get seriously hurt. That would not help the mission.

"There is a worn path on the flooring, see it? Follow it. You'll be less likely to trip," The Grey Mantis said.

"I see it," the girl replied.

The night was coming alive with the anger of the Gore Mongers behind them. They were halfway to the nearest tear in the fence. The Grey Mantis risked a look over his shoulder. The thugs were pouring out of the metal shack single file and seemingly without end. Grey Mantis knew he could handle himself against a dozen or more but eventually they would overwhelm him. Trying to protect the girl would only make things more difficult.

"Faster, Sierra. We need to make that tear!"

"I'm not walking over here!"

Something plinked off the railroad tie behind them.

It was an arrow.

Someone was shooting arrows at them. At least it wasn't a bullet.

"What was that?" she asked.

The Grey Mantis did not respond but increased his speed. If there was someone waiting for them on the other side of the fence he wanted time to face them down without Sierra. Was Jersey Sven so forward thinking that he would guard his exit? Or was he so sure in his supremacy in the city that he thought no one would dare attack him?

Plywood wired to the chain link fence made seeing beyond the tear impossible so the Grey Mantis jumped through the hole.

He was alone.

No one was in sight. The Grey Mantis held the rip in the fence open wider for Sierra. She stepped through easily then looked around.

"No car?"

"It's on the other side of the rail yard. Come on." The Grey Mantis looked for something to block the exit or tie it shut with but found nothing.

"More running?"

The Grey Mantis ran. Sierra followed. It wasn't a great distance they had to travel to get to the car but it did mean running around half the train yard to get there. The Grey Mantis hoped that Sierra was some kind of long distance runner at school. Even then she would certainly tire before they reached the destination. Sierra was breathing harder.

Maybe there was another choice besides escape?

There was a pop-burst of air from the fence to their left. The Grey Mantis's hand shot out plucking a dart from the air. It was a dart trailing a long line of wire.

"Dang!" someone out of sight cried from the fence-line.

"Wha..?"

A second pop, this one taking The Grey Mantis by surprise. It struck him in the arm then pain fired throughout his body. He could not move; he felt like he was on fire. He could hear Sierra screaming at someone to stop. Stiff as a statue, The Grey Mantis tipped over onto his side, then settled on his back. Jersey Sven came into view holding a kind of gun Robert had never seen before. The wires coming off the barb in his arm were coming from the end of the gun.

"Never seen someone catch a taser before, man. You are fast! Ain't as fast as electricity though, are yah?"

Fresh pain poured over and through The Grey Mantis until darkness took him.

• • •

"Please wake, Mr. Mantis," someone sobbed.

Robert felt his body jerking. His muscles were beyond his control. Random groups: pectorals, quadriceps and calves just cramped violently and refused to let up. He opened his eyes and saw a girl with her hands bound behind her back lying next to him. They were both on their sides, facing each other.

"Help me," the girl pleaded.

She looked familiar. She seemed important.

Were they in a car?

"Jersey, the guy is waking up," a male voice said from overhead.

No not a car, something bigger.

Robert turned his head to see the brute holding a baseball bat that had spoken.

"So put him out again," a distant voice commanded.

The bat came down and popped Robert in the base of his skull. He fell into the black.

"If you kill him…"

• • •

"We were gonna let you go with yer Dad, little girl, but he had to be a damn idiot. I'd love to know where he found the masked fool."

"I know, right," a second voice added.

Robert decided not to move. He could still feel Sierra breathing close to his face. Her respiration was up. She was terrified and rightfully so. It was a man sitting opposite where Robert was laying that spoke.

"Now we're gonna sell ya to the Koreans or the Chinese or the Russians maybe. Lotta buyers for some young tail. Your daddy really screwed the pooch on this one, princess."

"You got nothing but pain in your future, kid," the man with the bat said behind Robert.

By the way he spoke, Robert could tell he was smiling. They were doing their best to scare the girl witless.

"Takes a real man to scare a captive girl," Robert snarled.

The bat-man exhaled in surprise a second before Robert rolled and kicked him in the face bouncing his head off the steel interior. Before he could do any more fire seared through his body from a single point in his ribs.

Taser…

• • •

Robert imagined that if he were on the rack he wouldn't feel much worse. He opened his eyes and found himself in a room with concrete walls and steel piping above him. His hands were handcuffed. There was a chain suspending him over the wet cement floor, looped around a large pipe ending in an iron housing in the wall. If he stretched, his feet grazed the floor.

Sierra was not in sight.

Who knew what they were doing to her.

Maybe nothing. Maybe they wanted to keep her in good shape to fetch a higher price. That was a slim hope to hold onto but better than nothing. *Maybe Zeke was right when he said that he should have gone to his father to get the money. This rescue attempt certainly wasn't going as planned.*

Robert closed his eyes and regulated his breathing. He brought his knees up to his chest, slowly he straightened his legs until they found purchase on the large pipe that he swung from. He yanked and strained and shook the chain and handcuffs every way he could think of. Nothing moved. Nothing shifted. All he did was get tired and bloody his wrists for the effort. Robert eased his legs back and just hung, swinging slightly.

There was no doubt in his mind what was coming next. The door opened and three men he had never seen before came in. All wore black tee shirts and slacks. Each had a gun slung under an arm. They were two Caucasians and one Latino. All hard men judging by their expressions and slim, muscular builds.

"Hope you ate your Wheaties, man. Yer gonna need your strength tonight," the red-head said.

"We did. Big bowls," the man with an overbite chuckled.

The Latino stepped up to Robert. He found it odd that they had left his mask on. The Latino rotated his shoulders while looking up at Robert. He must have won the coin toss then, Robert thought. The Latino cracked his knuckles and spat in Robert's face.

"You're going to be eating out of a straw for a long time after tonight. So make it count." the Grey Mantis smirked.

Each man took a turn treating Robert like a punching bag for over an hour. He didn't make a single sound. It disappointed all of them.

When he passed out, they left him swinging and bleeding over the concrete.

• • •

Knives made from ice slashed across Robert's face in the hundreds. His broken nose screamed loudly at the liquid assault. While the Robert part of his psyche sat shivering, Jei, of the blood circle and pain-forged, snapped to and was on his feet taking in the surroundings.

He was not alone. There was a man some twenty feet out of reach. His hands were wrapped like a fighter's. Off to the right was a skinny male, little more than a boy, running with a steel bucket in one hand. *He was smart to run*, Jei thought. *I would have broken that offending arm of yours had it been within my reach.*

"The mighty Grey Mantis has joined us!" a loudspeaker blasted.

There were four spotlights shining down on the hardwood-floored area. It was impossible to see the speaker.

The man with the wrapped hands and baggy shorts smirked.

"There isn't a lot of time so let's get right to it, Mantis. You had your fun and put some serious pain on my people in the train yard. Now you pay for the ride. This was none of your business, jerk-off. We got a nice big event here tonight and you are going to be in the center ring. I need to make sure that you are as good as Sven here claims you are. I think he's exaggerating but I've seen what happened to the Gore Mongers.

"This is your opponent, Razor Cobb. He was the champ of this circuit for a few months. It seems he has healed from his shame and wants that title again. Razor, tear him apart, kill him, I don't care, and a spot is yours again on the circuit.

"Mantis, beat Razor and you live for the next fight. It's that simple. Show me what a tough guy you are and I might not kill you. Let's get it on, boys." Laughter echoed in the fighting circle before the loudspeaker went dead.

"To be clear, I am taking Sierra out of here before midnight," The Grey Mantis declared.

Once the shock of the ice-water subsided, The Grey Mantis nose throbbed it was just broken. Worse still were his ribs. Broken by Jersey Sven and battered by this operation's flunkies, The Grey Mantis's ribs pulsed with constant, fresh agony.

The opponent rolled his shoulders and fired a few fury-packed shin-strikes. He was likely a kickboxer of some sort. Thai boxers worked the body a lot with knee and shin strikes.

"Let's go Grey Mantis," Cobb ordered with great sarcasm.

Robert sighed.

"You can walk away and find another circuit to test your might. Remain, and become a cripple."

The kickboxer walked straight to The Grey Mantis.

"Shut up and fight," Cobb snapped.

The Grey Mantis hopped up and down a few times and shook his hands out to get all the circulation shooting through the veins as fast as possible. He was certainly going to have keep moving if he was going to live through this, never mind win.

Cobb held his fists out in front of him as he closed in. The Grey Mantis shifted his weight from his lead foot to his rear always keeping most of it on the rear. He sidestepped to avoid being dropped in the opening dance. Both fighters sought potential tells and were wary of feints. Cobb's patience was finite. He dashed forward, launching punch after punch.

There was hesitation in his firing sequence when The Grey Mantis did not behave as he expected. The Grey Mantis did not dash away to keep out of range. He stepped close, inside Cobbs' guard, and parried or deflected the strikes. In a furious exchange of blows Cobb found every strike blocked and counter punched to the inside of the biceps and a final heel palm that shattered Cobbs' nose.

The Grey Mantis felt the knee strike sink into his ribs, lifting him off the ground and dashing him to the blasted wooden floor. He rolled clumsily to his feet, panting hoarsely.

"I can't believe you just broke my damn nose, big-man. Unreal," Cobb said. He placed his fingers on each side of his nose and snapped it back into place. After inhaling sharply he spat blood to the ground.

There was nothing The Grey Mantis could do to fix his ribs. His breathing was going to be an issue.

"You should not have entered my circle, Razor Cobb."

Roaring, Cobb shuffled forward. Each kick The Grey Mantis intercepted with a kick of his own. Cobb shot in, launching flurry after flurry of strikes with powerful elbow blows mixed in trying to confuse and disorientate. Mantis Fist kung fu specialized in close quarter combat and striking before one is struck. It only enraged Cobb and allowed The Grey Mantis to insert his own chain-punching techniques, focusing on the broken nose. The resulting tears blinded and slowed Cobb so that blocking and entering his guard was that much easier.

The Grey Mantis focused his shots on the nose and temple. Simultaneously, he landed a heel-palm under Cobb's jawline while The Grey Mantis took an elbow to the cheek. Both fighters crashed to the floor, barely moving.

Wheezing, head spinning, The Grey Mantis slowly rose. Cobb was slower to get to his feet.

"Submit, Cobb. It is over. Why fight?"

"I got to get up, stupid. This is it for me. I can't do nuthin else. What am I if I ain't fightin'?"

Both Cobb's eyes were swelling shut. Tearing made vision impossible.

"Too much on the line, man."

"Submit. I cannot hold back. There is more at stake here than mere ego," The Grey Mantis warned.

"Damned if I'm goin' down 'gainst you, punk!"

Cobb fired kick after roundhouse kick forcing The Grey Mantis to intercept-kick or block. He too had no choice but to come on, to draw closer and make it all the more dangerous for him to take on the fury of the kickboxer. The Grey Mantis shot in, struck the throat, making Cobb's trachea spasm. The shock froze the Thai boxer long enough. The Grey Mantis landed a dozen strikes, chain-punching to the face, blasting Cobb to the ground until the only movement was the jerking of his unconscious form.

The Grey Mantis stood over the form of his defeated adversary panting. The pain was like a spiked ball deep inside behind his ribs. He wondered if he was bleeding internally.

Robert heard both doors close. One man from each door approached him. One had an athletic build and wore a tee shirt and jeans. The other was moving slower but still with purpose. It was Jersey Sven.

"Another round, Sven?" The Grey Mantis chided.

"You bet. Just not tonight." Sven fired a taser.

The Grey Mantis had barely registered the presence of the gun and felt his body burn and lock up.

"You passed the test, Mantis. Tonight you get to fight in the main event. No way yer walking away from that, tough guy," Jersey Sven laughed.

The second man came into view over The Grey Mantis.

"Let's get this done. There's still meetings and kiddies to sell," the man smirked and fired his taser into The Grey Mantis.

"Night-night, Mantis."

• • •

The crowd muttered amongst themselves. It didn't sound like there was a very good turn-out. Jei-Robert tried to remember where he was fighting and who his opponents were but came up with nothing. The floor was covered with sand. That could mean any of a dozen places he had fought before. Sometimes he was drugged and dropped into the circle when he started regaining consciousness and sometimes he walked out. It depended on how foul a mood Ran Li, his master, was in on a given day. Or how much trouble Jei-Robert had given him on that day.

It was a fine line that Jei-Robert walked every second of every day of his second life. If Jei failed in training or obedience, if he lost a match, there was the chance that Li would send his killers to America and murder his first parents and brother. Jei would continue to fight regardless but he would live knowing it had been his decision to fail that caused his families death. To do well was to hear the lie that one day he would be released if he made enough money for Li in the Blood Circles of China. Robert knew that every time he beat an opponent to the floor he lost a little more of

When he beat an opponent to the floor he lost more of who Robert had been.

who Robert had been and inched closer to where Jei-Robert was heading. It wasn't just the idea of getting his parents killed that made Robert cry, it was the idea that he was losing himself to save them.

The crying stopped after the first five years. Becoming Jei was like sliding into comfortable shoes by then.

This was not China, Grey Mantis realized. This was becoming another changing point in his life he noted. The smells and the sounds were wrong. Everyone was speaking American English and not a cacophony of Asian dialects.

The Grey Mantis opened his eyes. He was not alone. He could see five others milling about. All with an athletic build. Voices behind him suggested at least that number was there as well. It was going to be a group effort then. Jei had his share of multi-opponent contests before. It was an interesting challenge. I wonder if there are going to be any allies in his go round, The Grey Mantis thought.

He slowly rolled over then rose to his feet. His body shook under the strain of standing. He was thirsty and hungry. His broken ribs were taped as was his nose. How long was I out? Jei wondered. There were another six milling about behind him. None of them wore a mask but Jei still wore the mantle of The Grey Mantis.

Strange. They want to make sure it's a good fight.

"Attention ladies and gentlemen. If I could have your ear for just a moment." The voice was on the intercom.

The twelve athletes stood on a sand covered floor. A cement wall formed a complete circle around them. Jei guessed it was two hundred feet in diameter. He had fought in smaller arenas. Most were just the red circles the promoters sprayed from a can. The only walls were the rabid audience betting on the first to spill blood and the last man standing. The cement barrier was about six feet tall with another five feet of glass or plexiglass keeping the fans from getting any blood on them. There was a limit to how realistic they wanted their experience to be after all.

The fighters assembled around him were not so different from any other he fought in the past save for their race. There were only two Asians present. Three Latinos, three blacks and three whites plus Jei was the make-up. One white and one black were both over six feet tall. A few were Jei's size but most were shorter. Everyone had tattoos and scarring in great number. The one thing that every single fighter had, besides an apparent contempt for mask-wearing mystery men, was the look of one used to pain and strife in their eyes. They were all fighters. There was no doubt.

The Grey Mantis began to rotate his neck and then his shoulders. His nose was swollen shut but hurt less. His ribs were like knives stabbing into his organs. If he had to guess he figured it was no more than a day since he started his quest to rescue Sierra.

Zeke must be going crazy wondering where she is right now.

"We have a special treat for you tonight, ladies and gentlemen. In the center of the pit we have a celebrity of sorts. He's known on the street as The Grey Mantis. He is a master of the martial arts as all of his opponents have already learned."

The Grey Mantis tried to peer through the glare of the spotlights blazing down on everyone in the pit. It didn't matter over much. He had seen every kind of crowd you could imagine. Rich men or poor men, everyone here had one thing in common. They all wanted to see blood and live through the fighters down in the sand and muck as they broke each other open. No price was too high, no fight too one-sided. As long as they got the blood they paid for; it was an evening well spent.

"Tonight we have assembled eleven past champions of the pit. Some of you will no doubt recall those that have fought for you in the past. At no small expense we have brought them back from around the globe for your fighting entertainment tonight. Given The Grey Mantis' recent victories in New York we promise you an amazing display of martial ability," the loudspeaker said.

"Some of the more carnivorous of you might not think that eleven champions against an unknown will be enough to get your blood moving! Fear not!"

From equidistant points on the perimeter of the pit weapons came over the Plexiglas barricade. A few swords, kama, tonfa, simple clubs and a few broken bottles. Every fighter raced, some fought, to get the weapons offered. Not surprisingly there were only eleven offered to the pit. The Grey Mantis did not move from his place but continued to slowly stretch.

"It seems our x-factor fighter feels he doesn't need a weapon!"

The crowd booed.

"I wonder what the other players on the board will think of that?" the speaker said from the darkness.

The hidden audience laughed and whistled.

The Grey Mantis simply began snapping punches in quick succession.

"Fighters of the pit. Your objective is very simple: be the last man standing. No holds are barred. He who stands last will receive his weight in gold! Good luck. Now fight!"

Battle cries and kii-yais exploded and the carnage began in the pit. The audience broke into applause and laughter.

A heavily tattooed Latino charged at The Grey Mantis with a tonfa/nightstick in hand. He swung wide to increase the damage and Jei shot in chain-punching until the nightstick fell from his hand. The fighter had just begun to fall when a sword wielder came up from behind.

The Grey Mantis ducked and felt the spray when the sword ripped open the Latino's face. Well within the swordsman's guard The Grey Mantis landed a ridge-hand to the groin and followed up with a heel palm to the man's nose as he doubled over. Jei did not check to find out if he had killed the back-stabber. He took the sword, a *jian* native to China and ran at the giant Caucasian with a dragon tattoo dominating the right side of his bare chest.

The giant turned to the oncoming Grey Mantis and roared a ferocious battle cry before reaching out to crush the oncoming foe. The *jian* sang as it tore through the air, his right hand and lower abdomen. The giant spat blood and bent over holding himself with one hand. The Grey Mantis leapt up onto the hunched, tattooed man's shoulder and leapt with everything he had.

He reached the top of the plexi-glass and with great effort pulled himself over. The tuxedo-clad gentry screamed and dove over themselves to get out of the way of the crazy masked man with a sword.

"Calm down, ladies and gentlemen. It seems one of our fighters has decided to make up his own program. Rest assured that security has the matter well in hand," the loudspeaker related in a barely jovial inflection.

The Grey Mantis landed on a chair, straddling a woman while he balanced on the arms of her chair.

"Good thing the chairs are fixed to the floor. Excuse me, ma'am," the Grey Mantis apologized.

He kept the *jian* in a reverse grip to keep from accidently slashing any of the bloodthirsty audience as he ran. He kept his feet on chair arms and backs making impossibly good time getting to the back of the seating area. A man in black, talking into his sleeve, ran along the back walkway behind the audience. He reached into his auburn suit coat and pulled out a handgun. There was no way that The Grey Mantis was going to get within slashing range before getting shot.

"Back in the pit, fighter!"

The Grey Mantis jumped over the last four rows and threw the *jian*. It swept end over end and ran through the security guard. Had he not brought his arm up to protect himself it would not have pinned his arm to his chest. He howled as The Grey Mantis came on him and snapped a front kick to his midsection. The gun dropped. The Grey Mantis caught it and used it to backhand the guard. He then ejected the clip and stuck the pistol in his belt.

"No guns. Now where is the girl?" the Grey Mantis demanded.

"What are you— " He screamed as The Grey Mantis twisted the *jian* slightly.

"I am looking for the girl Sierra Buckingham. Hurry now!" the Grey Mantis repeated.

"Holy… she-she's in the ballroom on the first floor, the Daybreak Room I think, with the other kids, getting ready to go," the guard confessed.

"Which way? The way you came in?"

Sweat poured off the guard. He flipped his sweaty head in the direction he had come from. "Take the first ramp and go all the way up. Can't miss it."

The Grey Mantis took a hold of the sword handle and shoved the guard off the sword with his foot. He fell with a groan and just writhed as The Grey Mantis stepped around him and ran.

He had never taken to the sword. His own hands always seemed the most reliable weapon but he had given the training with a number of swords due practice. Another guard in a tee shirt with an earpiece appeared from the crowd that was now scrambling to escape. Word was moving through them faster than Jei could run.

"Back in the pit, stupid," the guard fired his taser.

The Grey Mantis dodged and leaped at the shooter. On the way down he slapped the side of the *jian* across the guard's face and ear. The guard crashed into the wall and slid to the floor clawing at his ear. A kick to the base of the skull and The Grey Mantis was back to running.

Everyone that had been seated around him were all up and racing for safety in a number of directions. Whatever was happening in the pit below was less interesting than making sure their butts were safe and not near any crazed martial artist with a sword.

The Grey Mantis ran while keeping himself below head level so no one could see him coming and act crazy, or in the case of security, actively seek him out. Jei didn't know if the hired help would hurt non-combatants to get at him but he wasn't willing to take any such risk.

A woman, well dressed in an expensive black gown, tripped and fell to the ground. No one stopped to help her. She was getting kicked and stomped by the time The Grey Mantis got to her. He took her arm and helped her to her feet. Her nose was bleeding and her make-up ran unchecked down her face. She began to thank The Grey Mantis until she saw the mask and things came together for her.

She screamed and ran off to be carried away with the charging crowd.

He stuck his head up for a second just to see where the exit was and how much longer he was going to have to remain hidden in the crowd. There were twenty feet yet. The Grey Mantis heard before he saw, the guard charging and punching his way through the crowd straight at him. The Grey Mantis managed to shove away a middle-aged man with a vast nose and small chin smoking an expensive cigar in time for the lineman-sized guard to bowl into him.

Jei got his hands up in time to block most of the blow. It sent him backwards into the cinderblock wall. His sword was knocked free by the brute before he could orient himself. He thrust a handheld taser unit. The Grey Mantis redirected the weapon, hammered away at the big man's jaw hinge, then hyper-extended his arm until the taser fell free.

The crowd had thinned noticeably in his general location. Dashing for the exit was considerably easier. There was definitely a panic in the pit seating. Those who might be busboys, managers, security guards and former fight fans were running in every direction. The Grey Mantis kept his head down and made his way using the most direct route to the first ramp. Most of the people were racing up that same ramp.

The ramp led up to a parking area. Everyone else that made it this far was running for their cars. Jei looked around and quickly found what he was looking for: a doorway with a sign that read "The Sunrise Room" dining hall with an arrow pointing to a metal door.

"Don't move!" a voice yelled behind him.

The Grey Mantis ducked low and kept running. With his hand on the door it blasted open and more security poured out before him. They lined up beyond his ability to see through the door. A hand-held taser went up and The Grey Mantis trapped and hyper-extended the guard's arm. The guard screamed and tried to back away while dozens surged forward. He was cast down. The Grey Mantis took the taser and leapt to the side.

Every man that came through the door received a mark for their time. In general it was a zap or strike forcing them to drop their weapons and decide if they were getting paid enough.

It was then that the security guard from the pit below moved within striking distance. There was no more time to be nice. There were simply too many. Some were armed with firearms but none had fired. Was he so lucky that the headman here, whoever he was, wanted The Grey Mantis alive to fight for him? That had to be it. What a sentimentally-fatally-flawed man. Finally the guards stopped pouring into the small corner of the parking garage.

The Grey Mantis was surrounded. All remained just outside of taser range.

It felt like a tiger actively gnawed on his damaged ribs.

"You are surrounded twenty to one. All of us are armed. I'll say this once. Drop the weapon, and lay down on your face. We will use whatever force we need to secure you."

Jei leveled his eyes at the speaker.

"I am here for your victim's release. Any who stand in my way, any who step into my circle, will never be the same. You have my word," The Grey Mantis declared.

Jei kept turning slightly, arms outstretched, ready to attack.

"Screw this. Take him!" the speaker ranted.

He did not want to make it too obvious what he was trying to do, so rather than fight right for the door he took the mob on a few degrees further north. There could be no striking to stun or trying not to hurt the prey at half power. There were too many. And they were too well trained. The advantage was that they would be less inclined to use the firearms for fear of hitting their own.

The taser worked well to keep his enemies at a distance but it was tricky to use and not serious injury his enemies. He wasn't really looking to rack up a body count. Additionally, he could not allow himself to be taken down. Sierra, along with any number of other children, was relying on him. That thought gave strength to his resolve.

The Grey Mantis front-kicked a guard's midsection making him double over. Jei leaped on top of the man's back and proceeded to step and hop from head to shoulder to back across the mob. Just as he was about to leap for the door that should have taken him to the main floor his ankle was grabbed. Then he tumbled and they had his wrist too. The Grey Mantis was cast to the ground. His sword was wrenched from him and the blows rained down on him.

A furious straight kick followed by a heel palm and elbow strike that dislocated a guard's jaw gave him the chance he needed to get to his feet. Everything was close range now. Good, because now fewer could reach him. But bad because the odds on avoiding getting struck were way down.

Every attack by The Grey Mantis was for a fast take down or to immediately cripple. Temple strikes, knee dislocating-kicks and solar plexus shots were what he attempted. It took all his skill in close combat to parry, deflect and block the majority of the strikes that came at him. He stole a baton and gained a little more room to work.

A hand-held taser appeared and The Grey Mantis blasted the hand that carried it with the baton. He caught it before it fell to the ground. With baton and taser The Grey Mantis shocked and smashed his way through those few that remained to try and keep him from reaching the stairwell. He swung the metal door open and sprinted up the stairs. People were still rushing to get away from the parking level. Certainly the police were going to arrive soon. Fortunately the Sunrise Room was as close as the guard said it would be.

A guard stood in front of the double doors that lead to where he prayed he would find Sierra and the children. The guard reached into his jacket and The Grey Mantis hurled his fighting baton. The guard cleared his coat but took the baton in the face knocking his head into the door behind him. He crumpled to the floor. The Grey Mantis looked down on the handgun.

Jei-Robert took the handgun and baton but left the Taser, then entered the Sunrise Room.

• • •

Given his life, Jei-Robert had not spent a great deal of time in banquet halls or fancy dining rooms since his abduction at age ten. This one did not seem terribly large. It might have held a dozen long tables and a dozen seats at each table with a raised platform in the far back where the guests of honor might dine if there were one. Today there was seating for thirteen children aged six to ten, he estimated. Most were girls: all were in tears. Sierra Buckingham sat at the center, behind the table. All the children were on the far side of the table.

Jersey Sven stood behind Sierra. He had a handgun in his belt. He leaned heavily on the high backed chair and looked like he was rode hard and put up wet. Which was pretty close to how The Grey Mantis felt. Before the dais was a man he had not met yet. He wore a black suit but no tie. His hair was slicked back and tied in a ponytail. Both hands were in his pants pockets, his shoulders slouched. He stepped forward a few feet and tilted his head.

"Wow, do you look like hell. I'm kinda glad that I left the mask on. Bet you look like a bucket of puke under there."

"Surrender Sierra…"

"…Buckingham and stay they hell out of your circle. Yeah, I know. You use that to death, man. But then if I had taken as many hits to the head as you have tonight I might be a bit on the punchy side myself.

"Tell ya what, since we're stating the obvious. Toss the gun aside or Sven will start plugging the kids, starting with the Buckingham kid."

"You are wrong here. These are people, not things," The Grey Mantis stated.

He tossed the gun to the floor as directed.

"C'mon, we all gotta do something. You have no idea how much cash there is in selling people. Besides, these are just kids. Let the parents have more. Or not. I could really care less. Look, man. Work for me, you'll be rich beyond your imagining. Train me an army. Is there anything I can offer to get you to stop damn well hounding me? This is getting pricey even for me."

Blood began running out of The Grey Mantis's nose. He said nothing.

"Is it worth all this pain yer in? Oh, forget it."

The man in the suit grew a pistol from his waist even as The Grey Mantis drew and hurled the wooden baton. Fire and stars exploded in The Grey Mantis's head. The world went sideways and he hit the ground hard. His body rose with all the speed he could manage though his head was slow to catch up. The Grey Mantis stumbled to the man in the suit who lay on his back with both hands cupping his nose. Blood trailed down his face. His right hand sought the dropped pistol. The Grey Mantis ground his heel into the hand on the gun. The man in the suit howled. The man in the suit punched but The Grey Mantis felt nothing. His body moved of its own accord. The Grey Mantis caught the offending hand and twisted it so the man had no choice but to stand up screaming.

The wrist snapped.

The Grey Mantis started chain punching and did not stop. Not even after the man in the suit stopped trying to resist.

"Mr. Mantis! Stop!"

Was that Sierra shouting?

"I don't think he's… he's not fighting anymore," the girl said.

She stood on the near side of the long table now. All the other children had stopped crying and looked with watery eyes. Some harbored fear in them.

The man in the suit's right foot continued to move, like the body was yet being struck.

"You did it. You got to us."

"Are you okay?" the Grey Mantis slurred.

Blood ran down the side of his face. The bullet had only grazed him. It was hard to focus.

"I think we're all okay. Are you okay?" Sierra asked.

Jersey Sven was nowhere to be seen.

"I will be. Do you hear sirens?"

"Yes."

"I'm going to go. The police will be in here soon. Don't be afraid, okay?"

"Thank you, Mr. Mantis," the girl thanked him.

Many children echoed the sentiment.

The Grey Mantis retrieved the guns, ejected the clips and tossed them in the garbage can as he left. He would stick to the shadows to make sure the police found the children then remove the mask and blend in with the departing crowd.

It was a long time since he felt good about fighting.

This felt right.

Robert was pleased.

The End

ABOUT THE GREY MANTIS STRIKES!

My love for martial arts movies goes back to my childhood growing up in Canada watching Bruce Lee and Chuck Norris on Saturday afternoons. They were my first superheroes. Then came the ninjas and Sho Kosugi and all the clones of all three. They were the first though. Bruce Lee had an energy on screen like a super nova, you can feel it through the TV screen. The dude was electric.

I dabbled in a lot of things when I took a shot or two at writing super hero fan fiction. It did show me that I could write what I loved the most. Maybe make a dime or two doing it. Why not?

Since then I have discovered all the usual characters like Donnie Yen, Steven Segal, Jackie Chan, Jett Li, Sammo Hung and most recently Daniel Wu. Asia has offered me poetry of martial motion that thrills like few other things. It's a vicious violence throwing at us all the severe archetypes that make my kind of fiction so great. It was really only a matter of time until I found the Grey Mantis working the wooden man in my imagination.

There was that crappy Green Hornet movie that came out a few years ago that set things in motion. Visually I really liked the way the duo look. Their skillset drew me to them as well. It didn't hurt that Bruce Lee played Kato on the show from the 60s. I had been desperately wanting to create my own pulp hero for the longest time. There didn't seem to really be a masked martial artist running around in the modern day as far as I could tell. So I thought maybe I'd fuse the Hornet with Kato and see what I get. Some drawings were what came to me initially. Slowly the pieces started coming to together, almost of their own accord. I wanted a heavy influence of China in the story but I knew I wanted him in America. This story, *The Grey Mantis Strikes!*, is the first story where the bits start coming together for me.

Few characters I've written were as fun or as easy for me to write.

I had a great time writing him. You can bet your dojo I'm gonna to do it again.

Thanks for reading.

• • •

C. WILLIAM RUSSETTE - had comic books *Lucifer Fawkes: Blood Flow* and *The Blind Ones* published through Rorschach Entertainment. Pro Se Productions published a number of his short stories. Pro Se also published a tale of monsters in the modern day called *Shamanskin*; it was Russette's first novel. ALL-STAR PULP COMICS from Airship 27 Productions included a short Black Bat comic written by C. William Russette. Airship 27 also published a Crimson Mask story for an anthology. Emby Press published the first Night Reaper story in their anthology *Super Hero Monster Hunter: The Good Fight*

C. William Russette co-operates a studio on Facebook by the name BAD TIGER STUDIO and lives in Pennsylvania with his wife and son.

Like this book? Here's what's come before...

During the golden days of American pulps hundreds of masked avengers were created to battle evildoers around the globe. *The Black Bat, Moon Man, Domino Lady*, and the *Purple Scar* to name only a few of these amazing pulp heroes. Now in each all-new volume four New Pulp writers introduce to pulp readers brand new pulp heroes cast in the mold of their 1930s counterparts.

In each volume of *Mystery Men & Women* find four brand new action-packed stories starring four original heroes to thrill and excite pulp fans everywhere as brought to you by Airship 27 Productions.

MYSTERY MEN
(& WOMEN)

www.ingramcontent.com/pod-product-compliance
Lightning Source LLC
Chambersburg PA
CBHW051125260626
47170CB00005B/1663